California Sunsets

The Davenports, Book 3

~ Erin and Jay ~

Bella Andre & Nicky Arden

CALIFORNIA SUNSETS
The Davenports, Book 3

Meet the Davenport family! Six brothers and sisters who call picturesque Carmel-by-the-Sea home. Successful, brilliant, and passionate, the only thing they all still need is the perfect partner in love and life.

Erin Davenport always imagined she'd end up with a quiet man. Someone like her.

Then she met Jay Malone.

He's the loudest, pushiest, most sales-oriented man she's ever met. A top Hollywood agent, Jay's bought a waterfront house in Carmel, and everywhere Erin turns, he seems to be there—big, gorgeous, and pulsing with life. He goes through women like candy, and Erin has no intention of being his latest treat.

Jay can sell anything to anyone. He turned a hot young surfer into an A-list movie star, so why is it so hard to sell himself to Archer Davenport's sister? Erin isn't like anyone he's ever known. He's been in Hollywood so long, he's accustomed to being surrounded by some of the most beautiful, talented women in the world. But Erin attracts him in a way no other woman ever has. She's gorgeous and rarely bothers with makeup or fancy clothes. She's a brilliant writer, but happy to work for the local newspaper.

She's the woman he's been looking for all his life. But can he convince the emotionally risk-averse writer to take a chance on their love story?

A note from Bella and Nicky

Thank you so much for continuing to be a part of our romantic adventures with the Davenports in beautiful Carmel-by-the-Sea! Writing this series has been so much fun, and while we could never pick a favorite Davenport, this book had us laughing the entire time we worked on it. We hope it gives you all the feels—the passionate romance, the laughter, and the sizzling heat between Erin and Jay.

We can never thank you enough for reading our books! You inspire us to create more new stories, and we absolutely love it when you get in touch over email or through social media to let us know how much you're enjoying our books.

Happy reading!
Bella Andre & Nicky Arden

P.S. Please sign up for our New Release newsletters for more information on upcoming books: BellaAndre. com/Newsletter and nickyarden.com/newsletter

Chapter One

When Erin Davenport walked into Anna's Coffee Shop on Tuesday morning, Tessa and Mila had already settled themselves at their favorite table. Mila was wearing a smart navy blue suit and had a particularly brilliant smile on her face, which usually meant one of two things: a really fun night with her fiancé, Herschel, or she'd sold another house.

Before Erin had a chance to ask her which it was, Mila said, "Today isn't a coffee day, ladies, it's a champagne day. Guess who just sold a waterfront home on Scenic Drive?"

Erin stroked her chin, pretending to ponder the question. "Dan Ferguson? I hear he's the best Realtor in Carmel."

"Very funny," her sister said, flipping back her long blonde hair, which was bleached lighter than normal from the July sun. Since Dan Ferguson was Mila's mentor and had trained her, it was a mild jab at best.

Tessa shook her head at them, a slight frown worrying her usually smooth brow. She was getting better, but she still wasn't completely accustomed to the way the Davenport siblings liked to tease each other. Erin regarded her new sister-in-law for a moment. Tessa was dressed in what looked to be vintage blue Levis and a pretty pink pastel shirt that no doubt she'd found at one of the thrift stores she loved to visit. Even in a casual, comfortable outfit, she was absolutely glowing—there was no other word for it. Despite her more introverted nature, she'd managed a very public wedding to Erin's A-list celebrity brother Archer at a grand, sprawling castle in Scotland, which had been splashed across every media outlet from digital to cable to print. Erin had noticed the way she'd avert her gaze if she saw their wedding pictures on the front cover of an entertainment magazine, but she never said anything, and in Erin's opinion, Tessa had handled the transition from a very private person to the wife of a big celebrity with true grace. Although, based on the way her paintings were starting to sell, Erin thought she was going to have to get used to the limelight. To everyone's joy, but possibly Archer's more than anybody, a Tessa Taylor-Davenport painting was becoming a real collector's item and the demand—and price—for her work was soaring.

Erin ordered a cappuccino and as she took her seat next to the two women she loved so much, she was perfectly willing to listen to Mila, who was just about bursting to tell them about her latest sale. "Go on."

Mila grinned. "It's that house you love, Erin. The one on Scenic Drive with the deco windows and all the Carmel stone. I don't want to boast, but the commission was a nice chunk of change."

Erin felt her jaw practically hit the floor. "I can't believe that house was for sale and I never even knew it." Even in her wildest dreams, Erin couldn't have afforded that home, but she loved it so dearly there was a tiny part of her that thought the house was waiting for her. That she didn't even know it was for sale was like a betrayal.

A little secretive smile played around Mila's lips. "That's why they pay me the big bucks, sis. I have my finger on the pulse and I get the scoops. Like you, at the newspaper, except with multimillion-dollar properties." She paused to enjoy getting in a little jibe of her own, and let the small smile grow. "Plus, it turned out the new owner is friends with another of my clients, and they gave me a recommendation. It was such an easy sale too."

"Who bought it?" Erin asked. How lucky they were to have that house and how she hoped they would treat it right. She sighed. She wasn't wealthy like some of her siblings and could never afford her dream house. But she didn't envy them. She was truly happy at her job as a reporter for the *Sea Shell*, Carmel-by-the-Sea's local paper, and not earning a big wage was okay with her. She'd created a life she loved and that suited her quiet nature. She couldn't imagine anything worse than having millions of screaming fans chanting her name, like her rock-star brother Damien, or being hounded by paparazzi like Arch.

Now Mila couldn't stop the grin from all but exploding on her face. She glanced at Erin in a very significant way. "Actually, you know the new owner."

"I do?" A spark of joy went through her and she reached out and grasped her sister's hand. "It's not Smith Sullivan and Valentina, is it? It would be so great to have them in the neighborhood, especially now that they're expecting a baby. And Arch—"

Mila shook her head. "Not even close. Well, actually, sort of close. Try again."

Her sister was clearly enjoying stringing this one out. Erin racked her brain. Who did she know who could afford that place and wouldn't have told her about it? "Is it another actor?" Mila shook her head. "A director?"

Again, Mila shook her head and Tessa chuckled, happy to take a backseat while Erin tried to read Mila's mind.

"One of Damien's friends? It's not a rock star, is it?" Much as she loved her brother, a rock star wouldn't be right for that house. She shuddered as she imagined a wild band trashing the grounds with their all-night parties or knocking through walls to create some ultramodern space.

Once more Mila shook her head, looking smug. "Try agent."

At the way Mila's eyes were glinting, Erin felt her excitement dim as though a big cloud had passed in front of the sun. "Oh no."

Mila nodded. "Oh yes. Julius Malone, our old friend Jay, bought that house. He'd told me he was interested in the area and when this became available, I called him right away. I knew it would be perfect for him."

"But I love that house," Erin said again, feeling even more forlorn. She didn't know why it seemed worse that Jay of all people should have it, but it did. Well, that wasn't true—she knew exactly why. Jay was a brash bulldozer. Not at all the kind of guy who'd treat a historic home like that with any respect.

Tessa said, "Jay is a good guy, Erin. I know he can be a bit. . . much sometimes, but he has a good heart. He's more than an agent to Arch. He's a true friend."

"He's also very hot *and* single," Mila added quickly.

Erin rolled her eyes. As if.

But Mila continued, "I saw the way you two were dancing at the wedding." She left the last comment hanging in the air.

Tessa giggled. "I agree with Mila. Even though I'd never look at any man besides Arch, obviously, Jay is very hot. I'm afraid I didn't notice the two of you dancing together, but Mila said there was some real chemistry."

Erin didn't choose her men based solely on looks, the way Mila had for most of her life. It wasn't until Herschel Greenfield had come along that Mila had found herself drawn to something deeper. Erin wished her sister would drop the subject of Jay. "Mila's just teasing. There was no chemistry." She had to admit, though, that dancing with Jay had been more fun than she'd have thought it would be.

Mila gently prodded her in the shoulder. "You've known him for years. I don't know what you've got against him."

Erin shrugged. Why did she struggle so much with Jay? He had some good qualities, but he was the very definition of an alpha male. Even though she was used to alpha men in her family, it was different when they were her father and brothers who were so protective of her—almost too protective sometimes, which was why it often sucked to be the youngest Davenport *and* a girl. She'd also had a terrible run-in with an alpha male at college, a memory she kept buried way beneath the surface. Something about Jay's confidence struck a difficult note in her, something she'd rather not face.

"It's not that I have anything against him," she said finally. "He's all the things that make him a great agent. He's just so loud and pushy and in your face. I feel lost when he's around, as though if I speak, no one can hear me."

The smile dropped from Mila's face. "You're right

about his persistence. He's like a dog with a bone when an idea gets hold of him. He didn't shut up about making a movie about Hersch's life until we finally agreed. Though, in fairness, it's going to be a really good movie."

"Oh, I'm sure of it," Erin said. As a reporter, she knew that Herschel's life story would touch the hearts of everybody watching it. He had gone through a major trauma when his space shuttle had splashed down in the ocean, and he'd almost died. With Mila's help, he was getting over his paralyzing fear of the water.

"I guess I'm drawn to persistence in a person," Mila said. "You should see how well Hersch is doing with his surfing. He just doesn't give up. I can see the moments when he's having to fight his demons to get out there, but he does it." She paused and gave Erin a searching look. "Sometimes you just have to get out there."

Tessa caught the look and softened her voice. "Jay has been very supportive of my career as well as Arch's. And you know, he's got a surprisingly sensitive side." They both stared at her until she added, "He just hides it well." A crease formed between her eyebrows. "Personally, I think Jay dates women who don't challenge him."

Erin was surprised at how much Tessa had seen, because she herself was considered the perceptive one of the family. But she had to give full credit to her new sister-in-law, because that's exactly what she thought about Jay too. The guy who thrived on a challenge avoided them when it came to women. However, Tessa hadn't been around Jay for as long as they had. She didn't know his dating history. Jay's girlfriends were all models and all had a certain look: very tall, very beautiful, very thin. While Erin was absolutely certain there were loads of women modelling who were also extremely intelligent and well informed, Jay never chose those ones. She suspected he didn't want to be challenged by a woman whose opinions might clash with his own. So he dated a string of women who were interchangeable and, apart from their undeniable beauty, sort of forgettable—at least, the ones she'd met over the years.

When she said so, Mila laughed. "Sadly, that's true. He even demonstrated it to us once."

Tessa glanced between the sisters as though they were teasing her. "I don't believe you."

Erin couldn't resist the opportunity to make the two women laugh. She put down her cappuccino, stood, and tried to make her five-foot-three frame as tall as possible. She pushed out her chest and swaggered up to Tessa, whose pretty blue eyes had widened slightly. She tilted up Tessa's chin with one finger. Then she said, in a husky voice that badly imitated Jay, with her best smoldering gaze, "Has anyone ever told you that you have the most beautiful blue eyes? No, don't look away. It would be a crime. Like covering up the Mona Lisa."

Mila laughed so hard she clutched her stomach. "It's true. That's what he does. Jay says it works often enough that he's never changed his pitch. Except sometimes he compliments a woman's smile, or her skin. He's so used to making deals that he even looks at getting laid as closing the deal."

Tessa stared at Mila, aghast. "But you're in sales and you're not like that."

"I am altogether classier than Jay. But I do think he is mellowing, Erin."

Tessa looked over at Erin as she seated herself once more. "I don't know. I could see you with someone like Jay. Don't they say opposites attract? I mean, look at me and Arch."

Erin shook her head. "You guys are the unicorn romance—the perfect couple."

"And what about Mila and Hersch?" Tessa continued, a sweet, sly grin forming at the corners of her mouth.

Erin threw up her hands. "Okay, okay, you've given me two examples of people who lucked out. I'd say that's way above average."

Mila shook her head. "Actually, if you count all of Smith Sullivan's siblings and cousins, it seems that finding true love isn't all that crazy, even when the odds seem stacked against the couple."

Erin sighed loudly and rolled her eyes. "The Sullivans are the ultimate anomaly. All so blissfully in love. I mean, I'm thrilled for them, of course, but I'm just not convinced it's going to happen for everyone. Especially me."

"Good things come in sets of three," Tessa said quietly.

Erin didn't share her optimism. She wasn't like Mila, who was more than happy to be the center of attention, and she wasn't an artist like Tessa, who had to accept some degree of public interest in her work. No, she was much quieter than both these women and sometimes that meant she faded into the background. But the background was where she liked to dwell. There she could people-watch and try to understand her fellow humans a little better. Those observation skills made her good at her job, writing about people all day long in the newspaper. Even if she wanted to step into the limelight, it would never work. No, it was best to remain exactly as she was. Single and quiet and in the background, watching and learning. The true love Mila and Tessa had found was nowhere in sight, and that was fine. It wasn't her turn.

She played for a moment with a silver ring she wore. "I would never, ever in a million years be with Jay."

"When did you get to be so tough?" Mila wanted to

know. She put her coffee mug down and turned to Erin as though there were something she was missing.

The only person she'd nearly told about that awful experience in college was Mila. But she'd never quite found the words. Instead, she'd buried that memory deep, deep down and felt most of the time as though she'd recovered and moved on. . . except that pushy alpha men who tried to get close to her tended to get pushed away fast.

Erin took another sip of her cappuccino and decided to divert the attention back to the house sale. "Well, maybe I'll be invited to the housewarming party and I'll finally see inside that house."

"No need to wait. I have to drop off the extra set of keys. Do you want to come and have a private viewing?"

She couldn't imagine anything she wanted more. So long as she didn't have to see the new owner. "Will Jay be there?"

"No. He's in LA until tomorrow. That's what he told me."

Erin couldn't turn down an opportunity to see inside the home she'd admired from afar for so long—especially before it got into the hands of Jay Malone and he filled it with lingerie models. She had a relatively flexible schedule at work, and today the editorial meeting wasn't until one.

The temptation was too great to resist.

"I'd love to," she said with a grin.

Chapter Two

Since Erin had walked to their morning coffee date, Mila drove her to Jay's new house. She always felt at home in her sister's SUV because it was the perfect encapsulation of Mila's personality: smart enough that she could impress clients and take them to view houses, but with plenty of room for surfboards and wetsuits. Anywhere Mila could be herself, Erin felt more like herself, too.

What, she wondered, made her so interested in the idea of a home? For as long as she could remember, Erin had felt a deep curiosity about other people's homes—how they were decorated, the objects chosen to fill the rooms—even what was in a stranger's fridge. Partly it must have been down to her natural inquisitive nature as a journalist, but maybe it was more than that. Her parents, Howie and Betsy, had created a beautiful home for their six children. A true family home. Perhaps, deep down, Erin possessed an innate desire to do the same.

As the house came into view, Erin could hardly

believe she was about to see inside. She didn't know why she loved *this* house, of all the gorgeous houses on Scenic Drive. It wasn't the flashiest, it wasn't the biggest, but to her it was perfect. Made of Carmel stone that almost glowed when the sun shone, it had been built in the thirties and reflected the Art Deco craze that had swept the town, with its sensational Deco-style windows. As it was built on a corner lot, nearly every room would have ocean views. She couldn't imagine anything more peaceful.

Mila parked and they headed up the path to the house. As Mila unlocked the door, excitement bubbled up in Erin. She stepped inside and sighed with satisfaction. It was as gorgeous inside as she'd imagined. As she'd suspected, the living room looked directly over the ocean. There was a beautiful stone fireplace, high ceilings, and since no one was living there yet, it was empty of furniture. Her imagination began to run wild and she knew exactly how she would decorate this place if it were hers. It begged for comfy Mission-style furniture, maybe a Tiffany lamp or two. Soft, warm lighting and huge bookcases to line the walls. And over there was the perfect place for a cozy armchair, where she might unwind in the evenings with a good book and a glass of good red wine. Mila gave her the spiel about square footage but Erin was too busy soaking in the atmosphere of the place to care about numbers. Down the hallway, she was delighted to find a room obviously built as a library, with floor-to-ceiling built-in bookshelves. Would Jay put his comic books in them? Or his model train collection?

There was a beautiful big gourmet kitchen, and across the hall was a room that looked out into a private garden filled with lush plants and silvery succulents.

Mila said, "This will be Jay's office," though it was pretty obvious it had been set up by the last people as an office too. There were still marks in the carpet where the desk had been, and enough power outlets in the wall to run the technology for a pretty big company.

"Do you know why the previous owners sold this place?" Erin asked. "I can't imagine ever wanting to leave."

Mila gave a shrug. "They wanted something bigger, if you can believe it."

Erin shook her head. This place had more than enough space for everything she'd ever dreamed.

As they climbed the oak staircase to the next level, Mila said, "There are six ensuite bedrooms. I wasn't sure Jay would want that many, but he seemed really pleased. He said he can invite friends and family and maybe some of his top clients to stay."

Erin's eyes grew wider as they walked into the master bedroom—probably the nicest room she'd ever seen in her life. Period. It was positioned to have the most glorious view of the ocean, with its shimmering, green-tinged waves and rocky alcoves, all framed by the green leaves of ancient trees. There was something incredibly romantic about the Deco arched windows framing the vista. It was as though she'd stepped inside an old novel full of martini glasses and swing dancing and late-night cigars. The crown jewel was the beautiful Deco fireplace in one wall, though it had been converted to gas at some point.

"Wow," she breathed and then glanced at Mila. "I think this bedroom is bigger than my whole apartment."

"I know, right?"

Mila didn't live in as small a space as Erin did, but her two-bedroom fairytale cottage would fit inside Jay's new house about four times.

She was about to ask to see the rest of the bedrooms when the front door banged shut.

She gazed at Mila in horror and grabbed her arm. "Who's that?"

Mila looked worried. "The only other person who has a key is Jay. He must have come back early. I'm sure he won't mind, Erin."

Now she heard footsteps on the stairs, almost like a horror movie, except this wasn't a scary monster—it was a brash Hollywood agent. She was shot through with mortification. Jay was about to discover her snooping around his new home.

She'd almost prefer the scary monster.

Sure enough, Jay's tall, broad-shouldered frame filled the doorway. He'd yet to take off his Ray-Ban sunglasses, and he cut a striking figure in a pair of designer jeans and a polo shirt that showed off his powerful arms. He walked straight into the bedroom, finally lowering his sunglasses. He didn't look annoyed or even surprised to see them. If anything, he looked pleased.

"Mila, Erin, good to see you. I saw your car out front."

Erin was absolutely tongue-tied and could feel herself blushing. To be found touring his house when he wasn't even there seemed completely inappropriate. But Jay didn't seem the least bit put out. His rugged face was tanned, his expression confident. Although she didn't find him to be as good-looking as her sister and Tessa did, she could see the appeal for some people. He had an intense sexuality about him. He had started to go bald early and so kept his head shaved. Somehow it made him look more virile.

Mila shook Jay's hand warmly. "I was just dropping off your extra set of keys and Erin was with me, so I gave her a tour." She shot a quick look at Erin and added, "But I need to get going. Can you show Erin around? She hasn't even seen the garden yet."

Erin started to back away and was about to say she'd rather catch a ride to her editorial meeting with

Mila, when Jay replied, "Sure. I'd be happy to." He gave Erin a wide smile, showing off his straight, white teeth. "You're the first person to see my new house. I can't wait to hear what you think."

His tone was so earnest and he was so obviously delighted that she didn't have the heart to refuse.

★ ★ ★

Jay felt like pinching himself every time he walked into his new home. The light-years between where he'd come from and where he was now shocked even him. And of the few who would appreciate the house as much as he did, he suspected Erin was one. He bet she would appreciate the quality and the old-school charm the way he did.

When the front door closed behind Mila, he grinned at his unexpected guest. "This is my favorite room in the house. The best views are from this bedroom. And believe me, the sunsets are amazing. Incredible. I mean, I walked in here and all I could think of was hot sex."

Erin's mouth fell open and she took a step back. "Jay!"

"What? Am I oversharing? Surely we've known each other long enough for you to know I'm not a virgin." He laughed, a little taken aback by Erin's reaction. Sometimes he said things without realizing how they might be taken.

"Definitely oversharing," Erin said in a prim and proper way. He found himself grinning down at Archer's kid sister. In truth, he'd always thought of her as someone a bit younger to tease. Although now, looking at her standing in the middle of his empty bedroom with a slight blush on her cheeks, he felt a flicker of something else, something he'd denied to himself over the years, shutting down the thought as soon as it appeared.

But with her petite frame silhouetted against the window, he realized Erin Davenport was beautiful. Really beautiful. How had he not seen this so clearly before? He frowned at himself. Surely he was not attracted to Archer's kid sister. He liked Erin, he respected her intelligence and the way she saw things that other people didn't notice, but no way could he ever have feelings for the sister of one of his top clients. Archer would actually kill him and bury his body in the Big Sur wilderness, and he wouldn't blame his client and friend. They'd been through a lot together. Archer probably knew more about his personal life than he was comfortable with. Jay knew that his string of women was longer than most, and even though he always tried to keep things casual, to be absolutely clear that he was married to his work and his clients would always come first, he'd left the odd broken heart in his wake.

He stood by the window for a moment, still a little

stunned that this was really going to be his view every day, then turned to Erin and suggested they continue the tour. He walked out of the bedroom and she followed more slowly. He couldn't stop himself from asking if Mila had told her there were six bedrooms. Erin nodded.

He knew he sounded as though he were bragging, but every time he was reminded of the house's size, he flashed back to his childhood home—a roach-infested apartment with no dad around and a drug-addicted mother who was barely hanging on. They had mostly lived on the meals he'd learned to cook when he was about seven. Probably about the time he learned to hustle. He could usually get an extra-large portion of the school lunch by making nice to the lunch ladies. He soon learned which grocery stores threw out produce that was going bad or packaged goods that were stale. And, while he wasn't proud that he'd had to steal money from his mom when she was passed out, he'd managed to keep them both alive.

Until he couldn't.

He pushed the unhappy memories away, wondering why his mind would even go there when his life now was everything that frightened and unhappy boy had dreamed of. For a fleeting second, he wished his mom were still alive. He had so much money now he could have put her in rehab, got her the help she needed. Though, deep down, he knew it wouldn't have succeeded.

He walked Erin down the hall and pointed out the bedrooms and the bathrooms, each of which had been painted in a different color. He was hoping she might share her ideas about the place. Erin had great taste. In fact, she was one of the classiest women he knew.

Instead, she just nodded again, then glanced at her watch. "I should really get going. I have an editorial meeting."

His spirits drooped a little. "Come on, the *Sea Shell* can do without you for ten more minutes." He didn't know why, but he didn't want to be alone in this big, echoing house that had no furniture in it yet. He liked having Erin here; the Davenports were as close to family as he'd ever had. It made him happy that the first two people who'd seen it with him were the two Davenport sisters.

When they got to the fifth ensuite bedroom she asked, "What do you want all these bedrooms for?"

He gave a stock answer. "Friends and family. Really special clients." He didn't share that secretly, he dreamed of filling these bedrooms with children. He didn't know where or when he was going to find the kind of woman he actually wanted to settle down with, but he had this feeling that it was the next step for him. Jay had always liked to have the next step planned out.

She gazed around. "It's architecturally brilliant, but strangely, at the same time it feels more like a family home."

Jay smiled a small smile. Once again, Erin had seen through him. He shrugged. "Maybe. But the minute Mila showed me this house I knew it was The One."

She looked slightly puzzled. "Really? I wouldn't have chosen this house for you."

He felt a little taken aback, almost offended. "Why not?"

She seemed to choose her words carefully. "It's not flashy enough."

His eyebrows shot up. "I'm not always flashy. That's so not fair."

Humor lit up her hazel eyes, which were fringed with thick, fluttery lashes. "Yes, you are." She began to tap the fingers of her left hand with the index finger of her right. "You drive the most expensive car I've ever seen—all your clothes are custom made—you never buy a T-shirt off the rack—you fly to Milan once a year for suits and shoes."

He laughed. "Come on, short stuff. You know that's just for my image. As I told Arch when he first asked me to be his agent—when I had zero experience and he didn't have much more as an actor—in Hollywood, and frankly in life, image is everything."

They walked down the stairs and Jay lingered by the library archway. "Apart from the master bedroom, this is my favorite room in the whole place."

Erin's face said it all.

"What? You think I don't read?" Again, Jay found

himself offended just by her expression.

Erin looked a little flushed. "Come on, you're a movie guy."

She wasn't to know, but Erin had hit a real sore spot. Jay was self-educated, and in fact had taught himself to read using cereal boxes and his mom's gossip magazines.

"Do you know how many scripts I read in a week?" Jay shot back. Then he softened. It wasn't the first time someone had believed him to be all talk and a fat wallet. "But that's not all. I have enough books to fill this room twice over. In fact, I'll have to have more bookshelves built in the living room."

Erin still looked a little incredulous, so he explained how he'd started reading scripts at an early age, then progressed to devouring every screenwriting book before discovering the literary greats of the twentieth century. "It wasn't long before I was going even further back and enjoying Plato and Socrates. Now I read a lot of modern philosophers."

He could see Erin absorbing this information and he stiffened, waiting for another jibe. Instead, she said, "I can't wait to see your library. I guess some of the philosophers were also great negotiators, and so are you."

He stared at her for a moment, searching her expression for a sign that she was teasing him. But her eyes were wide and earnest. It was the nicest thing she'd ever said to him, aligning his work and his outlook with those of the great philosophers. Heck, it was probably the nicest thing *anyone* had ever said to him.

He smiled at her and tried to push down that flash of attraction that was growing now. He studied Erin again, the strawberry blonde hair tied up in a messy ponytail, no makeup, casual clothes. She was nothing like the models he was used to dating, who shapeshifted according to the latest fashion, surprising him by turning up to dinner with a blunt bob and bleached eyebrows or transforming from a curly redhead to a siren with straight jet-black hair. For the longest time, he'd found it seductive to be kept on his toes this way, but looking now at Erin—the familiarity of her, how comfortable she was in her own skin—he realized it was sexy as hell. He had always respected her smarts and the way she could read people. It had made him extra careful about keeping up his tough front when she was around. He didn't want her sussing out his more than humble beginnings.

He took a deep breath and told himself to snap out of it. This was Arch's little sister. About as close to a NO GO area as it got. Besides, if Erin was starting to see that he was more than her big brother's Hollywood agent, he didn't want to say anything clumsy that might change her mind. The way she was looking at him now felt too good to jeopardize.

Chapter Three

From his bedroom window, Jay watched Erin walk at a quick pace down Scenic Drive on her way to work. Beyond her diminishing figure was the stunning view of Carmel's beach and ocean—worth every one of the many millions he'd spent on his new place. He had barely thought twice about parting with so much dough—this house was everything he'd dreamed of since he was a kid. It had been especially fun showing Erin around. The ten minutes he'd spent talking to her had been the most interesting he'd had in months. He certainly hadn't got intellectual remarks from the last woman he'd dated, whose only opinion about his new house was that it was *roomy*, but in all fairness, her brains hadn't been her chief attraction.

He'd made a point of never dating actresses—they could be clients one day and he never crossed that line. So she had been another in a long line of lingerie models who showed no hint of wanting to break into Hollywood.

Erin might not be centerfold material, but watching her walk down Scenic Drive, he was aware again of that nagging pull of attraction. She might challenge him and offer him stimulating conversation in his own home. It was something to think about. Except it wasn't. She was Arch's little sister. He allowed himself to watch her until she was out of sight, and then went over the furniture and interior design plans. He wanted to be fully furnished and move-in ready asap.

When the doorbell rang an hour or so later, he almost didn't answer it. Hardly anyone knew he was here, but since he was always available to his clients, there was always the possibility that one of them had tracked him down. He jabbed a couple of buttons on the unfamiliar security videocam until it flickered to life and there was Archer Davenport, grinning up at the camera as though it was there just for him.

Jay grinned back, put down the script he was reading, and headed for the door. He always had time for Archer. He was one of his most lucrative and, frankly, favorite clients. Also, they'd been a team from the beginning. As he walked downstairs his mind flashed back to the very early days of his career and the day Arch had first brought him home for Thanksgiving.

At that time, Arch had been a struggling actor and, like many hopefuls in LA, was a waiter trying to break into the movies. He'd discovered a part that was perfect for him, but he'd yet to secure an agent—and no agent, no part. That's where Jay came in. He was also working at the restaurant. They'd become good friends, charming the all-female tables and sharing tips, and, after mulling over Arch's dilemma, Jay had had one of those lightbulb moments. He figured that since Arch had natural talent, all he needed was the prestige of an agent. Why not Jay? All he had to do was to create a fancy-looking letterhead and start telling everybody in Hollywood how great his clients were.

So that was exactly what he did. He took to the role like a fish to water, knowing that confidence and self-belief and a lot of hustle was the recipe for success in Hollywood. Arch and Jay worked into the small hours of the night making the most of Archer's meager credits to create a stellar resume. He'd starred in the high school play and the way Jay sold it, he sounded like he'd brought down the house on Broadway. He'd done a couple of commercials, one for tube socks and one for an acne cream, and again Jay made him sound like a major celebrity.

Arch wavered a couple of times, but Jay wouldn't let him back down. He'd said, "Archer, Hollywood is all about creating an image and selling it. That's all we're doing with you." And then, "You're sure you can play the part?"

"Yes," Arch had said without hesitation.

Jay leaned forward, excitement buzzing through his bloodstream like he'd mainlined sugarcane, and said, "Can you blow them out of the water with how well you nail that audition?"

Arch had jumped to his feet and thrown his fist in the air. "Hell, yeah."

"Then I accept you as my first client."

Arch got the part and kept Jay as his agent. Soon, Arch's career was doing well enough that they could both quit the restaurant business. Jay scooped up a few more talented hopefuls and the rest was movie history. As the two of them told that story over the Thanksgiving table, everyone had laughed. But Jay also recalled with acute embarrassment how intimidated he'd been by the Davenport family. Mila, with her flashy surfing career, and even fifteen years ago, Damien was already on his way to fame and fortune. But they had been so warm and welcoming that he'd soon begun to feel at ease with this family in a way he'd never experienced before.

It was a happy memory and as he opened the door, he greeted Arch with a big grin. "Good to see you, man." He extended his hand for a bro handshake and then a quick manly hug—two claps on the back.

"I saw you drive past earlier," Arch said. "Figured I'd better get a tour of the house before you head home to LA."

Jay's grin faded. Was that how Arch saw him? As somebody who was going to use this gorgeous waterfront place like a weekend getaway? The longer he spent here, the more he felt as though Carmel-by-the-

Sea could be a fresh chapter for him, in this home he never would have dreamed would be his one day, back when he was a kid and had nothing.

"I figure I can do a lot of my business here and pop back to LA when I have to." He paused and then grinned again. "It's a lot nicer here, I think you'll agree." He took a step back and invited Arch into the Art Deco foyer.

As he gazed around, the expression on Arch's face said it all.

"I am definitely paying you too much if you can afford this," Arch said, laughing half in amazement. "I'm supposed to be the movie star and this is bigger than my place."

Jay couldn't help but feel a stab of pride, but he covered it with their well-worn banter. "Face it, bro, I'm better at business than you are."

"That's true. Also, I wouldn't have the modest wealth I've managed to accumulate if it wasn't for you."

He grinned. "My thoughts exactly."

He began his second tour of the day, noting that Arch was much less enthused by the built-in shelving in the library than Erin. He couldn't wait to fill those shelves with books. When he got to the master bedroom, a massive space begging for an enormous bed, he took a good long minute to enjoy the view. "No place like home," Arch said, gazing out at the ocean.

"There's just something about Carmel that nowhere else tops. Maybe it can even crack a tough LA nut like you."

Jay wasn't a sentimental guy, so he kept quiet, but inside he was thinking that Carmel-by-the-Sea had already hooked him. Was already reeling him in.

Turning to gaze around the bedroom, Arch raised an eyebrow and asked, "Okay, no bed yet. But where's Miss November?"

Jay grimaced. "It was Miss April, and she's no longer in the picture. We weren't compatible."

"Don't tell me you're turning over a new leaf?"

Somehow, Jay didn't find the comment funny. In fact, it had been playing on his mind all morning, ever since Erin had teased him about dating lingerie models.

Arch said, "I was just joking, but you're not laughing."

All Jay could say was, "Maybe I am." He looked around the room. "You're the third Davenport I've had in my house this morning. Mila was showing it to Erin when I got back early from LA."

Arch gave him a hard look, his earlier playfulness draining away. "I get that you just moved here and you're single, but Mila's all but engaged, and as for Erin, don't even think about going there."

Jay laughed easily. "Believe me, I respect my gonads too much to put them in jeopardy by going near one of your sisters."

He said the words with conviction, but in truth he had to admit that for the first time since he'd met her, he'd seen Erin not as Arch's cute and nerdy kid sister, but as an interesting woman. Which was weird. Too weird to keep thinking about. He wasn't the kind of guy to wade into murky territory—not even in his own thoughts. No. He was confident about making fast decisions. They'd almost always been the right ones.

So why did it feel like his head and heart were playing tricks on him? And why wasn't Arch's warning having its intended effect?

He quickly changed the subject to something safer—business. "How are you getting on with *Shock Tactics*?"

Arch flexed his impressive biceps. "I'm working out like a maniac. Tessa was hard enough on me when she was helping my broken leg heal, but now she seems to have taken it upon herself to be my personal trainer, and that woman is tough as anything. She's breaking me." Arch said this with such affection that Jay couldn't help but smile. They both knew Arch could have chosen any of the top personal trainers in the world to prepare for this role, but instead he'd chosen his new wife to take on the task.

"Whatever Tessa is doing, it's working. You're ripped. They're barely going to need any prosthetics to beef you up."

Arch nodded. "That's the idea."

"How's the script looking? Have they made any significant changes after the table read?"

Arch shrugged. "It's pretty good. Better than I thought it would be."

"I'm telling you right now, this has all the makings of a *Terminator*-style classic." He tapped his nose. "I can smell a hit."

Arch, who usually laughed at Jay's unwavering confidence, opened his eyes slightly wider. "Really?"

"Really." He couldn't explain how he did it, but it was a kind of superpower, being able to spot a hit. Of course, there was the odd fluke, but his track record was remarkable. And his gut was telling him that he and Arch were both going to make a nice chunk of change when the movie—and its sequels—went on to become legendary. As he liked to tell anybody who'd listen, especially his clients, that was why he got paid the big bucks.

Arch looked thoughtful. "What about this biopic of Herschel Greenfield? You think that's going to be a hit too?"

He was less sure of this one. But he knew one thing—the story needed to be told. "When I first saw Herschel Greenfield at Tessa's art show, there was something about the guy. He's a real American hero, but he's humble too. The guy's seen things that only a handful of people will ever get to see or experience. He nearly died coming back to Earth. And it's not fiction, it's real."

Arch nodded slowly. "I think the heart of the film is his honesty about being afraid to get back in the water. And how learning to surf helped him overcome that."

Jay absolutely agreed. "And the fact that you can surf makes you the perfect person to play him."

"Plus, I have easy access since he lives nearby and is crazy in love with my sister. Also, I genuinely like and respect him. He's brilliant, but never shows off, and his fitness is off the charts. Do you know how many Iron Man competitions he's done?"

Jay grinned. He was thrilled that Arch and Hersch were getting on so well. It would make it much easier for Arch to take on the part. He was probably picking up Hersch's mannerisms and way of speaking without even realizing it. He doubted that the Herschel Greenfield biopic would ever become a massive hit, but it would be worthwhile, and definitely profitable.

When they'd finished the tour, Arch turned down coffee, which was pretty much all Jay had in the house, and said he had to get home. "It's workout time."

Jay walked him out and they clapped each other on the back. But as he was leaving, Arch said, "This is a great house you've got here, and I'm super happy to see you in the neighborhood." He paused for a moment. "I'm sorry about Miss April. It would be nice to see you share this place with someone new." Arch gave him a penetrating look. "Someone *completely* new."

Jay gave a slightly forced laugh. "Copy that," he said as he waved good-bye.

He knew what Arch was implying—that if he had any thoughts about making a move on his sister, then stop, pronto. But something about being told not to do something was enough to push Jay in the opposite direction. He did not like being told what to do.

As Jay closed the front door, he turned to take in his new house and found his mind returning to his childhood home. They'd barely had any possessions, but they always had a TV. His mom would pass out watching old romantic movies, but he'd sit there until the credits rolled. He'd fallen in love with movies when dreams were all he had. And now he was living the dream. But it wasn't a dream, it was reality. And maybe, like those movies, the women who could pose for centerfolds or sell lingerie in fancy catalogs had been a dream too, and at the age of thirty-five, he was finally waking up. He didn't want women he chose because of their looks and hot bodies. He wanted somebody real. Somebody he could talk to.

He liked the way Erin had challenged him today, the way she'd made assumptions about him—that he was shallow and incapable of reading a book all the way to the end. He wanted to show her that there was more to him. Frankly, he'd never had to try very hard with women. Now, he realized he didn't want that anymore. He wanted someone like Erin.

He closed his eyes briefly. Someone *like* Erin, someone *completely new*, he reminded himself, even as deep inside a little voice suggested that maybe the woman he really wanted *was* Erin.

And didn't that make his life a whole lot more complicated?

Chapter Four

Erin had stayed much longer than she'd intended to at Jay's and now she had to hurry if she was going to pick up her dog Boswell and get to work on time. She followed a fairly loose schedule, as she was often out reporting on events or talking to the local residents, so she tended to come and go as she pleased, making sure she hit all her deadlines.

But today was their editorial meeting, and she was never late for that. Her editor did not take kindly to people showing up late to her meetings.

As she entered her one-bedroom apartment, she tried not to notice how small it felt after Jay's mansion. Buzzy bounded over to greet her and she bent to pat him. He had been a rescue dog, featured in the *Sea Shell*, and she couldn't resist rescuing him herself when she saw his photo. He was a mix of breeds, but closely resembled a cockapoo with his shaggy, toffee-colored hair and large, soulful eyes. It had been love at first sight.

"Hello, you," she said affectionately. "We're off to

work now. I just have to grab a few things."

Buzzy barked happily. He was excited to go any-where Erin went.

As she moved about her apartment, she tried again to take pleasure in how compact it was. To Buzzy, she said, "We don't need an ensuite bathroom, do we now?" And then, "This Formica countertop is practical. The whole place is quick to clean. And who needs a home gym when you have hills to walk and waves to surf?"

Buzzy barked his agreement.

"Okay, my view is of a schoolyard and not as in-spiring as the ocean, but I'm happy to have it." When Erin bought the place, she had been worried that the noise of the children might disturb her on days she worked on her articles at home. But on days their laughter and singing travelled on the breeze, she found it made her happy. She would let herself imagine what it might be like to walk her own child across the road to school and wave good-bye at the school gates. These reveries always made her smile, although she never let herself get carried away. She was about as single as they came and for now, that was just fine.

She clipped on Buzzy's leash. "I have you, and that's enough," she said, rubbing his soft coat.

But for the first time, she wondered if that was still true. She looked around her apartment again and realized it felt a little lonely. What would Jay make of it? If he were here, he'd be sure to take up all the air in the room, like he always did, but strangely, she thought he might fit in. He always did at the Davenport family home.

She had mixed feelings about Jay ending up with her dream house, the one she'd never been able to walk past without imagining herself inside. On a reporter's pay, there was no way she could afford that house—even if she saved every cent of every paycheck for the rest of her life. But Jay had simply said, "I want it," and it was his. If she had chosen a different career, she might have been in that position too, but she'd always known her path wasn't like those of her movie-star brother or her rock-star brother or their agent-to-the-stars friend. She didn't want to be a top Realtor like Mila or a house builder or an app developer like Nick and Finn. She was a writer. It was all she'd ever wanted and in her small way, she was proud of what she'd accomplished.

Like all Carmel locals, she'd loved the *Sea Shell* since she was a little girl and had been thrilled to begin working there as an intern when she came back to Carmel with her English degree from Stanford. She'd worked her way up to the role of main reporter and one day she hoped to be the editor of the *Sea Shell*, maybe even own it. That was a dream she could conceivably accomplish with a lot of hard work—to say nothing of determination to make it on her own. She didn't want to ask any of her rich relatives for help. That was important to her too. Whatever she accomplished, Erin wanted to do it with her own talent and her own money.

As she locked the door behind her, her thoughts turned to the meeting ahead. Pat Sinclair had been a top editor at the *Chicago Tribune* and then, burned out from stress, she'd arrived in Carmel-by-the-Sea with her wife for a holiday and fallen in love with it. When she'd taken over as editor of the *Sea Shell*, no one could believe it. Erin had given the woman six months before she ran screaming back to the bright lights and buzz of Chicago, but it hadn't worked out that way. The editorial standard had definitely risen since Pat had taken over, but she'd kept the heart of the *Sea Shell*—the local stories, the Dog of the Week, the weekly advice column—and if anything, the paper was a lot better now than it had been. Erin admired the heck out of her and wanted to learn all she could from Pat while she helmed the paper.

Erin let the midmorning sun warm her cheeks and thought how lucky she was that her job let her bring her dog to work. Buzzy loved the *Sea Shell* office. It was situated on a cobbled side street with a walk-in front office where people could place classified ads or drop off press releases for local events.

They walked in and Buzzy sat immediately, his whole hind end wagging as he waited for the treat that

Bobby, the receptionist, kept for the dogs who came through the door. As soon as Erin crossed the threshold into the editorial office, a wave of happiness filled her as she took in the familiar sight of the desks cluttered with multiple computer screens and stacks and stacks of paper. To an outsider it might have looked a mess, but everyone who worked there knew exactly where everything was. It was like a family home in that way, with all its quirks that made little sense to anyone but its family members.

Pat came out of her office, already going over the week's schedule as she walked to the conference room. She ran a hand through her short mop of salt-and-pepper hair. As always, she was chewing nicotine gum, caught as she was in a perpetual struggle to quit smoking that she never quite seemed to nuke. Pat liked to blame her wife, to whom she'd been married for ten years, and who staunchly refused to give up the habit. Next to her was tall, shy Clark, the photographer, with whom Erin had become firm friends over the years; Louis the editorial assistant; and Carrie, the junior reporter and copy editor. Erin took her place at the long table they used for editorial meetings, among other things. She sat next to Pat, who was looking more irritated than usual.

Carrie wanted to pitch a story about a school funding shortfall, but Pat was scowling. "We need something new, something exciting," she said, interrupting Carrie. "We could have had a scoop on the *huge* story of an A-list actor getting married secretly right here in Carmel before flying off to *Scotland...*" She paused and shot Erin a hard look.

Uh-oh. Erin got a sinking feeling in her stomach.

"But sadly, that opportunity passed us by." She grabbed a pen, holding it like a cigarette, and began to twiddle it between her fingers.

Erin gulped and felt guilty. She admired Pat hugely and knew she was lucky to have such an incredible mentor, but surely she could understand that Erin couldn't—wouldn't—betray her family just for the sake of a scoop. Erin had been in a tough position, caught between her job and her duty to her family, but family would always win.

She stayed silent. Pat hated to hear excuses.

"Luckily," Pat continued, "I've managed to get something of a scoop myself."

At this, Erin perked up. A distraction from her misdemeanor. Perfect.

"I've had my ear to the ground and word is that another Hollywood hotshot has just bought one of the most expensive homes in Carmel." Pat's mouth twitched in its telltale way when she had a good story. Erin felt her heart sink into her sandals. She knew exactly what Pat was about to ask.

She turned to Erin. "Jay Malone is the latest in a string of Hollywood celebrities to buy a place in

Carmel-by-the-Sea. There's a good story here, Erin, and I want you to find it. What is driving this move? Who *is* Jay Malone? I want a full profile."

Erin felt backed into a corner. This was her punishment for not giving the *Sea Shell* the story of the year by offering up Arch and Tessa's secret wedding in Carmel before they jetted off to Scotland for the lavish public celebration. Jay wasn't family, so in Pat's mind he was fair game. Since he'd been Arch's agent forever, Pat knew Erin could get access. And who better than a family friend to get to the heart of a story?

She thought that Pat understood deep down that Erin had done what was right, but she couldn't let it go unchallenged. Interviewing Jay was her punishment. She got that, and the journalist side of her felt that Pat had handled the situation well. She only hoped she'd do as well when her time came to be editor.

But the idea of interviewing Jay made something stick in her throat. She didn't like to use her family connections in her work, and she was certain that Jay was far too busy making multimillion-dollar deals to spend time being interviewed for the local paper.

She swallowed. "He's probably very difficult to get hold of and won't be in Carmel very much—"

But Pat cut her off with an upraised hand before she could come up with any more lame excuses. "It's your job to convince Jay Malone to spare you some of his precious time."

Erin persisted, "Perhaps one of our freelancers might have a better chance? Jay is more likely to talk to someone he doesn't know—he's professional like that."

Pat shook her head. "Erin, I assigned the story to you and I expect a full profile for the next issue." She glanced down at her papers. "Now, what's the story with the school funding crisis?" she asked Carrie, and Erin knew she'd better get an interview with Jay. Or else.

Her mind turned to the tricky task ahead. How to even approach Jay for what ultimately amounted to a favor? What could she say? *Hey Jay, can I please invade your privacy because we have a personal connection and my editor wants your profile in our weekly community newspaper?* Jay's previous profiles had been in *Rolling Stone* and *Vanity Fair*. And once, memorably, in *GQ*, where he and Archer had done a joint interview.

She doubted he would be very impressed by the likes of the *Sea Shell*.

* * *

By the next evening, Erin was still processing Pat's request while balanced on a wave. Like a lot of her family, Erin tended to work out her problems on the surfboard. There was something about being out on the waves, sometimes near people, sometimes alone, but always separated from others so that her board felt like her own tiny island. She had to focus on her footwork, on wave patterns, on what other surfers around her were doing, but behind all that busy work, her brain could mull over whatever was bothering her.

She wasn't sure why it felt like such a big deal to interview Jay. She perfectly understood Pat's position—that Erin had withheld the scoop of the century from the *Sea Shell*. While Pat would probably have done the same thing in her place, and protected the privacy of her beloved brother, she still had to make an example of Erin.

Erin totally got that. But of all the punishments Pat could have come up with, did it have to be an interview with Jay Malone?

She'd thought about calling Mila to see if she wanted to surf with her, but somehow she knew she needed to work these problems out herself. Mila was already too invested in Jay—to the point of suggesting he might be a possible suitor. She didn't want to give her big sister any more ideas.

The best surf was not far from Jay's house. She could still recall that day not so very many months ago when Jay had been out surfing with them, and had said to her so confidently that one day he'd own one of those waterfront properties they could see from the waves. She remembered mocking him at the time. Those properties hardly ever came up for sale, and when they did, they tended to go so fast that Erin, who kept her ears pretty close to the ground in Carmel-by-the-Sea, often didn't even hear about them. So to discover that he'd made good on that promise, and in such a short time, was quite astonishing.

She shook her head as she rode in, gazing toward Jay's beautiful house. She might be astonished, but she wasn't surprised. Put her very determined sister together with the most single-minded man she'd ever met, and it was inevitable they were going to get what they wanted.

She paddled out and rode back in again, and out and in again, and then she just sat out for a while, watching the sun go down. It was so beautiful she didn't mind that she was getting cold, even in a wetsuit over her old black bikini. She hadn't reached for her surfing gloves or booties, though, which she now regretted. It was time she headed back.

She was still riding the waves when the lights came on in Jay's house. He was home.

Okay, she couldn't call herself a journalist and be such a weenie she couldn't ask a celebrity for an interview. She had to get a grip. She'd just catch another couple of waves, and then she'd text him. She'd keep it professional, making it clear she wasn't asking for a personal favor—even though obviously she was—and if he said no, at least she'd have tried.

Pat could not ask more of her than that.

* * *

Jay had once been the kind of workaholic who put other workaholics to shame. He'd learned to manage on four hours of sleep a night, five if he was sleeping in, and when he wasn't having to comply with his body's irritating need for rest, he was either working, working out, promoting the list of clients he had, or doing his damnedest to increase his list. When he looked back on those years, they were a blur. And then one day, he'd ended up in the ER thinking he was having a heart attack. He was only thirty-one, and after ruling out a heart attack, to his great relief, the ER doc had sat him down and read him the riot act.

It turned out his diagnosis wasn't that unusual: He was suffering from stress and burnout. Humiliatingly, what he'd thought had been cardiac arrest was in fact a panic attack. Naturally, no one, but no one, knew the truth. When he'd emerged from the hospital hours later, embarrassed and chastened, the doc's words rang in his ears.

"It was a panic attack *this* time. Consider it a warning. You keep going at the pace you are, and the next time you're in here it will be a heart attack for sure. You want to be dead at forty? Keep on doing what you're doing."

It was the kind of dialogue his actors said in movies, not something Jay Malone had ever expected to hear in real life.

However, he'd listened. It hadn't been easy, but

slowly he'd begun to change. He started eating better. He kept up his weightlifting routine, but dialed it back from seven days a week to three, and instead added in swimming, surfing, and wilderness hikes. He would make the effort to take in the beautiful vistas while he walked, listen to the birds sing. Sometimes he even stopped to smell a rose, or pat a dog. He had learned to reconnect with life.

It wasn't just his body that needed a change, it was his mind too. He'd always been a reader—it was how he'd educated himself. But instead of racing through Plato and Aurelius and Dickens in one sitting, as though he were taking a university of life crash course, he made the effort to slow down and absorb more of what he read. He expanded his choices, reading for pure pleasure rather than self-improvement. Sometimes poetry, sometimes a novel, sometimes a book on history or biology or astronomy, especially now that he was working with Herschel Greenfield.

To his surprise, he'd found he enjoyed old English detective novels written by people like Wilkie Collins and Agatha Christie, and passed whole evenings turning the pages with a small Scotch in hand (well, he couldn't be a complete angel). He let his staff take on more responsibility. He also changed his relationship to his phone. From being always on, he selectively switched it to Do Not Disturb. There were a few exceptions, of course. Archer Davenport and Smith

Sullivan could phone him day or night and he'd always pick up, but there weren't many other people who made that list. Not many at all.

By that time, he was already successful enough and rich enough that he didn't have to keep working if he didn't want to. But he did want to. He loved his work and the thought of giving it up never crossed his mind. Now, a few years later, he still worked hard, still enjoyed the finer things in life, but he made darned sure to take time for himself. Life was precious.

This evening was one of those prized quiet ones when he didn't have an event to attend or an important meeting and since his day was packed tomorrow, he was relaxing in the new leather chair in his library and re-reading Stephen Hawking's *A Brief History of Time*. Herschel had offered to clarify some points he hadn't understood the first time around.

That was another thing that had changed since his time in hospital. Before the panic attack, he'd exerted so much effort in trying to pretend he always knew everything. Now he'd learned that no one knew everything, and to his mind, a mark of wisdom was not being afraid to ask questions.

He settled his new silver-rimmed reading glasses on his nose, glanced with pleasure around his library, now stocked with books he loved or books he intended to read. His gaze moved to the window, where he noticed a lone surfer out on the water. He loved this view so much, he was always keeping track of who was out there and what they were doing. There'd been a group of them earlier, but now there was only one.

He could tell she was female, and as he watched, he suddenly, instinctively knew it was Erin Davenport.

Something about the way she moved, the way she stood, was as unique as a fingerprint. As she rode closer, her wet hair streamed out behind her, and even though he couldn't make out her face, he could picture the concentration etched across her usually smooth and unruffled brow.

He smiled. It was strangely comforting to know she was out there, enjoying herself. She was a superb surfer. Technically adept and elegant with it, too. As he watched, he came to realize how much Mila, who had been a world-famous champion surfer, had overshadowed her sister's abilities. Erin wasn't a pro-level surfer, but she was a darned good amateur.

How had he never noticed that before? And how much more had he never noticed?

He went back to his book, but every few minutes he checked on Erin again. She was still going, riding those waves with a confidence he admired. The more he watched, the more he finally saw how often Erin was overshadowed by her overachieving siblings, and yet it slowly dawned on him that hers was the voice he had unconsciously listened to all those years when the Davenport family were exchanging views—or arguing.

It was Erin who made the most sense.

He put his book down, unable to concentrate. She'd been out there a long time. The last of the sun was being swallowed in a teal horizon—she had to be getting cold. When he grew truly worried, he took action. He went up to the master bathroom and chose one of the super plush, fluffy gray towels from the custom towel warmer that he'd decided to always keep turned on. Tucking it under his arm, he headed out, crossed the street and reached the beach just as Erin was coming in.

As he walked closer, he could see she was shivering as she pulled off her wetsuit. Underneath she had on a black bikini and even in the dim light, he appreciated the curves of her petite frame.

Trying to be a gentleman, he averted his eyes and spoke in a low voice so as not to startle her. "Hi. I was getting worried about you."

She jumped slightly and turned, her eyes widening with recognition. "I got carried away." She shivered again. "Stayed out too long."

Without thinking to ask, he wrapped the still-warm towel around her shoulders. "You must be freezing," he said by way of explanation, trying not to notice how sweet she looked swamped in his oversized towel.

"Oh, wow," she said, pulling the towel tightly around her. "Thanks. You read my mind."

Briefly, he wondered if she was as conscious as he

that she'd been standing there in a bikini, but then shoved the thought from his mind. As she shivered again, it was all he could do not to scold her for staying out too long. What had she been thinking?

Instead he said, "Why don't you come to my place for hot chocolate? Warm up."

She looked a little embarrassed. "I don't want to bother you. I'm fine."

He held back a grin. Erin was so different from her siblings he sometimes forgot she was a Davenport and as stubborn as the rest of them. "Erin, your lips are blue and you're shivering. I'm not taking no for an answer."

He bent to gather up her things and then began the short walk back up to his house, trying to ignore how good it felt to be the one who could offer Erin some comfort.

Chapter Five

Watching Jay take down a tin of Ghirardelli chocolate powder and then select a copper pan from his extensive collection, Erin asked, "When did all your stuff arrive?"

"Yesterday and today. I worked with a designer Mila recommended and chose most of the stuff so it just had to be delivered, and I sent some of my personal possessions here too. It's been pretty intense, but I like to get things done fast."

With enough money you could get anything done, but even so, she was impressed. The house didn't look lived in, exactly, but it looked settled. Like a home.

In a huge bouquet of flowers on the kitchen island, a card read, *Welcome home.* She didn't even need to read it. She recognized the personalized cards that went with her sister's housewarming gifts.

Even his kitchen was completely outfitted, and she'd bet Jay hadn't taken a buggy around Safeway to stock up on food either. Erin laughed. "I feel like I'm on *MasterChef.*"

He grinned at her. "One of those guys is my client.

I asked him for a few tips once, but he refused to give me any." He tipped milk into the pan and then stood for a moment, staring at the range. "I'm gonna be honest. I haven't attempted to work this thing yet." He gestured at the extraordinary range, which looked like it cost more than her entire apartment. "Why don't you go have a hot shower while I figure it out?"

Erin laughed. Of course he didn't know how to work the range yet. He probably hadn't made his own hot chocolate in over a decade. A shower sounded like heaven right now, but accepting a warming drink was one thing. Getting naked in his house was another entirely.

"Don't be polite," he said, firmly but not unkindly. "We've known each other too long and your lips still look a little blue."

She hesitated, then said at last, "Okay, if you're sure you don't mind."

Upstairs, she chose one of the guest bathrooms, instinctively steering away from his gorgeous ensuite. Still, there was nothing shabby about the guest bathrooms either. She sighed as she stepped into the hot, pounding rain shower. Erin couldn't believe where the evening had taken her. She'd meant to surf for an hour max, just long enough to clear her head about Jay and the newspaper assignment. Now she was showering in one of his luxurious bathrooms, slowly feeling her body come back to life.

She'd been foolish to stay out so long and get so cold. Maybe even more foolish to allow Jay to all but rescue her. Still, she'd solved one problem. Now she wouldn't have to send him an awkward text to ask if he would mind being interviewed—she could do it in person.

And yet the bubble of nerves in her stomach hadn't disappeared. As she soaped her body with a creamy ylang-ylang gel, she was reminded of how odd she'd felt standing in front of Jay in her bikini, even though they'd been out surfing together on countless hot days over the years. She couldn't help but imagine herself through his eyes—eyes that had appreciated a hundred supermodels and lingerie models with their perfect, sculpted bodies. She wasn't ashamed of her own—she loved her small frame and her curves, but next to those gazelles she must have appeared unimpressive at best.

Then she shook her head. What did she care what Jay Malone thought?

She stepped out of the shower and rubbed her gleaming skin dry with another of his warm and fluffy towels. A pleasant tingling in her toes told her there must be underfloor heating beneath the slabs of white and gray marble.

As he'd insisted, she helped herself to the body lotion, feeling like she was in a high-end spa, taking the time to massage it into her skin. It smelled heavenly. But as she reached down to smooth it over her legs and thighs, the image of Jay's large hands came to mind. For a split second, she closed her eyes and imagined it was his fingers traveling across her skin. The image felt so good she shuddered with pleasure and then caught herself.

No, this was Jay. Her brother's brash, loud agent. What was she thinking? Mila and Tessa, as well as the hot water and steam, had gone to her head.

She dressed quickly, leaving her hair to air dry, and then made her way downstairs.

As she walked past the library, she couldn't help but peek in. The reading light was on and a book lay open on a side table, reading glasses beside it. She was almost certain she'd interrupted him reading.

Dammit, couldn't he have been doing something she really disliked, like watching sports?

Reading was her favorite activity in the whole world. She had a momentary vision of the two of them sitting in this library, both reading, maybe talking about what they read. Other women had wild sex fantasies about their men, but to Erin, the sexiest thing she could imagine was a man who read for pleasure. Then, that moment when they closed their books for the night and looked over at one another with a certain expression in their eyes, when all thoughts of reading would be forgotten.

She shook away the image and scolded herself.

When she walked into the kitchen, he said, "Perfect

timing," and poured warmed milk into two thick earthenware mugs, then gently dropped three marsh-mallows into the liquid.

When she took the first sip, she let out a deep sigh of bliss. It was perfect. Rich and creamy. She licked a melted marshmallow and a hint of chocolate from her lip. There was a pause and she searched her brain for something to say, sifting through subjects, but nothing felt right. For once, Jay was also quiet. It was weird, because they knew each other so well, but normally they were in a group. Until today they'd rarely—if ever—been alone together.

It was as though they were playing poker, both looking at their cards, thinking about what they might put down, what the other might have. But the trouble was the card she really needed to play was sort of a joker.

She might as well get it over with. "There's some-thing I need to ask you."

He looked surprised. "Okay. Shoot."

She took another sip of hot chocolate to buy herself some time. With her index finger, she poked at a marshmallow, watching it bounce up and down on the hot chocolate like a life raft. That way, she didn't have to look at him. "It's more of a favor, really."

"I'm listening."

"And it wasn't my idea."

"Noted."

Finally, she took the plunge. "My editor at the *Sea Shell* was understandably annoyed that I never told them about Arch getting married right here in Carmel."

"Your editor should know you'd never throw your brother under the bus like that," he said gravely.

"I think she does. But in her journalist's eyes, I denied the paper the scoop of the year."

She glanced up and saw that Jay was nodding and, without words, clearly understanding what she was getting at.

"She found out that you've moved here, and that you're Archer's agent." She paused. "She wants a profile piece on you. And she wants me to write it." She ended the last bit in a rush and waited for Jay's response. When it didn't come, she blurted, "You don't have to do it. The thing is, a lot of celebrities live here, and since a number of them are perfectly happy to be profiled in the paper, my editor insisted that I ask."

Jay was still silent. Erin could tell he was balking at the idea, but she wasn't entirely sure why. Yes, he was a busy man and wouldn't want to give up his valuable time, but he seemed troubled by the request. Strange. This was the man who loved an audience, who would talk to anyone and everyone. She didn't know what else to say, so she waited for Jay to speak.

Finally, after appearing to weigh a long list of pros and cons, he said, "I'd be happy to do it."

Erin blinked twice. Despite their long history, she'd been expecting him to say no. The little flutter in her chest told her that she'd been hoping he'd say yes. Was it simply because she didn't want to go back to her editor without a story, or was something else at play?

"Really?" she asked, not quite believing it. "I'd be so grateful. It might get me off the blacklist. Otherwise, I bet she assigns me to report on high school basketball. I don't even understand basketball."

Jay grinned. "Well we can't have that, can we? I'm free tomorrow, if you like."

Erin blinked again. Jay was *never* free. He must have sensed her desperation—since she needed this interview for the next issue, it had to happen this week. "Seriously? I know what that really means is that you're going to clear your schedule, and you've probably got several zillion-dollar contracts on the line for your clients right now."

"It's no big deal. I needed a breather while I moved in anyway. I'll tell my PA to keep everyone at bay for a while. They can wait a day."

Erin breathed out a huge sigh of relief. "I am so grateful," she said. "And would it be okay if a photographer came and took a couple of shots of you?"

"Of course." He was still smiling. "You never know—with all the movie stars moving to Carmel, I might pick up some clients."

She knew he turned away more clients than he

took on, but she appreciated his making it seem as though it were a mutual favor. She suggested a start time of eleven a.m. and he nodded.

"There's one more thing before I come tomorrow," she said.

He looked up, alarmed. "What is it?"

"Can I bring my dog? He usually comes to work with me and he hates to be alone."

Jay laughed, the alarm vanishing. "Of course. I love dogs. I've always wanted one, but I'm too busy."

With the business chat out of the way, they fell into their usual easy rapport, drinking hot chocolate in the kitchen and laughing about some of the funnier things that had happened at Archer's wedding in Scotland. Then suddenly she remembered his asking her to dance, and how comfortable they'd been together, how well they'd moved together. She hadn't seen that coming, any more than she'd seen that library coming.

In fact, she was beginning to realize there were aspects to Jay Malone that she'd never glimpsed before.

* * *

Jay offered to drive Erin home, but it turned out she had parked her car nearby. By the time they'd finished their hot chocolate, he felt so comfortable in her company that he'd been tempted to ask her to stay and hang out. He'd had a vision of them watching an old movie in his home theatre and it felt darned good. But then he remembered his earlier conversation with his oldest and one of his most valuable clients, Archer Davenport, who'd warned him to stay away from his sister.

Then there was the small matter of his own conflicted feelings. He didn't want to give Erin the wrong idea. He'd wanted them to watch a movie like old buddies, but what if she got the wrong impression? Or worse, what if, in the intimate setting, he got the wrong idea and let these new thoughts about Erin take the reins?

No, it was much better to say good-bye and tell her he'd see her tomorrow. Besides, he had an absolutely packed day of meetings to reschedule.

He wasn't sure why he'd told Erin he was completely free tomorrow. They both knew it was a lie. It was just that he'd been able to read her and could see how much she wanted to get back in her editor's good graces. He'd worked with enough journalists and enough media to know that stories were always time sensitive. He imagined even a weekly community newspaper like the *Sea Shell* tried to stay topical. Besides, it might be fun. It would be interesting to see Erin at work, to hear the kind of questions she'd ask him—especially with so little time to prepare. Maybe there was also a little pride at play. He wanted to show off his new house and, more than that, he wanted to fit in with his new community. It was important to him to be accepted in Carmel—it was already feeling like home in a way nowhere else ever had, even LA.

He quickly composed an email to his personal assistant, Gina, to reschedule all tomorrow's meetings. In less than a minute his phone flashed and he smiled. She was an excellent assistant.

Are you sick? Do you need me to call an ambulance?

He laughed out loud. Okay, he was a workaholic, but surely he wasn't that bad. He wondered what to tell her. He couldn't exactly say he was dumping meetings with studio heads to be interviewed for a community paper.

No, I have to do a favor for a friend.

It's not April Fool's Day or something, is it?

It's real. Huge thanks, you're the best.

Gina and her team would make everything work— that's why he hired the best and paid them well. Then, because he figured he'd earned the right, he went back to his library, settled in his favorite chair, put on his reading glasses, and picked up his book.

Chapter Six

Erin had tossed and turned all night, her mind racing. She'd sent Pat Sinclair a quick email telling her that she'd secured the interview for the very next day. Pat, in her usual way, didn't heap praise on Erin's head for doing such great work. Instead, she sent a list of questions she'd already prepared, which only confirmed Erin's suspicions that she'd never had a choice about this assignment. Erin had read them while she brushed her teeth. They weren't exactly the most hard-hitting newspaper in the world, but sometimes Pat's background at the *Chicago Tribune* showed and the questions were designed to get a subject to reveal more about himself than he'd like. Still, Jay was an old hand at publicity. He'd answer exactly *what* he wanted to in exactly the *way* he wanted to. And frankly, she'd probably let him.

If she'd wanted to be the kind of journalist who went for the jugular, uncovering corruption and lies and skeletons in the closet, she wouldn't have taken a job at the *Sea Shell* newspaper in Carmel-by-the-Sea.

What worried her more was dealing with Jay on a professional level. Whenever they spent time together, it was as part of a big, noisy group that almost always included all of her annoying brothers. She'd never been anything but the little sister to Jay. Now, not only had he pretty much rescued her from hypothermia while she shivered in her bikini, but she also had to show up the next day as if all that hadn't happened, and interview him.

When she was assigned these profile pieces, she usually crafted them carefully to show a side of the person that would make them an interesting part of the community. Their readers were more interested in understanding the real essence of the human being than how many Academy Awards they had, or what Clint Eastwood had said to them twenty years ago. Not that she wouldn't include those things, but she always searched for something a bit deeper and more relatable. Trying to pry more sensitive information like this from the overconfident Jay Malone was truly going to put her to the test.

Maybe that wasn't the only reason her mind had been racing. There was something else from the evening that had clung to her memory and hadn't let go. For a miniscule moment on the beach, she could swear that Jay had looked at her as a man looks at a woman for the first time. She'd tried telling herself that she'd imagined the whole thing, but each time she returned to the scene, there was heat there, something undeniable floating between them, teasing and forbidden. It was true she was starting to see a whole new side of Jay, what with his huge home library and his caring way of making her hot chocolate when she was cold.

She'd thought she knew him well after all these years, but now she had the sense she was just getting started.

By the time she arrived at Jay's house at eleven the next morning, she was pretty tired from her sleepless night. Luckily, her dog had energy enough for them both and rushed in ahead of her, tail wagging. The great thing about Buzzy was that he was absolutely convinced that every single person he met was his new best friend. If they didn't feel the same way, he would back away looking so hurt that he'd been known to turn genuine dog haters into people who asked to pet him. It was his canine superpower. But straight away she saw he wouldn't need to use his superpower on Jay.

After squatting to accept Buzzy's enthusiastic overtures of friendship, Jay glanced up at Erin, laughter in his eyes. He was dressed as though he'd come off the beach, in a navy polo shirt and chinos. Both designer, obviously. Still, he looked both relaxed and put together. Now she knew exactly why she'd asked if Buzzy could come along this morning. Yes, she normally brought him to work, but he was also talented at breaking the ice, and if there was any awkwardness when the two of them were alone, she could always fuss over Buzzy. From the enthusiastic pets he was giving, clearly Jay would do the same.

"I can't believe I've never been in town long enough to meet your dog." Jay shook his head in disbelief. "What's his name again?"

"It's Buzzy. Buzzy, this is Jay."

He glanced at the dog and then back at Erin. "You call your dog Buzzy?"

"His name's Boswell. Buzzy for short."

"Ah. Boswell, after the guy who wrote *The Life of Samuel Johnson*?"

Erin blinked. Nobody ever got that. She swallowed and then nodded. Then she had to ask, "Have you read *The Life of Samuel Johnson*?"

"Of course," he said, looking a little incredulous. "He's a fascinating character. I'll admit I haven't read all of Johnson's works—the dictionary, for instance—but his *Rasselas* was brilliant."

Erin needed to sit down. Who even was this man?

Jay was clearly a reader. Funny he never shared that with others. She'd always thought he was such an oversharer, but now she wondered if he only over-shared things he didn't mind people knowing in order to hide things that he kept private.

Maybe Erin had been unfair. She'd made so many

assumptions about him because he wore slick suits and was, in fact, a brilliant agent. He just went overboard sometimes by being tough and never taking no for an answer when he wanted something for his clients.

Fortunately, he didn't leave her any more time to dwell as he guided them through the house. As she looked around on this third visit, she saw that more items had been delivered and arranged. How many people, from interior decorators to movers, had been involved to make this move so quick and so smooth? Just a few days since he'd received the keys and he was already perfectly at home. So many people who moved to Carmel-by-the-Sea hired an agency that furnished the place for them in an identifiable Carmel Beach style, but his pieces looked as though he'd picked them out personally, or at least accompanied the designer when they'd chosen everything. She spotted a Tessa Taylor-Davenport painting—one of the sea scenes for which she was becoming justifiably famous—hanging in the hallway.

Jay opened the door to the study and said, "I thought this would be a good place to be interviewed. If I need to reference anything, it's all at my fingertips."

She nodded, pleased to find herself in such a businesslike environment after a night worrying about how to be professional. But she melted when Jay excused himself for a moment and then returned with a bowl of water for the dog.

"Is it okay if I give him a treat?" He held up a pack of organic dog treats that Erin recognized from one of the many exclusive pet shops in Carmel.

She nodded and then said, "You have treats? You don't even have a dog."

Jay laughed. "I know. But everyone else in Carmel seems to have one. I see them walking on the beach. Plus, I've never seen so many stores catering to dogs. I had to go in and buy some locally made, organic, vegan dog treats." A wry smile played around his lips.

Erin knew he was making fun of her hometown, but it was gentle, maybe even teasing. She smiled back. There *were* a lot of vegan dog treats sold in town.

"Besides," he went on, "I really do love dogs. I'd get one if I was ever in one place long enough. But, as it is, I get to enjoy dogs like yours. Right, Buzzy?" he said in an entirely different tone, rubbing the dog's head, who nodded, his tongue hanging out blissfully, and then daintily accepted the offered treat. Buzzy curled up on the floor, delighted. Erin smiled. Her dog was a great judge of character, and she felt soothed that he was immediately drawn to Jay.

Jay said, "Before we start, can I get your advice on something? It's about home decorating."

She laughed. "Mila's way better at this stuff than I am, but sure."

"I think I just need a second opinion. Something's not feeling right."

Buzzy, who'd made himself instantly at home, curled up for a nap, so she left him in the study and followed Jay out to the garden, which was a beautiful, enclosed space. It felt more like a French or Italian courtyard garden than a place adjacent to the ocean. There were roses and irises growing, and a wrought-iron bench next to a splashing fountain. He pointed to a gorgeous, sinuous sculpture sitting on a column under an arch of roses.

"Is that a Barbara Hepworth?" Erin might not be the artist that her sister-in-law was, but she knew the famous Cornish sculptor's work. She couldn't even imagine what Jay must have paid for an original Hepworth. But she kept that thought to herself.

"It is," he said, sounding pleased that she knew the artist. "I can't find the right space for it." He carried the piece around and set it near the bench, near the roses, dead in the center, talking all the while about how he would have a proper base made and how Barbara Hepworth's work was so organic and worked so well outside.

He was right, of course, she knew that, but after looking at every spot he'd chosen, she finally said, "You know, I don't think it works out here at all. It's such a sensual piece, I think it belongs in your bedroom."

As the words slipped out of her mouth, their gazes connected and a moment of heat arced between them. It flared bright and true and she suddenly dropped her gaze, embarrassed.

She knew she was right about the sculpture, but she wished she hadn't mentioned the bedroom. Or the word *sensual*. It seemed suggestive, as though the two of them might end up in the bedroom together engaging in sensual activity.

As if that could ever happen.

And yet Jay didn't look at all embarrassed. In fact, he was now looking at her as if she were Einstein and had just discovered the theory of relativity. "You're right. The bedroom. I never would have thought of it." Then his expression changed again, softening with what appeared to be admiration. "Come on, let's try it right now."

Erin laughed, relieved to feel the tension between them dissolving into something more familiar. That was the Jay she knew: desperate to do everything yesterday. His enthusiastic impatience was infectious and she found herself joining him in all but running up the stairs with the Hepworth.

As soon as she walked into the bedroom, he looked at her with a huge grin on his face. "You're a genius. An absolute genius."

He moved one of the bedside tables to a blank wall opposite the windows and placed the sculpture there, and she nodded. "That's it. That's perfect." She could imagine how the light would change, giving even more movement to the piece.

He stepped back and nodded. "You're right. The sensuous lines are like the curves of a woman's body. This is exactly the right space for it."

He came a little closer to Erin and she felt herself take a sharp breath. For a second, she wondered if he was going to kiss her. But no. He just gazed at her earnestly for a moment and then quietly said, "You just see things the way they need to be. It's a gift."

They shared a look that seemed to go on for hours, so lost was she in the gray of his eyes, like the soft foam of ocean waves when they rolled at dusk.

A bark from Buzzy downstairs broke the moment. She shivered, not from cold, but from the startling realization that her whole body was tingling.

Jay smiled. "I think that's Buzzy asking if we're ready to get to work."

"He's a tough taskmaster," Erin said, relieved for the millionth time that Buzzy was in her life.

They went downstairs, and Jay made a pot of coffee and carried two cups into the study. He took a seat at a stylish desk that looked as though it was made of glass. The chairs looked fancy, but she found hers was actually comfortable.

"Do you mind if I record this?" Erin asked as she always did, setting her phone between them. Sometimes she needed to go back and get a quote exactly right or listen to something she might have misunderstood. But she also took notes in an old-fashioned notebook for the bulk of her story.

He told her to go ahead and they settled across from each other. She had all his attention as those gray eyes focused on hers.

Chapter Seven

Jay had been interviewed by some reasonably tough characters—hard news reporters trying to get the inside track on a former client's drug-induced spree of destruction, paparazzi trying to weasel romantic scoops on his A-listers—so to be interviewed by somebody he'd only ever considered as his best friend's kid sister should have been a breeze. And yet, as he waited for Erin to begin, he felt strangely on edge. Erin was a lot smarter than many people gave her credit for, a good listener, and often the quiet one in a noisy family. A family that was noisier, let's face it, when he was around. So he knew what she was like at a family breakfast, on the surfboard, and, if he was honest with himself, he'd enjoyed seeing her all dressed up and gorgeous at her brother's wedding.

But he'd never seen her at work.

It didn't help that they'd just shared a moment in the bedroom. It wasn't his mind playing tricks—she'd looked at him with a kind of tenderness he'd never seen enter her eyes before. There had been heat there too. A desire he'd been pushing away—for how long?

This was Arch's kid sister, he reminded himself. No-Go.

He turned his attention to the interview. He could pretty much imagine all the questions she'd ask him, questions he'd been asked a hundred times. What was it like working with top celebrities, how had he got into the business, and sometimes, painfully, that almost throwaway question: If I were looking to get into the business, or if my sister / brother / girlfriend / kid wanted an in, how would they go about it? He would feel the want emanating from the interviewer as they waited for his answer, hoping he'd give them the keys to the kingdom.

Truth was, there were no golden keys. Talent, hard work, and of course good looks could help, but so much of it was luck. Luck and pure hustle. These last two had been the magic ingredients that had worked for Jay's career.

This time, he decided, he would try to enjoy himself for once, and not feel as though he had to put up walls or be too careful about what he said. Erin looked so cute with her reporter's notebook, her phone set to record, and her dog, but as she met his gaze, her smile was a little cooler than it had been. It must be her professional smile. Interesting.

She cleared her throat. "I'm sure my first question will come as no surprise to you. We always ask everybody, what made you choose Carmel-by-the-Sea?"

If there'd been any residual worry that Erin might ask hard-hitting questions, it melted away. He gave her *his* professional smile and then launched into a well-rehearsed response.

"This is one of the most beautiful places I've ever been. I love the beach and the relaxed atmosphere here. LA can get intense, so to be able to retreat to somewhere peaceful with a slower pace of life is amazing. And then this house came up and I fell in love with it right away. Love at first sight, as they say. Plus, I've got a few clients in the area. A lot of people in my business find themselves up here, so I can fly between LA and here in my PJ."

Erin shot him a teasing look. "Your pajamas?"

"My private jet."

"Right. Cool," she said a little sarcastically.

Jay grinned. Her brothers owned or flew in private jets all the time, so she knew exactly what he meant by *PJ*. But she was having fun messing with him, and it was kind of hot to be teased. Usually, women were impressed by his jet. Not Erin. It was refreshing.

He realized then that she hadn't taken a single note. Clearly this was territory as familiar to her as it was to him.

Then she said, "I've known you for a long time, but I always do some background reading on my subjects before I interview them. Do you know what struck me? In none of your interviews do you say where you got your education."

He paused, weighing his options. He tended to overshare, but it was only ever about things he was happy for the world to know. There was a big part of him that he kept closed off from public scrutiny. Still, this was Erin and he wanted her to get a good interview. Maybe he could give her a little more than he'd usually give a reporter. Maybe it would also do him good to start talking about this stuff.

He took a breath. "I went to the school of hard knocks."

She chuckled a little. "Sure, I get that, but did you get a degree from Harvard Business School or—"

Before she listed every Ivy League school he could have gone to and didn't, he blurted, "I didn't finish high school."

Silence filled the room. He must have shocked her—heck, he'd shocked himself. He'd never told anyone that, let alone someone interviewing him. But as he met Erin's gaze, he saw that she wasn't shocked, merely interested in him.

"Really?" she asked. "I never knew that."

He shrugged. "It's not something I'm proud of." And yet saying it out loud, to Erin, made him feel lighter, freer, not ashamed. It was like a heavy burden was finally being lifted from his shoulders. And then he seemed to fall back in time. "I grew up in Los Angeles," he said. "LA is a city that is all about fantasy. It's Hollywood with its movie stars and fancy shops along Rodeo Drive. But then there's the side of the city that I grew up in. With its prostitutes and pimps and drug addicts and lowlifes. I never knew who my father was." He could almost smell the stale booze and pot smoke. "My mom never should have had a kid. She was wasted most of the time on booze and drugs and, well, she got by as best she could."

He realized he'd been staring out the window, talking without really thinking. The words were just sliding out of him, as though they'd been waiting years and years for the seams he'd stitched up so tightly to burst open.

He glanced at Erin. Again, she didn't look shocked. She was simply nodding as though she understood him. If she was figuring out that his mother turned tricks to make enough money to buy drugs and keep a roach-infested roof over their heads, she was getting the right idea. And yet, he didn't read pity in her eyes, because that would have stopped him dead in his tracks. Instead, he saw something like interest, and maybe a kindling respect? It felt good, but then he caught himself.

Why was he suddenly revealing his deep, dark secrets? Erin was a friend, but she was here as a reporter, not a confidante. He shook his head. She was the exact opposite of a confidante. She was doing a profile on him for the paper that everyone in town read cover to cover.

Erin must have sensed his inner conflict, because softly, she asked, "Did social services never get involved? Did no one see what was going on?"

He laughed, a short, humorless bark. "I was probably more scared of social services than I was of some of the creeps who hung out with my mom. Besides, she needed me. By the time I was seven, I was talking grocers out of food past its expiry date and just about managed to feed us both. Mostly it was milk and cereal. I learned to cut out the bad bits from bruised fruit and vegetables. I got lunch at school, so there was that. And I loved school. I loved learning."

He stopped again. What was he doing? No one knew how he had developed the gift of the gab by sweet-talking greengrocers out of their overripe bananas. He had a sudden flash of himself as a kid, skinny and scrappy and so darned hungry—not just for food, but for life. For living! If his mom had taught him anything, it was that he didn't want to end up like her. Wasting away.

Erin stayed silent, but it was a comfortable silence, one that told him he was safe here, with her.

He took a breath. "I would steal money out of my mom's purse when she was passed out, otherwise everything went on her habits. She wasn't a bad woman, my mom. She tried. That was what was so hard. In her way, she loved me. But her addictions were stronger than any love she had."

He paused, shocked by the stab of pain he felt at the memory. He hadn't let himself think so much about his mom in years.

"It sounds like you had to grow up very fast," Erin said, her voice still soft and full of understanding.

He had to stop spilling his guts and get this interview back on track and answer Erin's original question. "By the time I was fourteen, I knew I had to get a job. I went around the fancy parts of LA to every shop and restaurant, anywhere that might hire a scrappy kid, and one place, a real nice place, had a sign in the window for a dishwasher. I marched in there and said, 'I'll be the best dishwasher you've ever seen.' I sold them so hard I made it sound like it would be a crime if they didn't hire me on the spot. So that's exactly what they did. At first it was just an after-school job, but as I got older, I started working evenings, too. I began to understand that the diners were industry people. I recognized a few of them from TV and movies, but I quickly learned that the power people weren't the pretty faces on the screen, they were the producers. I worked so hard that when the owners said they wanted to promote me to full-time dishwasher, I said yes, but only if they would train me to be a waiter. Because waiters got tips, and even better, they overheard the gossip that was going on at the tables. I dropped out of high school without giving it much thought." He stopped again, trying to keep himself on track. He had a question to answer. "So by the time I was eighteen, I was waiting tables and charming Hollywood big shots. I made the fattest tips of all the staff. It meant my mom and I could live in a nicer apartment and eat decent food. But Mom was pretty far gone by then." An unfamiliar lump caught in his throat. It had been so long since he'd thought about the end of his poor, messed-up mom's life. "She died of an overdose before I turned nineteen."

"I'm so sorry," Erin said softly.

He nodded, took a sip of coffee and gave himself a moment. "But the one thing we always had was a TV, and sometimes if she was feeling good, she'd take me out to the movies and we'd sneak in without paying and live in a fantasy world for a few hours. It was my favorite time we spent together. I fell in love with movies and TV when I was a little kid with no hope. They showed me what life could be like. So by the time I was waiting tables, eavesdropping on the Hollywood bigwigs, I already knew the kind of life I wanted.

"A lot of people I worked with were actors, screenwriters, budding producers, and directors, waiting tables or tending bar until they got their big break. I got pally with a few of them, one in particular. He was about my age, already a crazy handsome guy, which I was never going to be, and we shared a similar work ethic. Unlike some of the others, he knew he wasn't going to get his big break because somebody liked his pretty face. He took acting lessons and went to every audition. He was one of the most focused guys I'd ever met. One day we were playing pool after our shift and he told me about this great part that he knew he was born to play. I agreed that he was perfect for it. But they wouldn't see him without an agent. We were both moaning about how unfair it was for people that weren't already established, and then I had one of those lightbulb moments. I threw down my pool cue and almost knocked the poor guy out as I yelled, 'How hard is it to be an agent?'

"And so we ran back to my apartment, spent the rest of the night putting together a cover letter and beefing up his CV, and I made up some letterhead with the name Exceptional Talent. We liked it because the initials were E.T., a movie that we both loved as kids. And it worked. It got him in the room. The studio called me—ha, I'll never forget it. Offered him the part and I negotiated a bigger paycheck than he was expecting. All those years of hustling paid off." He stopped and grinned. "I'm sure by now you've figured out the name of my first client."

"Archer Davenport," Erin said quietly. "My brother."

Chapter Eight

While Jay had been talking, Buzzy had sidled up to him and laid his head on his knee. He obviously felt the pure emotion in Jay's voice. As had Erin. In fact, she'd been completely transported by his sad but ultimately uplifting story of a tough childhood made good with hard work and raw ambition, and—although he'd downplayed it—a talent for Hollywood that was undeniable.

But more than the story itself, his personal revelations had her reeling. How could she not have known this about him? He'd been Arch's best friend for nearly fifteen years. Sure, she'd heard the story about them working together at the restaurant countless times. But they'd both always presented Jay as an up-and-coming agent who'd taken a chance on her brother.

Neither of them had revealed how big a chance they were taking on one another.

Now that she thought about it, this had to be one of the deep things that bonded the two men together for life. Which made her feel doubly concerned about the strange flip-flop her heart was doing as she stared at Jay's rugged face as if she were setting eyes on him for the very first time.

Yes, it was a shock to her that Jay had come from such humble and disadvantaged roots and, on the strength of his personality and his hustle alone, had made such an incredible success of himself. But Jay hadn't even made that point. Not once had he bragged about his huge list of wildly successful clients or the fact that he was a multimillionaire. A billionaire, for all she knew. This was a different Jay.

While he was speaking, she'd decided not to take any notes for fear of breaking the sense of trust they seemed to have between them. She had a feeling that the minute she reached for her notebook and pen and acted like a reporter, he'd remember she *was* one. Her article for the *Sea Shell* aside, she was fascinated by his story and wanted to hear all of it, or at least everything he was comfortable sharing. It must have been so hard for him to reveal the truth about his early life. Could it be he was saying these things because he wanted to give *her* the big scoop about who Jay Malone really was, when up until now his past had been completely shrouded in mystery? Or was something else brewing inside of him? A need for closeness with someone, maybe. Or a need to finally take the burden of the past off his shoulders by sharing it with her.

So she asked him more about those early days,

when he'd been a scrappy young agent, with just Arch as his client. She discovered that a major TV star and a bodybuilder turned action hero had also started out in that restaurant. It wasn't long before Jay left the restaurant business and Exceptional Talent opened its first small office, where he seemed to go from success to success. He talked freely and candidly and with obvious relief that the dark days of his childhood were out of the way.

When there was a natural break in the conversation, she asked, "Do you have any regrets?"

The question seemed to take him by surprise. She didn't even know why she asked—it wasn't on her list of questions. It was just that it felt like the right one at the right moment.

He gave her a rueful smile. "Yeah. I regret not finishing high school. I am self-educated in every sense of the word. I'm a big reader. I've learned a lot from books."

She nodded and said in understanding, "So have I. They're also my friends when I'm lonely and encouragement when I feel blue."

He leaned forward enthusiastically. "Exactly. Next to movies, books are the greatest."

She stared at him, feeling the true connection of one book lover to another. And then the stare deepened in intensity. Not only had she not known the real Jay Malone, she was noticing again how dreamy his eyes were. It was like they were suddenly back in the bedroom, talking about sensuous curves. Heat spread through her body.

Get it together, Erin, she chided herself. You're a professional. Act like it.

Clearing her throat, she said, "Okay, moving on to my next question. You're famous for repping some of the top young male actors in the profession, like Archer Davenport and Smith Sullivan, and they famously make a lot of action movies. But where are the softer movies for other demographics? How come you never put these clients in romantic comedies, for example?"

A funny look crossed his face, as though not only had no one ever asked him that before, he'd never even thought about it. And now that she had asked the question, she realized she already knew the answer. Jay was a hero in his own right. It took grit and determination to drag yourself up from such beginnings. A lot of people wouldn't manage it. No wonder so many of the movies he was involved with were about men overcoming great odds.

To her dismay, Jay now looked a little offended. "I put my actors in rom coms if it's the right movie for them."

She raised her eyebrows. "I seem to remember that when Archer broke his leg, you *threatened* him with a rom com if he didn't heal in time to do *Shock Tactics*."

His eyes twinkled and he held up his hands in mock

defense. "It's not easy when one of your top clients has a sister who's a reporter. Okay, I might have threatened Arch with a rom com, but I think he'd be a great romantic lead."

Erin wasn't buying it. "And yet, after he finishes *Shock Tactics*, he's going to do the Herschel Greenfield biopic. I'm guessing there's not much romance for Hersch in space."

Jay frowned. "Okay. Point taken. I don't have anything against a good romantic comedy. I'll keep my eyes open."

"I've also noticed you don't do any female-led movies."

Jay's frown deepened. "Do the readers of the *Sea Shell* really need to know this?"

"Your reputation is *brash bad boy*. The shark who always gets the big deal. Most of your clients are young male actors who are killing it. It's pretty understandable that our readers would want to know why you can't do this for female leads as well."

Quickly he shot back, "Any one of my clients could be the next big thing in Hollywood. Including my female clients."

Erin swallowed. It was obvious that Erin the reporter was overtaking Erin the friend, the listener. The interview was veering off track, and if she wasn't careful, she'd lose him altogether and Julius—Jay— Malone would clam up, snapping down that hard shell that concealed his softer—and yes, she had to admit it—dangerously attractive self. She wondered how much more he hid under that gruff, pushy exterior, partly as a defense. It couldn't be an easy life, repping prima donna clients and dealing with studio execs all the time. No doubt he'd been forced to develop a reputation as a hard-ass, even if that wasn't really him.

As if realizing they both needed a breather, Jay bent down and scooped Buzzy onto his lap. Her dog was more than happy to oblige and offered his belly for strokes, which Jay gave him with a giant grin on his face. It was so cute that she couldn't help but grin too, and some of the tension melted away. As friendly as Buzzy was, she'd never seen him adore someone he'd just met this much. She felt ashamed for giving Jay a hard time about the romance movies. If her dog could see in five minutes that Jay was a great guy, why had it taken her fifteen years to do the same?

"Why don't you get a dog? You could get a pet sitter when you're away for work."

Jay made a face. "I'd love to, but I travel way too much. I'm here one week, in LA the next, maybe flying to London for a meeting after that. It wouldn't be fair."

"I think you could make it work. And dogs obviously like you. I mean, Buzzy and Buster both like you," she amended, referring to the Davenport family dog.

Before she could say more, the doorbell rang.

Buzzy immediately leapt from Jay's lap and barked, letting everybody know they had a visitor. Because apparently the doorbell wasn't enough.

Buzzy raced to the front door and Erin said, "That will be the photographer." Relief flooded her body. A third person was exactly what this interview needed, and who better than her old friend Clark?

* * *

Jay answered the door to a tall, gangly young man. His glasses were slipping down his nose, but he couldn't do anything about it because his hands were full of camera equipment.

In a serious tone, the man said, "I'm Clark Barnstable from the *Sea Shell* newspaper. If you let me put all this stuff down, I can show you my press pass."

Jay could hardly hold back a grin. "It's okay. I'm expecting you. Erin's already here."

At that, Clark's serious expression brightened, and his large eyes filled with an eagerness that set Jay's teeth on edge. Clark's voice cracked a little as he said, "Erin's here?"

Oh boy. Jay had seen crushes before, but this one was acute. Clark's cheeks grew rosy and he nearly tripped over his tripod trying to get into the house as fast as he could.

Jay tried to keep his amusement in check. The poor guy. "We're in my study to the left. Need me to carry any of that stuff?"

"I can manage."

Clark hefted the stuff into the study and suddenly the room felt crowded. Buzzy circled Clark, whom he obviously recognized, demanding that as soon as his hands were free, a pat would be required.

Jay excused himself to make them all a fresh pot of coffee, and used the time to try to dislodge the hard knot that had formed in the pit of his stomach. When he returned and saw Erin and Clark talking, her body language made it clear that Clark's massive crush was unrequited. Erin was saying, "I thought we'd set up in here. What do you think?"

Clark gave a vigorous nod and Jay got the impression that if she'd suggested they take his feature photograph in the bathroom by the toilet, Clark would have enthusiastically agreed. Man, that kid had it bad. Still, Jay couldn't help a niggle of. . . something. It wasn't jealousy, obviously, but they worked together. The kid must see her five days a week and they'd go out on assignments like this one. They wouldn't be the first couple who had ended up getting together through shared circumstance. And then they'd stay together, because the love one of them had for the other would be strong enough to carry the whole relationship.

Still, he'd hate to see Erin settle. She deserved someone more. . . what? More like him? As soon as he had the thought, he banished it. Not only had he assured Arch that his sister was off-limits, but he truly believed it. Yes, he was seeing a side of her today that really impressed him. She was one of the most skillful interviewers he'd ever come across. But she wasn't his type. Not even close. Maybe they could become better friends. He had certainly revealed more about his past to her than he had any friend—including her brother. Talk about oversharing. She just made him want to talk to her. But what he'd failed to consider was that by talking to Erin, he was also talking to the readership of the *Sea Shell*. He'd have to think about the consequences of that later.

And yet he was glad she stayed as Clark set up and then took what seemed like hundreds of different shots around his study, where he'd already hung photos and movie posters from his clients' films. Erin suggested that they try the library, but Jay shook his head. He knew he was interesting because he represented hot actors—no one wanted to see that he read poetry or philosophy. He was happy to move to the garden at Clark's request, however. It was cool and peaceful in the shade, and he could hear the ocean in the distance.

While they were packing up, Clark said to Erin, "There's an auction this Saturday, if you want to come along."

"Auction?" Jay asked. "What kind of auction?" He loved auctions, and he still needed quite a few things for the house. It might be fun to go to a local auction and see what they were like.

Clark pushed his glasses up his nose. "It's photographic equipment mostly, but there will also be art and some antiques, I think."

"Cool," Jay said. "Where is it? I'm free on Saturday."

Something flashed across Clark's face, but he obligingly told Jay the name of the auction house and its address in Monterey before he turned his attention back to Erin. "Do you think you'll be able to come?"

"Probably," she said, with a small shrug and a smile. "Let's see how far I get with my deadline."

Jay tried not to frown. He was surprised Erin would want to spend her weekend at an auction with this gangly photo buff. Didn't she have better things to do? Still, he was intrigued. Not only by the auction, but also by what the relationship really was between these two.

With the interview over, Jay insisted on helping Clark carry his equipment back to his car. He tried not to be smug as he made light work of the heavy lighting rig. Clark thanked him, told Erin he'd see her back at the office, and drove off.

At the door, Erin turned to Jay with a smile. "I'd make tracks too, but it seems Buzzy has other ideas." She gestured down at Jay's feet, where Buzzy had made himself comfortable.

He laughed. "Come on, Buzzy my friend, it's time to go." He shifted his feet, but the dog only resettled himself. "Okay, okay," he said, "I'll walk you to Erin's car. You don't have to ask twice."

Buzzy reluctantly followed Jay as he strode out into the driveway.

At her car, Erin paused at the open door, a thoughtful expression in her eyes. Softly, she said, "Before I go, I have to know—why did you tell me all those things? I mean, it was a privilege to listen to your story—and thank you for trusting me—but you've always seemed to keep your past private. What changed?"

What *had* changed? But deep down he already knew the answer. He surprised himself as he shared it with her. "You asked me some pretty hard questions today, and even though I normally don't answer them, I did because it was you."

"I appreciate that," she said slowly, seeming to weigh his reply. "So, what do you want in return?"

He frowned. After everything he'd shared today, was that really what Erin thought of him? That he had some kind of ulterior motive? That everything was a deal?

His voice level, he asked, "What makes you think I expect anything?"

She rolled her eyes. "I learned lots of new things about you today, Jay, but a leopard doesn't totally change its spots. I've known you for years. There must be something in it for you as well."

As he shook his head, Jay felt his blood rising, but just as quickly he let it go. He had no one to blame but himself for Erin's cynicism. Jay had built his career on hustle; it was only fair that Erin would anticipate he wanted something in return. But he had some home truths for Erin, too.

Choosing his words more carefully than usual, he said, "Well, you asked pretty probing questions for the *Sea Shell*. Here's one for you. With your smarts and education, why aren't you working for the *San Francisco Chronicle* or the NYT?"

If Erin was offended by the question, she didn't show it. Instead, she smiled. "That's an easy one. I'm where I want to be. I love this town, I love being close to my family, I love the surfing. And I love the *Sea Shell*. People always say that they wait all week for a new issue and sit down to devour every page. I know we're not covering groundbreaking things most of the time, but people really like reading about the Dog of the Week and the local news."

It was such a sweet and earnest answer that Jay felt a new kind of warmth course through him. Without thinking, he said, "One day you'll own that paper."

Erin let out a little peal of laughter. "How did you know that's actually my secret ambition?"

He shot her a cheeky grin. "You think that after all these years, I don't know you that well?"

Erin blushed, a deep pink that traveled down her cheeks, her neck, all the way to the delicate bones of her clavicle. It was so sweet that the feelings he'd been trying so hard to push away all day rose to the surface.

Erin, he thought. Erin. *How have I never seen you properly before?*

As she stood by the door of her car, waiting for him to say something, the whole morning began to feel like they were on a date. And that could not happen. Ever. Archer—and probably the rest of the Davenports—would tear him to shreds. But more than that, the morning's foray into his past was a stark reminder that, regardless of his current success, Jay wasn't good enough for this woman.

He said good-bye abruptly, and with a quick farewell pet for Buzzy, headed back inside. He avoided the office and went straight out into the garden to collect himself. But before he had time to think, his phone rang, and his actual business life took over. As it turned out, it was a good thing he'd cleared his schedule, because one of his clients had just had a spectacular blowout with the director of the blockbuster movie he was starring in. Between dealing with furious studio executives, an equally furious star, and already inquisitive reporters, he had no time to worry about how much he'd overshared with the *Sea Shell*.

It probably didn't matter, anyway. With a sigh, he resigned himself to heading back to LA sooner than he'd imagined.

Chapter Nine

The *Sea Shell* might be a weekly, but because of the timing of her interview with Jay Malone, Erin was on a tight deadline. She only had the afternoon to write her piece if they were going to make this week's issue, and Pat Sinclair had made it pretty clear that she expected Erin to deliver.

She'd driven straight to the office, but as she sat at her desk, instead of reviewing her notes or listening to the recording, Erin found her mind wandering. She was jittery, and for once it wasn't because she'd drunk too much coffee. The problem was simple and she couldn't deny it any longer: She was developing feelings for Jay. Big time feelings. Her heart hadn't raced like this in a long time and the new, more real side she'd seen of him today excited her.

But then she admonished herself. This was Jay Malone. Annoying, loud Jay who was pushy and overly assertive. Jay, who only dated models twice her height and twice as beautiful. More than that, though Jay had always made her feel safe, she still hadn't lost her fear of being dominated by a powerful man. A fear she'd carried around with her since college. She knew Jay as a friend—but not what he'd be like as a lover or boyfriend. She figured he'd be too possessive and domineering—exactly what she *didn't* want in a man.

She turned her attention back to her article, but the fifteen hundred words she'd managed to type swam before her eyes. So she just sat for a few minutes and thought back on the extraordinary revelations Jay had offered her. She still couldn't believe that in all the years he'd been coming to the Davenport house for family gatherings, she'd never known a thing about his childhood or his humble beginnings. He just had such an aura of success about him that she'd figured he'd gone to some Ivy League school without ever asking. She'd been to Stanford and was used to the blazing confidence so many people had when they got into such a respected institution. But since she wasn't like that herself, it had been foolish to make assumptions about Jay. And what a shock to discover he hadn't even graduated from high school. His beginnings were more than just humble—they were, frankly, disadvantaged. And yet look what he'd made of himself. It was the kind of rags-to-riches story that people loved.

And yet, as much as her fingers itched to tell his tale in all its brutal detail, something was stopping her.

She recalled the moment when he'd said, "Do the readers of the *Sea Shell* really want to know this?" He'd been defending his choice of the kinds of deals he made, but this was a man baring his soul in a way he never had before in an interview. She knew that because she'd done her research and hadn't been able to find one darned personal thing about his life except for romantic links to a plethora of models. Although he'd told her that he'd spoken candidly because it was her, she couldn't quite believe this was the whole truth. Could it be that he'd become so lost in talking about the past he'd simply forgotten they were two professionals on the record? Had he felt, as she had, that the whole world had melted away until they were just two souls, showing themselves to each other?

She shook her head. No, she was getting carried away. This wasn't a scene from one of the romantic movies he never put his stars into.

And yet she couldn't let the thought go. If he'd opened up because it was her, as he'd explained, then he might have forgotten she was a reporter. If she told the world his painful story, one that he'd never revealed before, would he be filled with regret? See it as betrayal of a family friendship?

There was a reason she hadn't made a career of hard-hitting investigative news reporting. She didn't want to humiliate anyone or expose their secrets unless they wanted them exposed. And in this case, she couldn't be sure.

She blinked at the screen and read over what she'd

written about the house he'd bought, which definitely would be of interest to the people of Carmel-by-the-Sea, and some of the funny things he'd said—what it was like to move into a town where there were so many art galleries, fancy pet stores, and real estate offices. She smiled, seeing the town she loved so much through somebody else's eyes. Through Jay's eyes.

Her fingers hovered over the keys for a moment and then she continued to type, checking the recording on her phone every so often. She wrote about how he kept dog treats handy even though he didn't have a dog, because every time he was out walking through Carmel or across the beach, he met the greatest dogs and in this way he was getting to know the locals. She gave space to the highlights of his career, omitting the hard time she'd given him about not putting his actors in romances. The more she typed, the more the words seemed to pour from her fingers, and she entered that flow state where the story felt like it was writing itself.

She was just proofreading her piece before sending it to Pat for an edit, when Clark arrived with a selection of photos to run with it. She was intrigued to see what Clark had captured. Jay photographed well, with those intense eyes in the tough-guy face and the shaved head. He looked relaxed and truly at home in Carmel. The thought made her smile.

They agreed on one pose of Jay, not in his office as he had suggested, and not in his library as she had wished, but in that beautiful garden that was so tucked away from the world. In the space where he'd first thought the Barbara Hepworth sculpture might belong, Clark had taken a fun shot of him leaning over, with his elbow where the sculpture would have gone. The photograph was easy to caption: *Superstar agent Jay Malone contemplates what kind of sculpture to purchase for his new home in Carmel-by-the-Sea.*

She thought the picture evinced both Jay's cheeky sense of humor and the fact that he was settling into his new home, where hopefully he would buy art from a local sculptor. Her mind flipped back to the Barbara Hepworth. That beautiful piece had traveled a long way—all the way from Cornwall in England—and she shivered again thinking about the two of them in the bedroom picking the perfect spot for the sinuous piece. There must be a local sculptor who could fashion him something for the garden. Already she had some ideas of places she'd like to take him shopping. After admiring it for so long, she felt emotionally invested in that property. She wanted everything in it to be perfect. And there was a part of her too, who wanted that specifically for the young boy who never could have dreamed that one day he'd own such an impressive and beautiful home.

Pat's edits came back before she could leave for the day and, as always, Erin was impressed by the way her editor could so unerringly cut out wasted words or fluff and make the piece tighter. Along with the edits, she'd included a little note: *Great work, Erin.*

For Pat, that was gushing praise. Erin felt as though she'd been fully forgiven for not telling her editor about Archer's wedding. Even better, she hadn't had to sell out Jay in the process.

His story was safe with her.

Chapter Ten

Jay opened his copy of the *Sea Shell* with trepidation. The front page carried an article about school funding, but there was a little teaser of his profile, bottom right. As much as he wanted to know the local schools were well funded, he was way too curious not to flip immediately to the page where he was featured. The first thing he saw was the photograph, which had been set in the center of Erin's profile. He grinned, appreciating how it captured his more playful side. He was usually portrayed as serious, sometimes even menacing— especially when the article focused on how cutthroat he was when making deals. When he read the caption underneath, he chuckled and wondered if Erin might like to go shopping with him for a sculpture. She clearly had a good aesthetic eye, as well as a sense of humor.

The headline was innocuous enough: *Top Hollywood Agent Buys Dream Home in Carmel*. Then, with a sense of dread, he began to read. He didn't know what had possessed him to tell Erin all those intensely personal and humiliating things about his past. But there was something about the way she listened with such interest and no judgment. There had been no pity in her gaze, but a kind of understanding sympathy that made him keep going when he should have just shut the heck up. Plenty of reporters had tried to lower his mile-high walls—including the infamous Roxy Thanton from *Celebrity Tonight*, who'd also had a crack at Archer after he'd broken his leg. None had succeeded.

Until now.

How had a thirty-year-old woman whose hardest-hitting question was about not putting his leads in romantic comedies managed to draw out of him what he'd kept hidden from even the most intrusive of journalists? He shook his head. It couldn't have been Erin alone. No, he'd been listening to a little voice inside of him that said it was about time to be honest about where he'd come from. That it was okay. That it was time to stop hiding. But now, faced with the consequences of listening to that voice, he was worried.

It had taken years and years to become Jay Malone and now he'd undone all that hard work in one morning. He sighed loudly.

As one sentence flowed into the next, he couldn't believe what he was reading. It was beautiful, playful, thoughtful—and there wasn't a single mention of Jay's childhood. It was as though his life had begun when he and Archer met at the restaurant where they'd both been waiting tables. She'd put in the bit about him hustling to get the dishwasher job, and then when she'd talked about his agency, she'd described it as *fledgling* rather than revealing that he and Archer had cobbled together a CV, letterhead, and a company name. Beyond grateful, he couldn't keep the smile off his face. He still worked with those people he'd once had to hustle, and while nobody in Hollywood *wasn't* going to pick up the phone if Jay Malone called, he didn't want studio executives feeling like they'd been made a fool of. Those guys had long memories. Dealing with a *fledgling* agent was okay. Being tricked by a no-account hustler was an embarrassment.

Erin had saved him from himself. He wanted to wrap her in the world's biggest bear hug and squeeze her tight. And then he found he couldn't stop the image from developing. . . He'd hug her, feeling how small she was in his arms, how smooth her skin, how taut the muscles in her back. His hands would drop farther down, trailing over that soft, soft skin until they found her waist and circled it, drawing her in tighter. He closed his eyes. He could smell the coconut of her shampoo, feel the length of her strawberry blonde hair.

He stopped there. "Get a grip," he muttered. "This is Erin." *Erin!*

He shook the erotic image from his mind. All he needed to do was thank Erin for her discretion. He was about to pick up the phone and call her, or maybe arrange for a big bouquet of flowers to be delivered to her apartment, when his cell rang.

He gulped when he saw the display—did the guy have telepathic powers?

"Hey, Archer," he said, keeping his voice light and breezy, like he hadn't just been fantasizing about the man's little sister. "How's my favorite client?"

Archer laughed. "I know you say that to all your clients."

He grinned at that. "At the moment I'm speaking to them, every client is my favorite." However, he didn't pick up for all of them on the first ring like he did for Archer. He didn't need to tell the star of *Shock Tactics* that—they both knew it. They were also busy guys with no time to waste. "What's up?"

He was ready with pen and paper to take down whatever was vital from the call, but Arch surprised him. "Great job on the interview."

"Wait, you read the *Sea Shell*?"

Arch laughed. "Jay, *everybody* in Carmel-by-the-Sea reads the *Sea Shell*. I don't like to boast, but I thought my sister did a great job."

"I did too," he said, not letting Arch know how much she'd kept back. And how grateful he was. Jay kept waiting for Arch to talk business, but he never did. After a couple of minutes of catching up, he said he had to get going and congratulated Jay again on the profile.

Jay hung up a little bemused. He was not the kind of guy who underestimated *anything,* but clearly he hadn't quite grasped the local power of the *Sea Shell*.

He picked up the paper and read the other articles: The reopening of the town's oldest bakery after extensive renovations; a fire put out by a team of volunteers up in the valley after hiking teenagers lost control of their campfire. He turned to a full page devoted to a local animal shelter. It was becoming so full of homeless animals that it was running out of funding. There was a community-wide drive to try to keep it afloat. His gaze immediately landed on a real pity ad for a homeless dog. A scrappy little stray stared out at him with what appeared to be entreaty. The dog had the most soulful dark eyes, and as he stared at the photo, Jay couldn't help but think of that kid with a hard life looking for a break. That kid who'd been a scrappy little stray too.

He would have kept staring at that poor dog, but his phone rang again. He smiled when he saw the name. It had been a while since he'd heard from Smith Sullivan, who was currently working on a screenplay while he and Valentina looked forward to the birth of their first child. He couldn't imagine he was having any work problems, but Jay picked up his pen again as he greeted his friend and client.

"Jay," Smith said, "I just finished reading your pro-file piece in the *Sea Shell*. It was really great. Cool photo, too. Though you know you're going to have every sculptor in California trying to sell you something for your garden." He laughed.

Jay shook his head. "Smith, you don't even live in Carmel-by-the-Sea. How on earth did you get a copy of the *Sea Shell*?"

"I subscribe online. I wouldn't miss an issue of that any more than I'd miss an issue of *Variety*."

Again, Jay waited for Smith to talk business, but it never happened. Once they'd caught up on Valentina's pregnancy and how his writing was progressing, Smith said he had to go—they had a friend's birthday party to attend. After he hung up, Jay's bemusement deepened. He had to accept that everybody in Carmel, or who had any association with Carmel, apparently, read the *Sea Shell*. And maybe some of his clients valued their friendship more than he'd given them credit for. He smiled. He really did owe Erin a lot.

He picked up his phone and found her number. She answered after two rings. At the sound of her voice, he felt an instant warmth and connection and understood immediately why he had told her so much about himself. She was just so easy to talk to.

"I owe you the biggest bunch of flowers in Carmel. In California! How come you didn't include all those personal details I shared with you?"

There was a pause and then he heard the click of a door closing. He suspected she was still at the office and was giving herself some privacy. In a low voice, she said, "I wasn't sure you actually intended to say all those things for public consumption. Even I kind of forgot we were on the record and weren't just having a conversation friend to friend. But if you ever do decide you want to go public with the story of your upbringing and the heroic effort you put into carving out such a successful career, then I would love to write it for you. I think it could be really inspiring. Something that could touch a lot of people."

Jay let her words sink in. Instead of replying with the first thing that came to mind, as usual, he allowed himself a moment. The words *friend to friend* and *heroic effort* had had a strange effect on him. And he realized that, although he'd thought she'd saved him from himself by not including those details in the story, speaking it out loud was part of a healing journey. One where he accepted his upbringing and made peace with it. Otherwise, how would the good stuff be able to climb over his mile-high walls?

"I think you might be right—and you are the only person I would let tell that story. But I need some more time. Is that okay?"

Full of understanding, she replied, "Absolutely."

His gaze returned to the photo of the rescue dog and he smiled.

Erin asked, "Are you still there?"

"I'm just looking at the picture of your rescue dog

of the week. He looks like a feisty little scrapper."

He heard the rustle of paper as she turned to the same page. "Aww," she said. "What a character. It's so sad—I heard that if they don't find a home for him soon, they're going to have to put him down."

Jay didn't want to hear that. "You're kidding. Why?"

"He's young, but he's had a hard life, and apparently he's a little nervous, so people don't really warm to him. They can't keep him at the shelter indefinitely— there's not enough funding."

"I'll send them some cash as soon as I get off the phone." He paused. For once, money didn't seem like enough. Of course he would help solve the problem of funding. But it wouldn't necessarily mean that this cute mutt would find the right home. What if someone careless adopted him? Or someone who didn't have the right skills to help him feel at ease?

He looked back at the photo and again found himself speaking his thoughts aloud to Erin. "He reminds me of myself. A young scrapper who needed socializing."

With a chuckle, she said, "I don't know that you've ever needed help socializing, but I do know it's a nice evening for a drive. Maybe you should go look at him."

Jay silently shook his head. He didn't have the time—he had to get ready for his trip to LA to deal with the feud between his client and the director of the blockbuster he was shooting. There were a million things he needed to do before his flight. And yet he couldn't tear his eyes away from the dog. There was just something about him that had got Jay, hook, line, and sinker. Besides, as Erin had pointed out, it *was* a nice night for a drive.

"I'll go if you'll come with me." Yet another impulsive statement flying out of Jay's mouth when Erin was around.

She laughed. It was a soft, surprisingly sexy sound. "I'd love to."

And so, without quite knowing how it happened, Jay found himself picking up Erin from the apartment complex where she lived. She got into the Lamborghini and settled beside him in well-worn jeans and a casual cotton shirt, with sneakers on her feet and her hair pulled back in a loose ponytail. Normally the woman beside him was dressed in haute couture—Dior or Valentino—and they'd be heading to a hip bar or restaurant. Not an animal shelter. But as Jay stole furtive glances at Erin's profile, he thought she looked better than any other woman who'd ever sat there.

Chapter Eleven

Erin was more than happy to accompany Jay to the animal shelter. First of all, she absolutely loved dogs—all dogs, big and small and medium—so an evening surrounded by dozens of cute canines looking for new homes was as about as dreamy a proposal as staying in with a good book. She was also pleased that Jay was happy with the article, and that she'd done the right thing in holding back those personal details. She believed him when he said he'd take some time to think about sharing his story so that he could inspire other young kids like him. And she was thrilled he thought she was the right person for the job. She didn't like to admit it, but with Pat's praise at the paper being almost nonexistent, Jay's telling her she was an excellent interviewer meant a lot. He had so much experience with all kinds of media that he really knew what he was talking about.

She snuck a look at him as he drove, his rugged profile concentrating on the road ahead, and tried to imagine how different things might have been between her and Jay if she'd known the truth about his past. Not in a romantic sense, of course. That was out of the question. But maybe they would have become better friends, bonding over their love of books—and now dogs. She was so pleased that he might choose to take on a tricky dog in need of unconditional love—the kind of love that she was starting to realize Jay might need too.

She took a moment to appreciate the gorgeous sunset as they drove along the coastline. It didn't matter one bit that she'd lived here her whole life—the pinks and flaming oranges still took her breath away as they illuminated the white sand of the beach. The shelter was a little way out of town and she enjoyed the purr of the engine and the way Jay handled the powerful car.

When they pulled up at the shelter, she heard a chorus of dogs barking through the open windows. It was as though each of them was yelling, *Pick me. Pick me. Pick me.*

Jay parked and said, "Is this place really going to close due to lack of funding?"

"It's definitely under threat," she said, shaking her head. It made her so sad to think that some of these dogs might never find a home. "There's a big fundraising effort underway, but there's also a primary school facing some funding issues, and there's only so much money to go around. Even in a prosperous community like this one."

Jay nodded thoughtfully, as though he were making mental calculations about how much to donate. She was glad he was so game to use his wealth for good. So many people who amassed a fortune kept it to themselves, but she knew that, like her siblings, Jay wasn't one of them. As they entered the shelter, the sound of barking became close to deafening. Jay laughed and playfully covered his ears. However, the young clerk at the front desk was used to it and gave them both a friendly nod.

Erin greeted her and asked, "How are you doing, Emilia?"

She smiled. "Can't complain, Erin. Busy as usual!"

Erin said, "My friend here would like to have a look at the rescue dog of the week."

Emilia eyed him up the way a matchmaker might eye a potential suitor to see if he was worthy of meeting his match. He flashed her his most winning smile and then she gave a curt nod. "You got kids?"

"No. Is that bad?"

"No. It's good. Rocco needs attention. Wait here a minute—I'll go get him."

Jay watched her leave and then said to Erin, "I'm still not convinced I can look after a dog. I travel so much. But I'm super curious to see this little guy. Maybe I can donate what they need to keep him alive for someone else to adopt him."

Erin had a feeling that the minute Jay set eyes on this dog, he would make it work somehow. That's just what dog people did.

Emilia returned, leading a dog on a leash. He wasn't a big dog, and his hair was more like something you'd find on a welcome mat than a pet. He went to Erin first, sniffed her, and then went back to Emilia. Jay bent down and the dog's big brown eyes fixed on him warily. He was clearly nervous. His short ears lay flat to his head and his tail wagged, but in a very tentative fashion.

They stayed that way for a moment, just looking at each other.

Then, in a soft voice, Jay said, "Hey, buddy."

The dog took a few steps forward and stopped. Jay didn't move. He remained still and then the pup slowly came to him. As he did, he sniffed, and then sniffed again, and then the wiry tail began to wag like crazy. Jay laughed, petting him and playing with his ears, and the next thing they knew, the little guy was jumping all over him and nuzzling him.

Emilia turned to Erin and said, "That's amazing. He's scared of most men."

Jay grinned, clearly flattered. "He's a scrappy little tough guy with a soft center."

Erin couldn't help herself. "Just like you."

Jay turned to look at her, his eyes wide, and she realized that he was surprised to hear she thought of him that way. That she knew he had a soft center under all that bravado. She couldn't tell whether he was pleased or embarrassed by her remark. She figured he wasn't used to letting his guard down and it might take a while before he was truly comfortable with it.

"He's a great dog," Emilia was saying, "but he needs socializing. He's been here longer than most because he's not cute and cuddly. But he likes you." She laughed. The dog was licking Jay's nose. "Obviously."

"I wish I could take him," Jay said ruefully, "but I travel too much."

All Erin said was, "Jay. . . " and let the rest hang in the air.

Jay stared into the dog's soulful brown eyes. Then the dog put out his paws and lowered his body, his eyes never leaving Jay's. She practically felt the dog saying, *Come on, give me a break, please.*

Jay let out a sigh. "Somebody gave me a chance when I had no hope," he told the dog, "and it turned out pretty well. Let's you and me take a chance on each other." The dog licked his face and let out a little yip. Jay laughed and said, "I'll take him."

Erin watched as Jay paid the fee and filled out the forms to adopt a mongrel of unspecified origin that Emilia told him was mostly border terrier.

Emilia was pretty matter of fact through the whole process—she did, after all, do this every day—but Erin was impressed and wasn't going to hold back. As they were leaving, she said, "Jay, you saved his life."

But Jay only looked worried. He turned to her. "You have to help me. I don't know how I'm going to find the time this little guy deserves."

As though she could sense his buyer's remorse, she said, "You *know* I will. It's going to be okay."

Jay seemed to relax a little. A warm feeling suffused her body and she realized that he trusted her. Really, truly trusted her. It felt good.

He said, "I guess living with me can't be worse than getting yapped at by a hundred other homeless dogs every day."

She laughed. "Definitely not. He'll be living in the finest house in all of Carmel-by-the-Sea." Without thinking, she added, "I'm jealous."

Jay gave her a look she couldn't read and she wished she'd kept her mouth shut. She hoped he didn't think she wanted to live with him. It was just that his house was incredible. She decided to say nothing further, in case she dug an even deeper hole for herself.

Jay lifted the dog and tucked him under one arm. One well-muscled arm, she couldn't help but notice, and while he was searching his pockets for his car keys, the dog licked his neck and then his ear. Her heart melted. Just melted.

"Are you going to keep his name?" Erin asked. Secretly, she thought Rocco didn't suit the poor dog at all. "The shelter people give the dogs names if they come in as strays."

"I don't think so," Jay replied. "It doesn't suit him." He looked down at the dog. "Is your name Rocco?" The dog sneezed.

Glad they were on the same page, Erin helped put the dog in the car. He immediately pushed his head between the seats. A little dog drool dripped on the butter-soft leather and there were a few strands of hair left behind on Jay's designer polo shirt. He didn't seem to mind, and she suspected that both these things would do him good.

"We need to pick up supplies," Erin said as she settled into the passenger seat with the dog now on her lap. She directed him to her favorite pet store and he bought the fanciest dog food, the fanciest bed, the most ridiculously expensive leash and harness, and some complicated gizmo that kept the dog safely strapped in the car, as well as some chew toys and treats. This dog's life was about to get a whole lot better—all his doggie dreams were coming true.

With the car fully loaded, Jay turned to Erin. "Will you come with me while I take him for his first walk?"

She'd been having a hard time keeping herself from turning into a puddle of goo watching Jay spoil his new pet, and this request didn't help matters. He seemed surprisingly nervous, a quality she'd never encountered in him before. Frankly, it was endearing. As tactfully as possible, she asked whether he'd ever had a dog before. He shook his head and looked a little ashamed. She found it adorable, but wasn't about to let him know. Instead, she agreed to accompany the two new best friends on their first walk. She didn't even suggest that they pick up Buzzy first, who was waiting patiently for her at home. She suspected that for this first walk, it was important that Jay and the dog have some time to bond without distraction. She could stand well back.

Jay parked in his drive and as soon as he opened the car's door, the dog bounded straight out and Jay had to chase him.

"He might need a bit of training," Erin called, trying not to laugh. She watched Jay as he quickly caught up. It was turning out to be the cutest—and most unexpected—evening with Jay. He'd been a goner as soon as the dog leaned against him, as if he were saying, "I'm yours. And you're mine."

For a second, a thought flashed through her mind about saying that exact thing to Jay, but then she forced it away. Yes, they were getting closer, but they were far from *belonging* to one another.

Besides, the two of them could never be.

Jay motioned for Erin to catch up and she joined them as they crossed the road, then took their first steps together on the white sand. There were quite a few other dog owners on the beach, catching the last of the light. Jay was hypervigilant, sweetly protective, keeping the dog on the leash and poised at the ready with the poop bags he'd bought at the store. The dog was utterly delighted, trotting alongside Jay and yipping at the water. Those two were going to get on just fine, she thought. She definitely liked this softer side of Jay a lot better than the brash hustler.

They stayed silent, taking in the beauty of the beach and watching the dog absorb it all. But as they were walking, Jay suddenly stopped and banged his fist against his forehead.

"What is it?" she asked him.

"I'm going to LA for two days. I've just adopted a dog and I have to leave. What am I going to do?"

Erin tried to look reassuring. She knew what it was like to get carried away falling in love with a dog and forget all about practicalities. It was easily done. But maybe not for Jay, who was used to being the one pulling the puppet strings in Hollywood and keeping track of every deal and detail with his clients. He must be kicking himself.

She put a hand on his shoulder. "It's okay. Calm down. We'll figure it out. When do you have to leave?"

"Tomorrow!" he groaned. "I never do stuff like this. I wasn't thinking. I'm going to have to take him back to the shelter."

"You're just panicking," she said in as soothing a voice she could muster. "You've taken on a big responsibility, but you're ready for it. I can help you."

He said, "Obviously, if I had more time I'd hire the best dog-sitter in town, but I don't have the time to vet somebody. And besides, it's such short notice."

The dog looked up at them with those large, brown eyes as if he understood everything they were saying and was worried he was heading straight back to the rescue center. It was heartbreaking. Nor did it require any more thought. "I'll do it," she said.

He blinked twice, clearly astonished. "Really? I mean, would you stay in the house for a couple of days while I'm gone?"

She had to bite back her smile. Did he really think it was a hardship to stay in the house of her dreams for a couple of days with two of the sweetest dogs in the world? "I'd be happy to."

Two seconds later, she found herself in his arms as he hugged her tight. "You're a life saver," he said into her ear. Her lobe tingled where she felt his warm breath. He squeezed her tighter then, and as he did, she felt the strength in him, the heat coming off his body. The sea air whispered through her hair, telling her naughty secrets.

The hug lasted just a moment too long. And then he pulled back as though one of the dogs running around had just bitten his ankle. All business again, he said, "Great. That's great. Come on back and I'll get you a key and the codes to the security system."

Chapter Twelve

To keep the conversation light as they walked back to Jay's house, Erin asked, "Any more thoughts on what you're going to name him?"

He seemed to puzzle over the question and then smiled. "I don't know. I'm not asking you, or you'll come up with something literary and obscure." His smile turned into a mischievous grin. "It should probably start with a *B* to keep it in the family. Since we already have Buzzy and Buster, why don't we add more confusion? I could call him Baxter."

Erin nodded, the phrase *keep it in the family* ringing in her ears—because Jay *was* an old friend of the family. In fact, he *was* family to the Davenports.

Experimentally, Jay called, "Baxter," but the dog didn't even look at him, just kept running.

"Not Baxter," she said, laughing. She thought over some other names beginning with *B* and then suggested Bullseye.

He bellowed, "Bullseye!" The dog kept running. "Bartholomew!"

Not to be outdone, Erin yelled, "Blacktop."

He turned and looked at her with a raised brow. "Blacktop?"

She shrugged. "Like the cab. I thought maybe he would stop if you called."

They both looked at the dog. Nope.

By the time they'd got to Brigadier and Bullfrog, they accepted that they were running out of names and the dog seemed uninterested in all of them. He said, "I need to give this some serious thought. As you know, names are important. I don't want to yell out something that's going to embarrass both of us."

She nodded. "You and the dog will find a name that fits. Give it a day or two. You'll figure it out."

They'd arrived at his house and she could see Jay wanted to say something, but was hesitating. He'd get there in his own time. She was liking this new Jay, who took more than half a second before speaking.

Finally, he said, "I have a spare set of keys ready, but do you want to come inside for hot chocolate? I really want you there to help the little guy settle in."

Erin smiled. It felt good to be needed like this. Really good. She should get back to Buzzy, but she was also dying to see how the unnamed border terrier/mutt mix liked his new home. After living in a crowded cage in a shelter, he was definitely moving up in the world. So she agreed.

Jay opened the door and showed her the code to

the security alarm. But no sooner did he let the dog off the leash, rather than timidly staring at his enormous, multimillion-dollar new home, he took off to race from room to room.

Jay looked at her. "What's he doing?"

She shrugged, totally surprised. "I don't know. He's a terrier. Maybe he's searching out vermin."

"*Vermin?* For the amount this place cost, his search better be in vain. I guess if he finds any, I'll have to give him an enormous treat."

They both followed the dog's erratic movements around the house, and then he roared up the stairs at top speed. By the time Erin got to the top, right behind Jay, the dog was in Jay's fabulous bedroom. He had leaped onto the bed and settled himself right in the middle of it.

She couldn't help it—the giggles took over. "I'll say it again—some training really is in order."

Jay shrugged with a sparkle in his eye. She could tell he liked the feisty spirit of his new canine friend. "You're not wrong."

The dog leaped off the bed and ran down the stairs and into the kitchen. They followed at a more sedate pace and then Jay pushed a button on a fancy-looking control panel. Music came on. He said, "Maybe some tunes will calm him down."

Shania Twain sang, *Man! I Feel Like a Woman!* while the pup sniffed here and there. When Taylor Swift came on, Erin hoped that the rescue dog might settle, but apart from stopping to slurp some water from his new designer water dish, he kept moving. Poor little guy, it must be so strange for him.

A Willie Nelson song came on and the dog stopped. Cocked his head. And then began to howl along with the music. Erin and Jay looked at each other and burst out laughing.

"Is he a country and western fan?" she asked.

Jay grinned. "A Willie Nelson fan, anyway."

They waited, fascinated, as the pup continued to howl and then howled again, and then the song ended and The Yellowjackets came on. He sniffed around the room in complete unconcern. Jay then tried Frank Sinatra. Nothing. Other male country singers. Nothing. He went back to Willie Nelson, trying a different song this time, and the dog threw back his head and howled.

He looked at Erin. "I think you're right. He's telling us what he wants to be called."

"Willie?"

Jay was looking at the dog with a fascinated expression on his face. "No, I can't call my dog Willie, but I could call him Nelson. That's a fine name, even if it doesn't start with a *B*." He tried experimentally, "Nelson? Nelson, come."

The dog perked up his ears and turned around.

He tried again. "Nelson, come here." The dog ran toward him, tail wagging. Jay glanced up at Erin. "You were right. He let me know. His name is Nelson."

She nodded. "I like it. It suits him."

Jay nodded, clearly happy to have solved this one. "Are you sure I can't tempt you with a celebratory hot chocolate?"

Erin paused. She was starting to think that Jay could tempt her with just about anything. She looked at him for a moment—that rugged stubble, the shaved head, the easy golden tan were all familiar to her. But the softness in his eyes? The tenderness as he patted Nelson? All that was so new. And so sexy.

She had to be careful. She could feel herself getting carried away with it all—the romance of the sumptuous house, the sweetness of the dog. And Jay in the middle of it all, busy and happy and thoughtful.

She shook her head. No hot chocolate. It was too creamy and delicious. Besides, chocolate put her in a naughty mood. "I'd better be going," she said lamely. "Could I have those keys?"

Jay looked disappointed, but he quickly recovered and went to fetch the spare keys.

As she was leaving, he said, "Hey, I know you've done so much for me already, but could you and Buzzy come for a walk with us early tomorrow morning before I fly? You heard the lady at the shelter. She says he needs socializing and Buzzy seems like he'd be a good influence. Also, if you and Buzzy are going to stay here, we should make sure they get along okay before I take off."

She had to agree. Everything Jay said made sense. Plus, a small, niggling part of her was happy she would see Jay again so soon. But again, she pushed it away. Trying to imitate Jay's natural businesslike manner, she made a plan to meet him at the beach at seven in the morning.

They stood for a moment on the doorstep, and there was an awkward moment when she didn't know whether to just walk off or hug him or give him a fist bump. They were in uncharted territory here. Ever since that intense hug full of longing on the beach, she felt as though she had to be careful. She didn't want either of them getting the wrong idea. Jay was *so* not for her, and she was *so* not for him, even though she was finding herself more and more drawn to the man.

In the end, he solved the hug/no hug problem by reaching out and giving her a pat on the upper arm. "Thanks for your help, there, short stuff."

Just his use of that nickname seemed to reset the relationship and remind them both that she was Archer's kid sister. "Good night yourself, there, big shot." She'd started calling him that a while ago, sometimes reminding him that the initials were *BS*.

★ ★ ★

Buzzy wasn't very happy when she got home. He sniffed her, obviously able to tell that she'd been spending time with another dog. This must be how a betrayed woman felt when she smelled another woman's perfume on her husband.

She gave her sweet dog extra attention and a dog treat. "It wasn't like that, honest. You're my one true love."

When she got the leash and took Buzzy for his own walk—an extra-long one with plenty of ball throwing—she could tell that all was forgiven. But when they got back, she explained to him that he'd be spending a lot of time with Nelson over the next few days. She only hoped they'd get along. She couldn't imagine what would happen if her dog and Jay's didn't like each other. It could be the end of the budding friendship growing between her and Jay.

However, the next morning she discovered right away that her fears were unfounded. She and Buzzy walked down on the beach to find Jay and Nelson already there. Nelson came running toward her, obviously remembering her from the night before, and seeing Buzzy, he ran forward, tail wagging, pretty much his whole wriggling body and posture saying, *Please like me!*

Buzzy played hard to get and didn't immediately extend the paw of friendship. He walked around a bit, they sniffed butts, and then Buzzy began to run. His favorite thing was to run along the beach, ears flapping, tongue lolling out. Nelson took off in hot pursuit. For a little guy, he was really speedy. They raced around, jumping all over each other, circling each other, rolling in the sand, while she and Jay walked along behind them enjoying the spectacle.

As the dogs dropped to the sand side by side, panting, she said, "I think your socialization experiment is working."

"I think it's hero-worship, not socialization."

She chuckled, a little proud. It was true—the younger Nelson jumped up the second that Buzzy did. And then they were off and running.

"How was he last night?" she asked. "Any trouble settling in?"

"Fine. He slept like a baby. We both did."

He looked a bit sheepish, and she turned to him, shocked. "Julius Malone, did you let that dog sleep with you on the bed?"

Big, tough Jay Malone looked pretty embarrassed. "I put that expensive dog bed on the floor and he wouldn't get in it. He just sat there looking at me with his big eyes. And then he kind of started to tremble. What could I do? I'm sure he'll grow out of it."

If she knew dogs—and she did—that would not be happening. But Jay would figure all that out for himself.

Suddenly he asked, "Are you reading anything good at the moment?"

She was so taken aback by the non sequitur that

she stopped in her tracks and peered at him.

He laughed. "Is it such a weird question?"

She shook her head. "Not at all. It's just not one I ever expected to hear coming from your lips." A sudden shiver went through her at the thought of Jay's lips. They were full and a pleasing shape and for a moment she thought about what they might feel like grazing her neck, her collar bone... down, down, until—

She stopped there, chastising herself. What was her mind doing? *"Prodigal Summer,"* she blurted.

"Prod what?" Jay asked.

She stared at him. Was he teasing her? His eyes *were* full of mischief.

"Prodigal Summer," she repeated. "It's by one of my favorite authors, Barbara Kingsolver. I read her novel *The Poisonwood Bible* when I was a teenager and I've loved her work ever since."

Jay looked thoughtful. "I should read more female authors. What's it about?"

Erin blinked again. Had the man who scoffed at putting his Hollywood heartthrobs in romantic comedies just admitted he should read more female authors? She swallowed. Was Jay saying all this stuff because he knew what she wanted to hear? But then she shook away that cynical idea. Deep down, she could tell, he was being his true self. Not the bravado-filled tough guy he'd been putting out into the world.

She took a breath and felt the familiar joy of explaining why she loved a particular author or novel. "It's set over the course of one long, hot summer," she said. "And it weaves three stories of love against a background of forested mountains and struggling small farms. The ecological narrative is as compelling as the human relationships, and it just gets to the truth of things somehow. I haven't finished it yet, but it takes my breath away, it really does." A little wistfully, she added, "If only I could write like that."

"But you're an incredible writer. And you totally get to the truth of things. Look how you were with me. I've spent years and years concealing my upbringing, but five minutes with Erin Davenport and I'm spilling my guts. You've got something in you that makes people feel safe, and you tell their stories beautifully." Jay looked like he wanted to say more, but stopped himself. "What is it about you that makes me want to tell you all my secrets?"

She was so shocked by Jay's sweet words that she had no answer for him. Instead, she held his gaze, a moment trembling and shimmering between them that seemed to last forever. She couldn't hear anything but the blood pounding in her ears. Couldn't see anything apart from Jay's gray eyes, which sparkled with what looked to her like lust and admiration. She felt soft at the knees, as though she might swoon onto the sand at any moment. Just like Hollywood.

And then he came closer, strong jawline tilting, and for a split second she thought—*my goodness he's going to kiss me*—

When suddenly Nelson came bounding up between them barking his head off. He was already protective, or maybe even downright jealous. She laughed nervously and Jay joined in. She was darned grateful to that dog for saving her from herself. The moment had dissolved like a mirage.

Jay bent down and picked him up, and Nelson licked his face happily.

I kind of want to crawl into his lap and lick his face too.

Chapter Thirteen

Jay left for LA with a heavy heart, a small bag of essentials in one hand. Nelson had only just come into his life and already he was leaving him. He felt like the worst dog dad in the world. But at least he'd saved him from a humdrum life at the rescue center, squabbling over cheap chow and who got the chewed-up squeaky toy. And now he had the best dogsitter in the world, Erin, and a built-in new best bud, Buzzy.

Without having to ask, he knew that Erin would head over to his place as quickly as she could. She would sense that Jay was worried about Nelson being all by himself so soon after he'd been adopted. He didn't want Nelson to develop abandonment issues— he knew exactly how it felt to be on his own with no role model. So he was determined to be a reliable carer for Nelson, and when work forced him away, Erin was the perfect substitute. Probably even better, if he was honest with himself.

How had it taken him this long to really get to know Erin? He'd learned more about her in the last two days than he had in fifteen years of being her brother's buddy and agent. And he liked it. He liked her. He *liked* her. She was a super interesting woman in her own right—not simply the youngest Davenport sibling, lost in the noise of her big family. Even though they'd only just said good-bye, he was looking forward to the next time they'd be alone together.

Erin was getting under his skin, with her thoughtful manner and her sense of humor and the way she made him laugh so hard. All those dog names beginning with *B* that no one would ever use. Women he'd dated in the past never made him laugh. . . not that he was dating Erin, of course. But given how much time they'd spent together over the last couple of days, he was amazed that he was never bored in her company, never dying to get away and be on his own.

She was also incredibly sexy—although frankly, even that thought would get him in serious hot water with Archer. He had to stop his mind from wandering in this direction for both their sakes.

At least Nelson loved Buzzy. That was one thing he didn't have to worry about. It was too cute how his little guy followed Buzzy around, looking up to the bigger, more confident dog to see how things were done. It reminded him again of when he'd first had dinner at the Davenport family home. Watching Betsy Davenport was how he'd learned table manners. He shook his head. Maybe he was getting soft now that he was in his mid-thirties, but he was really going to miss Nelson even though they'd only spent one night together.

If only he could get the idea of spending the night with Erin out of his head.

* * *

Erin might be doing Jay a favor by house- and dog-sitting, but the truth was that when she walked into the beautiful home she'd admired for so long, the favor was all his. Although it was strange moving out of her own home just up the street for the two nights Jay would be in LA, she could fantasize that this was her place. She'd cook herself dinner in that impressive kitchen and sit in the library and read whatever book appealed to her from his well-stocked shelves. And as much as she'd love to settle down for the night in that big, beautiful master bedroom, as Jay had said she must, she'd told him she was perfectly happy with one of the guest rooms. He hadn't pushed the matter, just shrugged and said he'd leave it to her.

Part of the reason she didn't want to sleep in his bed was because she'd surely end up in the sexy-thought land that she was working so hard to leave.

Since Buzzy and Nelson had already decided to be best friends, it was an easy enough gig. As she walked around at her leisure, really taking things in, what surprised her was how comfortable his home was. It wasn't show-offy at all. Sure, in his office he had a couple of trophies and a framed picture of himself with some of his bigger clients, but everywhere else the house was understated—as though Jay was more interested in allowing his tasteful art collection to shine than in displaying his famous connections. And not a single piece of furniture was ornamental rather than comfortable. Each piece had been chosen to be used and loved rather than simply to impress, and she was beginning to wonder if Jay envisaged this place as being more than just an incredible bachelor pad. Maybe he had a family in mind.

But then she laughed at herself. She was getting carried away. Jay, who only dated lingerie models interested in the next big shoot, was about as far away from starting a family as a person could get. The gorgeousness of this house was definitely doing a number on her, because now she was imagining her own family in here. Two, maybe three kids sitting at the huge kitchen table, drawing or doing their home-work. Buzzy sprawled out happily in his dog bed by the stove, Nelson next to him in his bed. And then for a split second, she saw Jay's strong, sturdy outline, gently stirring a copper pan of hot chocolate.

Luckily, a bark from Nelson tugged her back to real life. She shook her head at herself. Just because this house was a romantic dream didn't mean that she was actually living in either one. Besides, Jay wasn't the kind to have children. Or was he? She was learning so much about this man she'd thought she already knew. Maybe he would keep surprising her.

But what did it matter if he did want to have a family? She was never, ever getting together with Jay.

She continued her solo tour of the house—solo except for the two dogs, of course. Her editor had agreed that she could work from home for the next two days so she didn't have to leave Nelson. Pat, like pretty much everyone else in Carmel-by-the-Sea, was a dog person and understood how important it was for Nelson to remain in the same place while he was still becoming accustomed to living with Jay. Not that he seemed to be having any trouble settling in. If anything, in the few hours she'd been here, it already seemed as though he'd been the dog of the house for years, not two days. He had good manners too. He didn't beg at the table and sat before she offered him a treat. No one could guess what his past had been. All Emilia from the shelter had been able to tell them was that he'd been found wandering with no collar on, and since he hadn't been chipped, there was no way to find his owner, if he had one. He'd clearly been living on the streets for some time. But now that he was settled in a house, Erin could see that at some point he'd been trained. Or else he naturally had good manners. Either way, he was a pleasure to look after. And it was nice for Buzzy to have company. Her dog didn't seem to mind the hero worship at all and was quick to put Nelson in his place if he got too rambunctious or enthusiastic.

On her lunch break, she took the dogs for a long walk on the beach and was surprised to spot her brother Damien jogging down the sand. He was quite far away, but she'd recognize his longish, curly dark brown hair and lean silhouette at any distance. Damien wasn't always good at communicating when he was back home. His schedule with his band was so hectic that it gave Erin vertigo just thinking about it, but Damien seemed pretty happy with his rock-star lifestyle.

As he came into view, she waved hello and Damien grinned, his dark eyes sparkling. "You got another dog?" he asked in lieu of a greeting, looking at the two friends as they played in the sand.

She shook her head and introduced Nelson, who sniffed Damien briefly and then quickly returned to playing with Buzzy. Erin smiled. Emilia had been right—Nelson definitely wasn't as affectionate with other men as he was with Jay. Buzzy, on the other hand, was super happy to see one of the Davenport men and rolled on the sand, offering his belly to Damien for patting.

When she told her brother that she was house- and dog-sitting for Jay Malone, he seemed surprised—and a little suspicious. "I didn't know you guys were that friendly."

Erin had to will herself not to blush. "We're not. I went to his new house to do an interview for the paper."

Damien told her he'd just read it and thought it was great. She thanked him and then said, "Anyway, I'm just doing him a favor." She shrugged, like it was no big deal, although the idea of sleeping in his house that evening was filling her with a delicious kind of dread at where her mind might wander as day turned into night.

"Didn't you always love that house?" Damien asked.

"Ever since I can remember. It's my favorite house in Carmel."

"Then that's a nice gig for you. Hope it won't be too hard to leave, though."

She shook her head. "I'm perfectly happy in my apartment. But I won't deny it's fun to hang out in in such a gorgeous home for a couple of days."

Damien squinted against the sun and gazed across the beach to admire its lines. "Sure is nice. I think Crystal organized a wedding for the daughter of the people who used to own it."

At the mention of Crystal Lopez, the wedding planner, she realized she hadn't seen her high school friend in too long. They were overdue for a girls' night and Erin couldn't imagine a better location than Jay's house.

She said good-bye to Damien, who she'd see at the family home for breakfast on Saturday, and then sent a quick text to Crystal to see if she'd like to come over to catch up. The reply came back instantly.

Would love to. See you at 7.

Erin grinned and then called the dogs. It was turning out to be a perfect day.

* * *

Crystal arrived at seven fifteen, full of apologies for being late. She looked around and then whistled through her teeth. "Wow, Jay Malone has done a great job furnishing this place. It looks even better than I remember."

Erin had to agree. Although she'd never seen inside before, she instinctively felt that Jay had brought something special to the house.

"I hate being late, but I was dealing with a nightmare father of the bride," Crystal explained, flipping her glossy dark hair over her shoulders.

"*Father* of the bride?" Erin's eyes widened. "I've never heard of a nightmare dad during wedding planning. I thought they liked to keep out of it and just show up with tears in their eyes to give their daughters away on the big day." She showed Crystal through to the sumptuous kitchen and opened a cold bottle of Italian Pino Grigio she'd bought from a nice wine shop earlier that day.

Crystal laughed. "If only. This one kept telling me, in no uncertain terms, that since he was paying for the wedding, he expected everything to be perfect." She explained that the man was very high up in the military and barked orders at her like she was a green recruit. "I genuinely thought that if he didn't approve of the menu, he'd make me drop and give him fifty."

Erin burst out laughing and poured Crystal a large glass of the crisp white wine. Since she could never truly switch off from reporter mode, she asked, "Are there any upcoming weddings the *Sea Shell* should know about?"

Crystal took a seat as Erin put together dinner and shook her head. "I don't think so. I'm sure the colonel would be only too happy to have his daughter's wedding featured in the newspaper, but I can't think what they've done to deserve it. I'll definitely drop you an email, though, if I come across anything really good."

Business out of the way, they settled back to catch up. Erin wasn't much of a cook, but she threw together a simple tomato and mascarpone pasta, which she served with a fresh herb salad. As the wine level grew lower, they discussed their dating lives, which was sadly a very short conversation. Erin hadn't had a date in longer than she cared to admit. Crystal had recently enjoyed what seemed like a super promising relationship with a guy she'd met online, until he turned out to be the groom in one of the weddings she was organizing.

"Ouch," Erin said, reaching for her friend's arm and giving it a squeeze. "What a jerk."

But to Erin's surprise, Crystal only rolled her eyes as if to say *men, huh,* and then chuckled. "You think I was stunned? Imagine how he felt. I've never seen anyone go so pale so fast. I thought he was going to faint. Sort of wish he had!"

"Did you out him to the bride?"

Crystal looked shocked. "Erin, I am a professional. But as it turned out, the bride caught him kissing one of her attendants. The wedding's been postponed while they get some counseling."

Crystal's story stayed with Erin long after her friend had gone. It was a stark reminder of how sneaky and selfish men could be, and it dragged up the bad memories of her first year at college, which she tried to keep buried at all costs. She shuddered as she remembered that dark night, the wandering hands and insistence that he should have access to her body. . .

As if he sensed her distress, Buzzy came running over, with Nelson bounding behind him. He nudged Erin's ankles until she bent and curled her arms around him. He licked her cheek tenderly and Erin realized it was wet with tears. "You're the only guy I need," she whispered to Buzzy. There was a bark from Nelson.

"Okay, and you, too," she said with a laugh.

She finished tidying up after dinner, and decided to end the evening with another stroll on the beach so that the dogs could have their final walk. It was still warm out and she enjoyed having the nearly deserted beach. The soft lap of the waves, the smell of the ocean breeze—this was her favorite place on earth and it never failed to soothe and calm her.

When they returned, she went upstairs and got ready for bed, delighted that she had this gorgeous place all to herself and could get an earlyish night with a good book in the super luxurious king-sized bed in the guest room. But Nelson had other ideas. No matter what Erin did, he wouldn't settle. He kept staring at her and then running back to the master bedroom. As if that wasn't bad enough, Buzzy joined him.

In the end she threw up her hands. "All right, I get that the routine is to sleep in Jay's bedroom, but a little flexibility would be nice." It was pretty clear she wasn't going to get that, not from Nelson. So with a resigned shrug, she moved her few belongings into Jay's huge bedroom and guided the dogs into their respective beds under the window. The Barbara Hepworth looked so perfect where Jay had placed it that it made her smile.

And then she stared at his huge, beautiful bed for a good while before finally pulling back the covers and slipping between the sheets. They felt sumptuous against her skin, like bathing in silk. He'd told her the sheets were fresh and she appreciated his thoughtfulness. Still, this was Jay's bed, Jay's bedroom, and being here felt strangely intimate. Erin opened her novel in case her mind entered dangerous territory. Trying to keep her thoughts on the complicated plot, she adjusted the pillow and soon found herself turning the pages.

Until the bed lurched.

"Oh no." But Nelson was already curled up at her feet. Even as she tried to push him off, Buzzy made himself comfortable on the other side. Wondering how on earth she would ever get these two to do her bidding, she decided that was a problem for Jay and switched off the bedside lamp.

Chapter Fourteen

Jay had spent a long and arduous day in LA, but in the end, peace had been restored between his client and the director of the big-budget action film he was starring in. Tempers had gotten out of hand, egos had clashed, the resulting firestorm hadn't been pretty, but it was nothing he hadn't dealt with before. He was able to get some concessions from the director that made his client feel like he'd been listened to, and while there was no way the bad-boy celebrity would apologize, he did promise that the next time he was unhappy, he would phone Jay before doing anything else. Then he took the star out to dinner and massaged his bruised ego a little more. Finally, he was done and was in his car and on his way back to his LA home with a busy brain and something of a heavy heart.

The day would have been a lot easier if he hadn't spent most of it thinking about Erin and Nelson. He'd texted Erin three times, which seemed a little crazy, he knew, but he needed updates about Nelson—how he was doing, whether he was eating okay, and did she think he was settling in. Erin's responses had always been quick and each time she gave him reassuring news. He even received a cute photo of Nelson and Buzzy on the beach. But still, Jay and Nelson had barely got to know each other. He would just hate for the little guy to be confused or sad.

As he drove down the familiar freeway, he found his thoughts turning back to Erin, who right about now would be getting ready for bed. He couldn't stop himself from wondering what kind of garment she slept in; what side of the bed was hers. One thing he did know for sure—she wouldn't spend the best part of forty minutes on a complicated skincare routine like other women who had stayed in his home. He loved the idea of Erin locking up the house, switching off the lamps, and getting the dogs ready to settle down for the night. She would probably spend too long reading in bed, unable to stop turning the pages, promising herself it would be just one more chapter, like he did.

He shook his head. How was the thought of Erin so comforting and so sexy at the same time? He'd never experienced anything like it.

He made a sudden decision. He didn't want to wake up in LA. He wanted to wake up in Carmel-by-the-Sea in his beautiful new house, with the view of the ocean and his dog curled up beside him. What was the point of having a PJ if he couldn't use it to get himself home? So, he turned the car around and headed for the airport and what he was already starting to think of as home.

It was late when Jay finally pulled into his driveway. In fact, it had been late when he left LA, enough that he didn't want to wake Erin to tell her he was back a day early. He disabled the burglar alarm and crept into the house so quietly that not even Nelson heard him. After such a long day, Jay was exhausted and headed straight for his bedroom. As he pushed open the door, he could see moonlight coming through the open windows, casting the room in a beautiful silvery glow.

And then he saw her.

Erin was lying in his bed, the two dogs asleep on either side of her. As he gazed at the three of them, something softened inside him and he felt like his heart was expanding outward, filling the rest of his body. She looked—perfect. He finally had to admit to himself that he wanted to find Erin in his bed a lot more often.

And by *often* he meant *always*. Instead of the dogs, *he* wanted to be the one sharing the bed with her.

Nelson stirred, opened his eyes, looked at Jay, and thumped his tail. Then he went back to sleep.

Jay had never felt like this about any woman and the depth of his feelings scared him. It took superhuman strength to stop himself from sliding under the covers with Erin and pulling her close. Her skin would feel buttery soft, her breath warm and enticing on his neck.

He shivered and had a stern word with himself. To follow his urges and slip in beside her would be an idiotic move—she was sleeping and he would never take advantage of her vulnerability. But what if he called her name softly, to let her know he was home, and she invited him into bed?

He stood there another moment, wondering if he'd do it, and then he realized that above all, he wanted Erin to feel safe and secure in his home. So he left her there, sound asleep, and forced himself to go to one of the guest rooms instead.

* * *

Erin woke the next morning thanks to Nelson, who was more efficient than any alarm clock as he rolled around on the bed far earlier than she'd have liked. Buzzy decided that if Nelson was up, he'd better be too, and so Erin was outnumbered by their canine enthusiasm for the day.

"Okay, you two," she said to the dogs as she stretched her limbs. "You win."

She swung her legs out of bed, not bothering to don a robe over the cotton shorts and skimpy T-shirt she wore to sleep. It wasn't until she got downstairs that she realized she wasn't alone in the house. The smell of coffee permeated the air and when she entered the kitchen, there was Jay, frothing a jug of milk.

He turned. . . and gazed at her skimpy nightwear in frank enjoyment.

She felt herself turn a deep shade of pink and half squeaked, "What are you doing here?"

"I got home late last night. I didn't want to disturb you, so I tried out one of the guest rooms."

Erin was mortified. Jay must have come to his bedroom first and seen her sprawled out and probably drooling in the middle of his gigantic bed. "You should have woken me. I didn't mean to sleep in your bed, but Nelson wouldn't sleep anywhere else."

Jay grinned at that and bent to pat the dog, who was jumping up and down all over him. "Nelson has good taste. That room does have the best views."

Erin swallowed. She was trying to act cool even though she wanted to run upstairs and throw every bit of clothing she'd worn on top of her nightclothes. "How was your trip? How come you didn't stay over?"

"It was so successful I didn't need to. Besides, I wanted to get back to Nelson as soon as I could. It was harder than I thought to be away from him." He paused and an intense expression crossed his face. Erin wondered if he was going to say something more, but he just nodded toward the fancy coffee machine. "Coffee?"

She nodded. "Black please. And strong. It's early for me. Can you let the dogs out while I run upstairs and get dressed?" She held his gaze, refusing to be embarrassed that she was half naked. He'd obviously seen way hotter women in a lot less than she was currently wearing, but she'd feel much better if she covered up.

"No problem," he said, and then, "Come on, boys."

He was clearly an early riser and so cheerful in the morning. Erin was more of a *Don't talk to me until the third cup of coffee* type. Still, she scampered upstairs and pulled on underwear, then her faded jeans and a T-shirt. She combed her hair, brushed her teeth and then rubbed some moisturizer across her face.

Feeling much more respectable, she returned to the kitchen, where Jay was busy feeding the dogs. He straightened and then went to the counter and passed her a ceramic mug steaming with hot coffee. She took a sip. It was no surprise to find the man made the best coffee ever. Strong but not overpowering. A bit like him.

She took a seat to enjoy it and watched the dogs eat their breakfast with pleasure.

Jay followed her gaze. "They really seem to like each other."

She smiled. "They do. You should have seen Nelson last night. When Buzzy wants to go out, he doesn't scratch at the door, he comes and nudges me with his head. Nelson started doing it too. It was the cutest thing. He's a smart dog."

Jay looked proud of his dog's burgeoning brilliance. "Good to know," he said. "And thank you. I'd much prefer a little nuzzle than scratching."

Erin felt a lot calmer now she'd had some coffee and was properly dressed. "So, tell me about your trip."

"The usual. A clash of monumental egos nearly derailed a film in a way that would have been detrimental to both their careers. I rode to the rescue, got my guy back onside, and then got the director to accept that maybe he'd been a little hard on him. They both agreed to put aside their differences and the movie's back on track."

"That's great." She suspected there had been a lot of delicate negotiation that he wasn't telling her about. Having grown up with four brothers, all of whom had very healthy egos and strong opinions, she could only imagine how tactful he'd had to be. Then she laughed. "I was just thinking about my brothers. My mom had the best way of breaking up fights and getting them to be friends again."

His eyes twinkled. "Oh yeah. I learned everything I know about conflict resolution from your mom. Betsy is one heck of an impressive woman."

She loved that he admitted this. She loved that he respected her mom. Again, there was that moment of connection between her and Jay that was so strong it scared her.

He was obviously feeling it too, because he turned away, opened a cupboard door, and pulled out a frying pan. "Can I make you breakfast?".

Something cold arrowed through Erin. His suggestion felt way too intimate. Something about a man cooking her breakfast in his own kitchen made her remember she'd slept in his bed last night—which of course she had, but in the most innocent way imaginable. She needed to get her bearings. She hadn't expected Jay to be here this morning and her defenses were down. All the way down.

She stood. "I need to get to work pretty early this morning. Thanks, though." She finished her coffee and went to put the mug in the dishwasher. Jay intercepted her move and took it from her hand. For the split second his fingers touched hers, she felt a desire so overwhelming she had to take a breath.

Jay took a few steps back, set the mug down, and said, "I need to thank you for helping me with Nelson. Why don't I take you to dinner?"

Dinner. Normally when a man asked her out for dinner, it was a date, but the way he framed it, it was just one friend thanking another for doing them a favor. Although of course she'd loved every minute of staying in his beautiful home with his adorable rescue dog.

"Sure, that would be great. I'd love to."

Jay grinned, obviously relieved she wasn't going to try and dodge his offer. "How's tomorrow night?" he asked.

Erin had to hold back a bemused expression. Tomorrow was Saturday, which was a total date night. And yet she had no plans. Neither, it seemed, did he.

She said she was looking forward to it and then gathered the rest of her things. Dinner with a family friend thanking her for doing them a favor, she told herself as she made her way home. That's all it was, even though deep down, her feelings for Jay were much more than friendship.

Chapter Fifteen

Erin dropped Boswell at home, then walked over to meet Mila and Tessa at Anna's Cafe. Tessa glowed in her quiet way as she told the sisters that a very prestigious art journal was doing a piece on her work this month. She was so modest that Erin felt she was almost embarrassed to share such exciting news, and probably would have kept it to herself if Archer hadn't already outed her on the family WhatsApp group. When Mila chastised her for downplaying the whole thing, Tessa simply shook her head as though she couldn't believe her good fortune.

"A year ago, I was a paid caregiver keeping my art a secret. I never thought I had any talent, never mind that people would pay to put my paintings on their walls or that a top art journal would want to feature me. So sometimes I feel like I'm dreaming and if I pinch myself, I'll wake up."

Mila had always had incredible confidence and Erin could see she was struggling to understand Tessa's point of view. But Erin got it. "Imposter syndrome."

Tessa nodded eagerly. "Yes," she said, "and then on top of it, I wake up every morning beside a gorgeous, loving movie star. Honestly, how can I not be dreaming?"

They all chuckled at that. While Mila also visibly cringed at the notion that her brother was gorgeous, half the population thought as much. Harder for Erin to get her head around was why you'd *choose* to live with Archer—she'd spent eighteen years sharing a bathroom with the guy. But apparently it was different if you were married.

Erin couldn't help sharing her own experience. "I'm having kind of a fantasy experience myself right now. I woke up this morning in Jay Malone's bed." She waited for the two women's exclamations of shock and surprise to subside, along with, in Mila's case, a certain smug *I told you so* expression, and laughed. "He wasn't there. I was sharing the bed with his new rescue dog, Nelson."

She nonchalantly took a sip of her coffee and let the other two digest this news. Mila got there first.

"Wait. I don't get it. You're telling me that *Jay Malone* lets you sleep in his bed when he's not there? And he got a *dog*?"

"Those two things are actually related. I was housesitting for him and looking after the dog he rescued a couple of days ago. And it's no hardship. Mila, you really did find him the perfect house."

Mila was never unwilling to take a compliment. Her lips curved in a very satisfied smile. "I know. Honey, if you had a few more millions in the bank, I would have loved for you to get that house, but since you couldn't afford it, and Jay could, at least it's sort of in the family."

Erin cringed. To the rest of the Davenports, Jay was family. But after the last week, to her he was anything but. She couldn't hold the truth in any longer. She needed to tell the women in her life how she was really feeling. Who else could help her deal with such conflicting emotions?

Mila was looking at her with what she could only call a penetrating stare, so Erin put her cup down on the saucer with a slight clink and said, "I am so screwed."

Tessa immediately looked sympathetic. "I'm sure you're not. What's going on?"

"I think I have feelings for Jay Malone." She didn't say it like *I like him and I hope he likes me*, it was more a cry of despair. How was it possible that the man who could not be a worse match for her was making her feel like a horny teenager?

Mila laughed, and her earlier smug look intensified—almost as if she'd been certain all along that this crazy pairing would work. "Don't look so tragic," she said. "I told you before I could see you two together. He's super hot, and he's in your dream house. Go for it. Have a whole bunch of hot sex and worry about the details later."

That was what Mila would do, but she wasn't Mila. She was Erin, the quiet one who lived in her head more than her body.

She glanced up to find Tessa looking at her with understanding. Much more what she'd been looking for here. "What made you change your mind?" Tessa asked softly.

"Jay surprised me," Erin admitted. It was simple and it was true. "But that doesn't mean he's the right man for me." She shot a penetrating look of her own in Mila's direction. "And I'm only interested in Mr. Right."

Tessa made a murmur of agreement. "I remember having those feelings about Archer. It wasn't that I didn't think he was right for me so much as he was a million miles away from me in every way but physical proximity. I tried to so hard to ignore my own feelings, never realizing that Arch was having feelings too. Is there any chance Jay feels the same way you do?"

She thought back to that moment on the beach when they'd hugged a little too long, and then again when a kiss had hovered just beyond reach and they'd both pulled away.

"Sometimes it feels like he's interested in me too, but I'm so far from his usual type that maybe I'm seeing things that aren't there just because I'm longing for them."

Mila said, "Maybe you need to let him know in no uncertain terms that you're available for plenty of hot sex and no strings."

Before Erin could even reply, Tessa shook her head. "Erin's already tangled up in emotional strings, aren't you?"

It was such a nice way to put it. Erin nodded. "I can't believe it. He's brash and annoying and pushy, but then you see him with his rescue dog and it's the most adorable thing ever. I think that's when I fell for him—when he took this scrappy dog that no one else wanted and saved him. And did you know that Jay Malone reads?"

"Oh," Mila said, understanding dawning. "A guy who reads is your biggest weakness in the world." She seemed to think about it for a minute and then said, "At least he's hot. Not like that drippy young photographer who looks at you with his tongue hanging out."

Shocked, Erin said, "Clark? We're just friends."

"Everybody in town knows that Clark wants to be a lot more than your friend. It's kind of funny to watch him follow you around, a bit like Buzzy does."

She didn't want to laugh at poor Clark, but even she could see it was sort of true. She was never sure what to do about him. They were friends and, okay, she knew that his feelings were warmer toward her than hers were to him, but on the other hand, he never tried anything and she didn't want to lose him from her life.

"But enough about Clark," Mila declared. "So you have feelings for Jay—both in and out of the bedroom." She put up her hands. "I say jump his bones and go for it."

Erin shook her head at her sister. Why was she not surprised that this was still her advice? She turned to Tessa, silently appealing to her to suggest something other than getting naked.

Although naked did sound good. More than good. Amazingly, skin-tingling good.

"You could try talking to him," Tessa suggested. "Tell him how you feel?"

Neither of those things seemed like an option. Erin felt more confused than ever. Jay was part of her life— her brother's agent and practically family. If she let him know that she was developing feelings for him and he didn't return them or didn't want to act on them— which was extremely likely—how embarrassing would that be? Family brunches would always be awkward.

No, she liked the way he'd reset things, calling her *short stuff*, and she'd immediately retaliated by calling him *big shot*. Just like when they'd first gotten to know each other and he'd teased her and she teased him right back. No doubt she was creating a fantasy in her head because he'd surprised her so much with his story about his past and his affection for the dog. Not to mention his well-stocked library.

Decision made. Their dinner tomorrow would be a friendly thank-you and she would bury whatever feelings were trying to bubble to the surface.

"By the way," Mila said, "I forgot to compliment you on your piece about Jay. I thought you did a really good job. You made him sound much more relatable than most profiles I've read."

Mila was never one to pull punches, so she was pleased that her sister thought she'd done a good job. If she only knew how much of that interview Erin had kept to herself. But she would continue to keep Jay's disadvantaged background secret until he decided it was time to share it. As she left the café, she decided it was good she was going to the auction tomorrow with Clark. It would take her mind off Jay and her eroding sense of self-preservation.

That man was messing with her head, heart, and body in a big way.

* * *

Erin had to finish another story about the local animal shelter running out of funding and just as she was wrapping up the final details, Clark appeared at her desk. He waited until she'd finished typing and then said, "Still on for the auction tomorrow?"

She might not have romantic feelings for Clark, but he was a good friend and the auction would be a good distraction—and talking point—for dinner with Jay later that day. She nodded and noticed that he seemed more excited about this one than usual. "What is it that you're after?"

He grinned, and she had a feeling she'd be bored for the next half hour as he waxed lyrical about the details of some obscure camera she'd never heard of and wouldn't recognize if she saw it. Sometimes she wished her work buddy was passionately interested in art or jewelry or antiques, but photography was his deal. The nice thing about tomorrow's auction was that it also included the former as well as the latter.

She promised to meet Clark in the morning and then wrapped up her story and sent it to Pat for an edit. For just a moment, she allowed herself to imagine Jay at his office, sitting in his very expensive chair at his very expensive desk, making decisions about big-budget Hollywood productions, Nelson curled up happily at his feet.

Chapter Sixteen

Jay hadn't really intended to go to the auction Clark had mentioned during his shoot for the *Sea Shell*, but after a long walk with Nelson on the beach Saturday morning, he found himself with the better part of a day free, which almost never happened. He was scheduled to be flying back from LA today, hence the empty calendar. He looked up the auction online and checked out some of the items. One thing caught his eye—a camera that had been used to make silent movies. The same model that had shot *Citizen Kane*. He was still looking for some quirky, interesting things to add to the décor of his home. A Mitchell Standard would be an amazing conversation piece.

If he was honest, a small part of him was determined to go because Erin would be there with her friend Clark. Not that it seemed like she had any interest in the poor guy, but Jay knew that men could be dogged in pursuit of the women they adored. It would be a chance for him to observe the two of them, to see if they were more than just friends. Also, he felt

protective of Erin. And although he tried telling himself
that it was none of his business, he wanted to keep an
eye on Archer's kid sister to be sure she wasn't making
a mistake.

No. It was more than that. Erin confused him. She
was getting under his skin in a way that left him
wanting more. So much more.

He headed out and thought again how much Carmel-by-the-Sea already felt like home. With the
sunshine warming him as he drove alongside the
ocean, it was clear that he was living in one of the most
beautiful places in the world.

He found the auction house and headed inside to
the buzz of people chattering as they maneuvered
around the antiques. Although he was keeping an eye
out for Erin and Clark, he soon got caught up in all the
quirky, fun stuff. There was a whole area of art,
jewelry, and furniture, but he was drawn to where the
cameras were displayed. He wasn't especially a camera
geek, but he loved everything to do with the movies,
and that silent-movie camera was calling him.

Brochure in hand, he was fascinated to read more
about the Mitchell Standard, the 35mm studio camera
introduced in the 1920s as a hand-cranked silent film
camera. According to the information provided, the
camera came with a four-lens turret, a matte box on
rails mounted to the front of the camera, and options
that included a film footage counter and an internal

matte disk with nine pre-cut mattes, including half-frames, circles, keyhole, binocular, and oval. He thought about how basic that was and yet how charming. It would have been really noisy, but that wouldn't have mattered in a silent film. It wasn't until 1926 that they had to worry about camera noise—and the stars' voices.

He was admiring the camera when Erin appeared at his side. He grinned at her and then noticed Clark trailing behind her, looking like a kid who'd just wandered into his very first toy store. His eyes were big and it was like he didn't know where to look next because he wanted to take it all in at once.

Jay was pleased to see Erin, so he was surprised at the slightly accusatory note in her tone as she asked, "What are you doing here?"

The same question, twice in two days. As if he had to defend himself. Jay kept his own tone light. "I'm interested in the Mitchell Standard. It's the same camera that was used to film *Citizen Kane*. Can you imagine? How fun would that be as a conversation piece in the house?"

She looked slightly taken aback, probably at his enthusiasm for a camera that was over one hundred years old.

But Clark got it. "That's going to go for a lot of money. It's a find."

Jay felt a bit crestfallen. "Are we going to bid

against each other?" It wasn't that he couldn't outbid a guy who made his living as a photographer for a weekly, but he didn't want to crush a young man's dreams either.

Luckily, Clark shook his head. "I could never afford it. Besides, I'm after a vintage Leica from the thirties." He wandered off to look for the camera he was hoping to bid on.

Erin remained silent, looking deep in thought, her eyes trained on the Mitchell Standard without really seeming to take it in.

Before he could stop himself, Jay blurted, "So, are you guys on a date?"

She looked shocked. "No. I don't date people I work with."

Jay looked over at Clark, all gangly and geeking out over the camera. "It's just that he sort of seems your type."

Erin scoffed, instantly looking suspicious. "What do you mean?"

Jay shrugged. He'd known her for so long. Did she really think he hadn't noticed? "You tend to go out with geeky guys who don't challenge you."

If she'd been a cat, Erin's back would have arched and she would have hissed at him. "You don't know that."

"Actually, I do. I've been in your life a long time. And I've got eyes."

She looked stunned for a second, and then put her hands on her hips. He was in for it now. "Well, Mr. Lingerie Model Dater, since you won't go out with a woman whose assets aren't on full display at all hours, I'd say the pot was calling the kettle black."

He almost laughed. "Lingerie model? Can you not even say the word *underwear* to me?"

"Of course I can."

"Then prove it."

For some reason she blushed. He'd only been joking about her saying it out loud, but she almost stammered as she half-whispered, "Underwear."

And then regret filled him. Regret at challenging Erin about her taste because clearly he was jealous—jealous of a geeky young guy who obviously had no chance with Erin. Regret at asking her to say *underwear* because now all he could think about was Erin in sexy underwear that he would very much like to peel off her. And yet he loved how she'd obliged him, how she'd said the word even though it embarrassed her. It made him wonder what else she might be willing to do just for him.

He barely stopped his train of thought before his body got in on the act and started to react. This was ridiculous. Erin was not a potential lover. He had to get that through his rebelling mind and body, no matter how hard it was.

And oh boy, was it hard.

Erin excused herself and went to rejoin Clark. Jay felt like a fool, especially since he had been looking forward to taking Erin out to dinner later to thank her for dog sitting. Now he wouldn't be surprised if she canceled.

He walked on around the auction house, but his heart wasn't in it anymore and nothing else took his fancy. When the auction started, he found a place near the front and then saw Clark and Erin join a little later at the back.

Clark had been right. The opening bid for the Mitchell Standard was pretty high, but Jay had already decided he was going to buy it and nobody was going to outbid him. He already had the spot picked out in the living room where it was going to stand. He'd treat it nicely, honor its heritage. He liked to think that he was helping to preserve a little piece of movie history, and one day he'd probably donate it to a film school or a museum or something. But for now, he just wanted to enjoy it. Apparently, it still worked. It would be really fun to make a movie on it. He was positive Archer Davenport and Smith Sullivan would get behind such a project.

He watched idly as other items came and went. And then the Leica that Clark was interested in came up. He was rooting for the kid, but Clark stopped bidding when the price got too high. He could see the absolute disappointment on his face, and some impulse that he didn't even understand made him discreetly join the bidding. He didn't even think Clark or Erin had realized that he was in it. And Jay didn't like not to win. So, in less than a minute the Leica was his.

With the auction over, he went to collect both his items, feeling pretty pleased with himself. The Mitchell Standard was being very carefully boxed up, and he was given a ticket to drive up and receive it, but the Leica they handed over to him. He was about to phone Erin when he caught sight of them ambling slowly away from the building.

"Hey, Erin, Clark—hold up," he called.

When they turned, he jogged forward and presented Clark with the camera. Clark's face transformed— first with shock, then with pure joy—and Jay felt a rush of happiness that he'd made this guy's day. It had been a long time since he'd hung out with people who didn't have more money than they could ever hope to spend, so it was refreshing to see someone so thrilled by a gift that was all but nothing to Jay.

Clark stammered, "I can't believe it. Wow. Look, let me pay you what I can."

But Jay shook his head. "It's my pleasure. And I get it. I like to think that these pieces of history are going to people who'll look after them and enjoy them."

Clark nodded enthusiastically. "I will take such good care of this. I don't know how to thank you."

Jay smiled. "Why don't you come and have coffee

with me? I'm new to town and don't really know many people."

At this point, Clark would probably have given him a kidney if he'd asked, so coffee was a no-brainer. During the whole exchange, Erin hadn't said a word. Instead, she was watching. But that was Erin all over. Quiet and observant.

As the three of them walked to a coffee bar that Clark knew near the auction house, Jay realized he was actually having a great day. He'd got himself a fabulous piece of movie history and had done a good deed for another human being. He was feeling pretty good about himself. When Clark insisted on buying the coffee, he let him.

While he was getting their order, Erin and Jay hunted for a free table, which wasn't easy on a busy Saturday. When one became free, they jumped on it and then waited for Clark.

Erin was so quiet he wondered if she was holding a grudge about his earlier comments. But then she said, "That was a nice thing you did for Clark."

He decided to tell her the truth. "He reminds me a little of me when I was younger. Full of passion, with some pretty geeky interests. So I knew exactly how good that camera would make him feel."

She laughed. "I never saw you as a geeky guy, but I think maybe you've just hidden that side of yourself pretty well." She gave him a smile that was almost coy.

"A master of disguise. You were born for the movie business."

Jay smiled back. "Hey, I'm sorry if I was out of line earlier. Who you date is none of my business."

Did he imagine it, or did Erin look disappointed?

But she only shrugged. "You're not wrong." And then she changed the subject. "So, what are you going to do with the movie camera?"

"I might make a silent movie. For fun. I bet Arch and Smith would be up for it."

She shook her head, laughing. "I can just see Archer hamming it up."

"Not just Archer. We should get your dad involved, too. Can't you imagine him all big and showoffy? In fact, all your family would love it."

"Not me."

He shook his head. She was telling the truth. "No, you'd be behind the scenes. Probably the screenwriter."

She smiled, as though she was pleased he understood her that way. "Definitely."

And then he had a thought. "Have you ever considered writing a screenplay?"

She tilted her head. "It would be impossible to say I'd never thought about it, since obviously there's an actor in the family, and he talks a lot about scripts. But I've never pursued it."

He didn't comment, just nodded, because Clark

was arriving with the coffee and he didn't want to embarrass Erin any more than he already had today.

As the three of them talked, Jay could see that Clark was hopelessly in love with Erin. But his earlier instinct about the two of them had been right: She didn't return that love. Even though she and Clark were close friends, it would never be more. Frankly, he was relieved, mostly because he didn't want her wasting herself on somebody like Clark.

It flashed through his mind that he would make a better match for her, but obviously they could never be more than friends.

* * *

Erin did what she did best: She sat back and watched Jay and Clark converse. She'd noticed before that Jay could get along with just about anyone. He was naturally charming, and though he was opinionated and talked a lot, he had a way of making other people feel at ease. Now that she observed him with Clark, who was his polar opposite, she realized just how much he did to make other people feel comfortable with him. She was beginning to wonder if that was what he'd done with her all those years ago when they'd first met. Had he made sure that as a big male, he wasn't at all threatening? Had he deliberately put her into the little-sister role because that would make things easier for her, and for him too? There were a lot of things to think about now that had never before entered her head.

Jay asked, "So, Clark, what are you interested in, apart from vintage cameras?"

Erin groaned inwardly. Jay was about to get Clark started on his favorite subject.

"I love *all* cameras," Clark said, pushing his glasses up his nose, as he did when he was enthused about something. "Not just vintage cameras." He leaned forward. "I'd love to be a camera operator for the movies, but I've never had enough money for film school."

Jay made a noise like a snort. "I never went to film school either. LA is all about appearances and connections."

Clark looked rather deflated. "Which I don't have."

"What have you done toward becoming a cameraman? I mean, apart from taking photographs for the *Sea Shell*, obviously."

"I just do that for money."

Erin took a sip of her cappuccino. Clark was kind of endearing, especially when he let his enthusiasm rip. She had sometimes wondered if part of her appeal for him was that her brother was Archer Davenport. Not that Clark would ever take advantage of the connection; maybe it was more that he felt she brought a little stardust into the room just by being the sister of a movie star. Clark told Jay about the short movies he made for fun.

And then to Clark's shock and her surprise, Jay said, "Why don't you send me a couple of your shorts? I can't make any promises, but I know of an entry-level position that might be opening up at one of the studios."

Into the stunned silence, Clark said, "Are you kidding me?"

"No. But it would mean moving to LA."

"It would be my dream job."

Jay smiled. "Well, let me see your stuff, and if I like it, I'll put in a good word for you."

Erin had always thought Clark had real potential, so while she was kind of irked that Jay was all but stealing the *Sea Shell*'s photographer out from under her nose, she was also pleased for Clark. She'd always known they'd lose him one day to bigger things.

Belatedly, Jay seemed to realize what he was doing. "Erin, am I landing the paper in it here?"

She smiled, letting him know she wasn't angry at all. "Yes. You are."

He shook his head. "Then I guess I owe you."

It was such an innocent comment, but something shimmered between them, something hot and sexy.

And then Clark burst through that moment, fumbling with his new camera. He turned to Jay. "I'd like you to be the first person I take a portrait of with this camera. It came with eight frames left on the roll inside it."

Jay smiled and said of course, but he wasn't going to steal the limelight. He shuffled closer to Erin, slung his arm around her shoulders, and pulled her in tight.

Professional that Clark was, he spent ages getting everything just perfect. Meanwhile, she felt the warmth of Jay's arm around her, could smell the spicy heat of his body, almost hear his heartbeat, they were so close. Her own heart began to pound wildly, and she realized she wanted the moment over but also for it never to end.

Clark frowned, and then got up, moving her head her head ever so slightly closer to Jay, and rearranging the casual way his arm was draped into more of a hold. Clark pushed the now empty coffee cups to the side so only the two of them were in the frame. That was exactly how it felt—as though the whole world had emptied out and it was just her and Jay. Clark took his time; this wasn't a digital camera he could click away on like crazy. He was careful and ended up taking only three photographs—but she'd bet each of them would be technically perfect.

Jay said thanks and then quickly let his arm drop. He moved away from her as though nothing had happened.

Had Erin temporarily lost her mind? Jay had just been casually posing for a photograph, not trying to get up close and personal. She chastised herself for getting carried away.

"I'll swing by at seven to pick you up for dinner."

Erin said that sounded like a perfect plan.

It was. All too perfect.

Chapter Seventeen

Jay had sort of been lying to Erin.

No, not lying, he just hadn't told her the complete truth. Nelson had definitely been missing her, but the worst part was that Jay had been missing her like crazy too. Because she was great to be with, and also because his body wanted what his body wanted. He swore to himself that was the only reason he couldn't stop thinking about her, that maybe he just had a little crush. But deep down he knew that wasn't true either. More serious emotions for Erin were taking root. But instead of grounding him, he felt as though he were holding a grenade that was about to explode and take them both down.

So, he continued to tell himself a story—that Erin was like any other woman. That the reason he couldn't stop thinking about her was that he hadn't slept with her and he wasn't used to not getting what he wanted. Maybe it was about time he dealt with that part of himself and grew up.

He'd make sure that tonight was only about saying

thank you. He'd wine and dine her and show her an amazing time—all without trying to get her into bed. Maybe this way he could train himself out of his feelings and get her out of his system. He needed to do something to fix how much he longed to be with her all the time.

Even as he was thinking this, he imagined an angel on one shoulder and a devil on the other. The angel was telling him he was full of BS, which was kind of funny because that was Erin's nickname for him. Big shot—which was a tease, of course.

Since he wanted the evening to be special, he'd chosen a restaurant on the coast that was so exclusive it had to be booked months in advance for even a remote chance of securing a table. But he knew there were always a few tables kept aside for special clients, of whom he was one. When he called the day before and asked for an intimate table with a view, they'd said absolutely and they'd be delighted to see him.

He should have been looking forward to dinner, but now that Erin was due at his place any minute, he felt a little apprehensive. As though he'd just made a huge mistake, but he couldn't figure out what it was. He tried to shake the unfamiliar emotion away. He was Jay Malone. He knew how to close a deal. And that's what this was—he was just saying thank you in the best way he knew how.

Except, as he shaved, it felt a lot like getting ready

for a date.

Would it really be so bad if it were? Maybe that's how he could get Erin out of his system: allow himself this one date and then move on and get back to being friends. He could still recall her body warm against his while Clark had taken a great deal of time setting up his shots earlier that day.

He pushed the memory away and thought about Clark instead. He'd been watching the guy, thinking his instincts were right. He'd bet those shots were great. Maybe he really could help Clark get on the path to his dream career. And then he remembered how pleased he'd felt that the man was so meticulous, because he loved sitting there snuggled up against Erin, enjoying her softness, smelling her scent... and for those moments, allowing himself to think about how much he wanted her in his bed.

* * *

Erin eyed her open closet, her gaze roaming over the modest selection of clothes. Jay hadn't said where they were going, but knowing him, it would be somewhere fancy. Maybe even flashy. However, Erin wasn't like Mila—she didn't have a closet crammed with designer clothes. In fact, she had a pretty small wardrobe because she only liked to own pieces that she truly loved. She pulled out one of her favorite dresses. It was blue-green and made of fine silk. She didn't have many opportunities to wear it, but since she'd been shopping with Mila when she saw it, her sister had talked her into buying it, insisting she'd always regret it if she didn't. It was one of the more expensive pieces she'd ever invested in, but Mila had been right. Every time she wore it, she had a good time.

There was also the small bonus that Jay had never seen her in it.

She took extra care with her appearance, carefully making up her face with a light hand so that her eyelids shimmered and her skin glowed. She even went to the trouble of putting in hot rollers so that her hair fell in loose waves around her face. She might not be a lingerie model, or any kind of model, but she looked her best.

As she slipped on some simple strappy sandals, she mused that at least she might be better read than some of Jay's usual dates. She was still pleasantly surprised by his library; at least they wouldn't run out of things to talk about. But why was she even worrying about that? It wasn't like this was a date... except for the butterflies in her stomach saying otherwise.

She was about to leave her apartment when he texted to say he was waiting outside. She grabbed her keys and stepped out into the warm evening. And there he was, waiting by the passenger side of his Lamborghini, looking particularly sexy in a sharp navy suit and crisp white shirt.

She laughed as he waved and said, "Your chauffeur has arrived." His eyes flickered over her briefly and then held her gaze. "You look breathtaking, by the way."

Erin smiled, thanked him, and then slipped into the car. If there was one thing Jay knew how to do, it was to make a lady feel good. Her earlier nerves about not looking like a model melted away and she decided to just enjoy herself tonight because it was a one-off—even though her body ached for it to be more.

The powerful engine roared as they headed off down the coast. Erin relaxed into the leather seat and let Jay do the talking while she admired the beauty of where she was lucky enough to live. After some time had passed, she began to have an inkling of where they might be headed, and when they pulled into a secluded spot high above the ocean, her hunch was confirmed.

She turned to him in astonishment. Le Nuit was a place she'd heard about, read about, but where she'd never imagined herself dining. "Jay," she said, "you have to book this place months in advance."

The grin he sent her was cocky—the Jay she liked least. "They know me here."

And that line told her more than she wanted to know. He obviously came here frequently. Who had he been with? Clients he was wining and dining, perhaps even her own brother, but almost certainly with other women. As they walked in, she knew she'd been right. She caught a flash of surprise on the maître d's face. It was quickly gone, but Erin got the message loud and clear: she was not like the usual women who walked in beside Jay. She felt uncomfortable but held her own, even as they were led to their table and she realized that the exclusivity of this place was its downfall—it felt sterile and snooty, and the other diners looked like they were more interested in being seen than in what was on their plates.

Jay nodded and said a quick hello to a couple of people as they walked by, and then they were seated at a round table for two draped in white damask. The owner himself came over, enquired after Jay's health, introduced himself to Erin, and then asked, "Champagne for the lady?"

Before she could even reply, Jay said, "That would be great. And I'll have—"

"Your usual Scotch, sir?"

Jay chuckled, obviously delighted that the owner of one of the top restaurants in California had memorized his drink order. "You got it."

Erin tried not to frown. It wasn't that she didn't want the glass of champagne, but it might have been nice if she'd been allowed to answer for herself. Still, she was nothing if not polite.

The drinks arrived swiftly, and Jay raised his glass. "To you, Erin," he said, smiling. "Thank you for all you've done for me over the last week."

She clinked his glass good naturedly, and as they took their first sip, a very good-looking man came toward their table. She recognized him—a movie star, and one she was pretty sure Archer didn't like.

"Jay, my man," he said, as if they were old pals.

"Tom, how's it going?" He didn't seem to mind the interruption. If anything, he was enjoying being recognized. Once again, this was the Jay that Erin liked least.

"Can't complain," Tom said, shrugging and then giving them a flash of his perfect white teeth. "We should have lunch."

"Absolutely. I'll get Gina to put something in the calendar."

The man nodded and then looked at her with his eyebrows raised. Jay said, "This is Erin."

"Good to meet you, Erin."

"You too, Tom."

He and Jay talked business for a couple of minutes. Erin studied her menu, feeling like a spare part, but when Tom drifted off, Jay said, "If you take my advice, you'll let them choose our meal for us. That's how you get the best food here."

She was game. She didn't recognize most of the things on the menu anyway. He ordered a bottle of wine that she knew would be expensive, from the number of French words he had to pronounce, and then they were just looking at each other across the table. An awkward silence fell.

She thought back to earlier in the day when he'd been so much more relaxed and more himself. "I have to tell you that Clark is in heaven about the possibility of that job in LA."

Jay chuckled. "You don't have to tell me. He's already sent me three short films and his resume. As sorry as I am to steal a good man from the paper, I have to tell you those shorts are good. He's got an instinct and an eye that can't be taught. I predict your friend Clark is going places."

She was genuinely happy for Clark. It was nice to see good things happen to a friend. "We have some freelance photographers, so the paper won't be without one, but I'll tell you right now—you're going to make an enemy of Pat Sinclair, our editor. She's pretty fierce."

"I'm sure I can handle her," Jay said with amusement. He was fully back to being his old self. Erin didn't know where to take the conversation from there, but luckily she was saved by the arrival of a tiny glass of what the waiter explained was clear tomato consommé.

As lots of small plates with tiny, very pretty things topped with foam were brought to the table in a seemingly never-ending relay, Erin found that, while she was enjoying the food, she couldn't quite relax. The restaurant was more about style than substance and, just as when she found this quality in people, it put her on edge. Still, it was nice of Jay to bring her to such an expensive place, so she told herself to just chill out and enjoy the evening as their conversation finally turned to books and LA and how much he liked his new home.

"It's such a beautiful house and you've done a great job making it into a home. I really enjoyed staying there."

Jay gave her a funny look and leaned in closer. "When I walked in on the three of you sleeping in my bed the other night—" He paused and held her gaze, and the intense expression in his gray eyes had her heart pumping a little harder. "I was very tempted to climb in as well."

She let out a long, trembling breath. She couldn't even speak. The deep emotions she'd been pushing down inside welled up and she couldn't deny her feelings for another second. Jay's gaze was still trained on hers and she had a feeling they both knew what was going to happen next.

She could barely taste the fancy little dessert they brought out, and both of them turned down coffee. Before she knew it, they were back outside looking at the water swirling and crashing against the rocks below them. Her heart pounded with a similar rhythm.

Jay turned toward her and she was positive he was going to kiss her. She was feeling a little wild—maybe it was the wine, maybe it was the setting, maybe it was because it had been so long since she'd been with a man, or because Jay was such a sweetheart with both Nelson and Buzzy. Whatever it was, she made the crazy decision that she was ready, not only to kiss him, but to go home and sleep with him too. In fact, she was so turned on by the prospect that she tingled all over and could hardly stand still.

She couldn't wait for him to make the move and was about to lean in herself, when Jay tilted up her chin with a finger. "Has anyone ever told you that you have the most beautiful eyes? No, don't look away, it would be a crime."

Her heart plummeted like a rock through water.

She pulled back and said, "Stop!" before he got out the rest of his awful line and embarrassed them both even more. She stared at him, horrified, all of her desire snuffed out like a candle in a cold draft. "This is what you always do, isn't it? This is your signature move to—" She made air quotes. "—*seal the deal* and get some unsuspecting woman into bed. News flash— I'm not an *underwear* model." She emphasized the word just to let him know she could say it to his face.

Instead of backing off and apologizing the way she expected, he almost leered at her. "I did see you in your bathing suit. You *could* model."

Erin shook her head, outraged. This wasn't the Jay she liked. This was the hustler. The big shot. And now she was on the receiving end, being hustled.

What had gone wrong? On some level, she wondered if he was nervous, and trying too hard, but she was too angry to think it through.

She took another step back. "Does talking to women like that ever work?"

He still had that cocky look on his face. "Sure. Like you said, I always seal the deal."

Erin's revulsion had to be written all over her face, because at last it dawned in Jay's eyes that he'd blown it.

"*Deal?*" she all but shouted. Her brothers had taught her how to hit a man without hurting her hand, so she could get in a surprise shot if she wanted to. But she stopped herself. She was better than that. More calmly, and very clearly, she said, "I am not a deal. Nor am I another notch in your bedpost."

Jay looked stricken. All the color had drained from his face and the cocky smile was long gone. He threw up his hands and said, "No. That's not what I meant."

"I can't believe I was almost ready to go home with you." She paused and let it sink in just how much he'd screwed up. "And now you'll *never* see me naked." With that, she stepped away, pulled her phone out of her bag, and called a cab.

Jay followed her. "Erin, come on—at least let me drive you home."

She kept her back to him. "No. I'm too angry."

Luckily, there were plenty of cabs nearby to pick up patrons from the very fancy restaurant, so one pulled up right away. She strode toward it, but Jay overtook her and managed to open the door for her.

She glanced at him as she got in and before he shut the door, he opened his lips. She waited for him to apologize. Instead, he said, "You know I can't resist a challenge. I'll have you in my bed before you know it."

She simply raised an eyebrow, letting him know she didn't care about anything he had to say. In a clipped, emotionless voice she said, "In your dreams."

Chapter Eighteen

Jay stood by the side of the road watching the taillights of the cab get smaller and smaller as Erin put space between them. *In your dreams.* He wondered if she would ever know how true those words were. Not only had he royally screwed everything up, but he was also definitely going to dream about her tonight, and the next night, just the way he had all week.

But now he'd made a complete mess of things, all because he was nervous and had acted like a clown.

He stood there long after the cab had disappeared from sight, powerless, rooted to the ground. He had to fix this, but he didn't have a clue where to begin. He was used to things going his way and he had taken that for granted when he should have been putting Erin's feelings first. This whole evening was supposed to have been about making her feel special and appreciated. Instead, he'd made her feel like just another in a long line of women.

The reality was that she was special. So incredibly special.

Slowly, he walked back to his car. He started the engine with a heavy heart. Even the car felt empty without her. He'd been so stupidly excited on the drive there, and now he didn't even want to go back to the house because somehow it already reminded him of Erin. He let the engine idle for a moment, wondering what to do. There was a restaurant and bar nearby that he knew well, The Ram's Head, which was part of a working sheep ranch. It had been owned by an A-list actor for years. Jay wasn't much of a drinker, but he headed there anyway. It was a secluded spot—perfect for hiding away—and it was only a few minutes' drive.

He went straight to the bar, happy to be anonymous, since no one who worked there knew him. He greeted the bartender and ordered a double whiskey, then after a beat added, "And keep 'em coming." A line out of a cheesy Western, but he didn't care. He felt exactly like that lonely drifter in every Western who walks into a bar and orders a drink to drown his sorrows. If this really were a Western, some gunslinger would walk in and pick a fight with him. Luckily, mostly tourists and locals had come out for a decent meal or a quiet drink. It was peaceful here. Not showy like the restaurant he'd chosen for Erin. It had seemed like such a good idea at the time, but now that he thought about it, Le Nuit didn't suit Erin at all. He should have taken her somewhere more relaxed and intimate. He should have brought her here.

He looked out at the rolling green fields full of sheep and then back to the tables around him. Everybody there seemed to be part of a couple, and they were all enjoying each other's company, talking with ease and laughing. That should have been him and Erin this evening. If he hadn't made such a mess of things, he could only imagine what they might be getting up to right about now.

The bartender was true to Jay's request and kept those double whiskeys coming, though he kept an eye on him. Probably making sure he didn't make any trouble. But Jay was just getting quietly, sloppily drunk.

The day had started so well. The auction had been so much more fun than he'd imagined and now he'd ruined the day. The whole damn weekend. To try and cheer himself up, he thought about the antique movie camera he'd bought, and how he wanted to use it to make a genuine black and white picture. It would be so cool to shoot something on the same kind of camera that had been used to film *Citizen Kane*.

He kept drinking and as he stared out at those fields of sheep, an idea for a movie came to him. He didn't usually come up with movie ideas, but he was pretty sure this was a good one. And he knew exactly the two A-listers he wanted.

He pulled out his cell and hit speed dial.

For some reason he had trouble getting the name

out. He'd never known *Archer* was such a difficult word to say. "I've got this great idea for a movie 'bout sheep."

Archer seemed a bit confused. "Jay? Is that you?"

"'Course it is. I'm telling you—I've got a great idea for a movie. There are all these sheep. In a field. It's a meadow—I mean, metaphor. Not an action movie. It's a metaphor."

"You want to make a movie about sheep?"

"That's what I said." He kept having to repeat himself and Arch seemed to be having trouble understanding. Finally, Jay said, "Never mind. I'll do you up a treatment, send it over in the morning, but pencil some time in. I want you—you an' Smith in the starring roles."

Archer said, "Why don't I come and get you? You can tell me about the movie while I drive you home."

"No. I'm good. Get a taxi."

He got off the phone and then immediately called Smith Sullivan, managing to down another double whiskey between calls. Again, he went through the explanation about the sheep and the metaphor.

Smith said, "You mean you want to make an art-house movie?"

Jay shook his head from side to side but stopped when he it made him dizzy. "It's a metaphor," he insisted. "All the sheep, in a pen. That's the human condition. But then the ram could have all the sheep and he only wants one. But she won't have him."

Jay felt sad, so sad, at the thought of that poor ram who only wanted one sheep, and she rejected him.

Smith asked, "Am I going to be a sheep? Is that what you're saying?"

"No. I was thinking… a shepherd. You and Archer. Both shepherds."

Smith said something to Valentina in the background and it kind of sounded like they were laughing. Did they think his movie was a comedy? Finally, irritated with them both, he said, "I'll get back to you tomorrow. Send you a treatment."

"You do that."

When Smith offered to send a car, it reminded Jay that he really needed to get home. Once more he said he'd take a cab. What was with Smith and Archer wanting to ferry him around? He was a grown man. He got up from the barstool and nearly fell on the floor.

The bartender offered to get him a cab, which he thought was very decent, but he said, "No, I'll walk." He'd find someone to drive him back for his car in the morning.

He wasn't sure why he felt this compulsion to walk, but he needed fresh air, and he wanted to smell the ocean. As he headed out, he looked up at the silvery moon and inhaled the salty ocean as he listened to the gentle crash of the waves. It was so beautiful.

But its beauty only served to remind him that without Erin, all that lay out there was a whole big world of loneliness. He wished Erin was beside him.

Why did he feel like he'd just made the worst mistake of his life?

Chapter Nineteen

When Jay got home, he was greeted by a dog bounding up and down, unbelievably happy to see him. At least he had Nelson, who didn't know what a screw-up he was. Even through his whiskey haze, he knew his dog would need an evening walk, so he managed to pull himself together enough to get the two of them out and onto the sand. The crisp salt air soon had a sobering effect, and by the time Nelson had tired himself out, Jay had concluded that the only thing left to do with this sorry day was to end it by going to bed. He dragged himself back into the house and up to the bedroom, where he instructed the smart speaker to play some Willie Nelson. The dog crooned as though he, too, had a broken heart, and Jay fell into bed without bothering to take off his clothes.

The next morning, he was awakened by the jarring noise of a phone ringing. He rubbed his temples, wondering where he was and why he felt so awful. As he lifted his head, he realized he was still fully dressed, and had passed out on top of the covers. When he tried to sit up, he also realized he had the mother of all hangovers. Nelson slowly opened one bleary eye and then shut it again. The phone continued to ring and Jay cursed under his breath. Unless it was one of his top clients, he had no intention of answering it. He searched around him and then squinted at the display.

When he groaned, Nelson lifted his head. "It's Smith Sullivan," he explained. "We always answer the phone when it's Smith."

Nelson gave him a bemused look, then went back to snoozing.

Jay hit the answer button and then Smith's voice boomed down the phone, all loud and cheerful. "I just want you to know I'm fully in with the role you offered me yesterday."

Jay rubbed his face. Yesterday's stubble met his fingers. He had no idea what Smith was talking about so he tried to bluff. "Right. The action film?" Had they been talking about a new action film? He was so hungover he couldn't remember.

Smith sounded like he was seriously trying to hold back laughter. "Yeah, it's going to be so good, out there in the grass with the sheep. All those sheep and that lonely old ram. You were inspired when you pitched it to me last night. I had trouble getting to sleep, I was so excited about it."

Jay was silent as he held up his throbbing head with the phone on one side and a hand on the other. "There were sheep?"

Smith finally burst out laughing. "There were *only* sheep. Valentina and I are still laughing. Jay, what on earth were you up to last night?"

"I might have had a couple of drinks too many," he admitted. He scratched his head. Sheep? He wanted to make a movie about *sheep*?

Then Smith turned serious. "I know you don't drink like that as a rule. What's going on?"

He and Smith went way back—almost as far back as he did with Archer—and right about now he was feeling sorry enough for himself that he needed a friend. He decided to tell at least the core of the truth to Smith Sullivan who, in love as he was with Valentina, was the perfect person to help him in this situation.

He swallowed, unsure of how to put such unfamiliar feelings into words. "I've completely fallen for a woman and she will have no part of me." He paused. It was strange to hear himself speak this way. This was not the kind of thing he'd ever said to anyone before and the words felt odd in his mouth. He needed to lighten the tone. "I'm not a hot A-list actor like you." This wasn't the reason Erin had rejected him, but his default defense was always to joke around.

But Smith wasn't having it. He'd known Jay too long and he clearly knew what a friend in need sounded like. "Have you shown this woman the *real* you? You play a good game, like I always used to, but look how much Valentina had to get past when she met me. I was an actor, always under the spotlight when she prefers privacy, and what's more, I was playing the role of her sister's love interest in a movie. And now I'm about to become a father, because thankfully, Valentina stuck around long enough for me to convince her that we had what it took to make it. You act like you're all about the big deal, Jay, but you're a good man underneath. Let her see that."

Despite how rotten Jay felt, Smith had managed to make him smile. Maybe he'd phoned to make fun of him—and who could blame the man—but there was kindness there too. He was checking up on his agent to make sure he was okay. And Jay appreciated that.

Plus, it was really good advice. "You might be right," Jay said, inwardly cursing himself for treating Erin like she was just another girl when she was anything but. Smith had his number—Jay had defaulted to his well-worn playboy dealmaker persona, the guy who saw getting a woman into bed as a challenge to be overcome. But he didn't feel that way about Erin, and she wasn't that kind of woman, so what had made him act that way? He must have known his behavior would drive her away.

Secretly, in the part of himself where he still felt like a little kid from a roach-infested apartment with no hope, just his own hustle, did he feel he didn't deserve a decent woman like Erin? Because he'd sure succeeded in blowing the one incredible chance she'd given him.

While he was thinking, Smith said, "And get that script to me about the sheep. I'm already doing some shepherd method acting to get ready for the role."

Smith was still laughing when he hung up.

Jay shook his head and vowed never to drink again. He needed to get on with the day and somehow make amends with Erin.

He managed to get to his feet, take the dog out, put on some coffee, and take some painkillers. He was about to head upstairs to a long, hot shower and shave off that sad stubble when his phone rang again. Once more he groaned. Archer Davenport. Another person he always picked up for.

As he said hello, Archer sounded in suspiciously high spirits.

"I didn't offer you a part in a sheep movie, did I?"

Archer was cracking up now. "Smith and I were so excited to be shepherds. And then it got a little confusing with the whole 'it's a metaphor' and then a ram entering the scene, or something like that."

Well, it was nice *someone* saw the funny side of it. He was feeling pretty humorless, himself. He was glad that Archer hadn't video called and seen the sorry state he was in, still wearing his wrinkled suit and barely managing to keep the coffee cup from shaking in his hands.

"Sorry about that," he said. "The evening got away from me."

Archer, as Smith had done before him, turned serious. "Smith says you're in love and that's why you got plastered. You were drowning your sorrows because she rejected you."

Jay's stomach lurched unpleasantly. In love? Those were words he hadn't admitted to himself. He just couldn't go there. This was *Erin*. There was something about her unlike any woman he'd ever known. And now he was on the phone with her *brother,* who had all but said he'd cut off a vital body part if he so much as touched her.

How had he gotten himself into this mess?

He managed, "I don't know about love. . . but she's not like the others."

Now Archer sounded just plain curious. "Who is she? Your heart never broke over any of the lingerie models you've dated." Quickly he added, "No offense. But you are a one-track kind of guy."

Jay winced. Those women were from another lifetime. "She's not like that. She's different."

"That's great. Who is it? Anyone I know?"

He shuddered. Holy hell—if her brother knew it was Erin, Jay would be in big trouble with his very talented and heavily muscled client and friend. So all he said was, "I screwed things up anyway. She doesn't want to see me ever again." Jay looked down at himself. If Erin could see him now, she would run a hundred miles to get away.

Archer was quiet for a moment, clearly thinking things through. After a few beats had passed, he said, "Jay, I hope you make things right with this woman. I never had a chance with Tessa until I told her how I felt. You have to get real and you have to be vulnerable. It's the only way."

Jay took a deep breath. Archer's advice was good, but if he knew that he was giving Jay advice on how to win his own sister. . . Well, his head hurt too much right now to even contemplate all the complexities of that. All he knew was that dating Erin had always been problematic. Now, it was just plain hopeless.

"Hey, man, you should come over for dinner tonight," Archer said. "Tessa will cook you something healthy to make up for your heavy night."

Jay hesitated—it was such a genuine offer of friendship that he was truly touched. But he couldn't imagine having dinner with Arch and Tessa while hiding the fact that the woman he was crazy about was Arch's sister, so he thanked him and said he already had plans for the evening.

Jay put down his phone and wondered what on earth to do with himself. Even on a Sunday, he nearly always had work to do, but today he just wasn't up to it. There were all kinds of things he could do, people he could call, but he didn't feel up to any of that either. He couldn't stop thinking about Erin. He wanted to apologize, but he didn't know how. He didn't even think he could face it today. He needed a day to lick his wounds, get himself back into fighting shape. Because he felt as though he was in a battle—a battle to win her back, or at least get them on the comfortable, friendly footing they'd enjoyed for so long.

It wasn't until Jay had showered and shaved and come downstairs feeling a lot more human and ready to take Nelson for a proper walk on the beach. He opened the door and noticed an envelope sitting atop his welcome mat. His name was scrawled on the front in unfamiliar handwriting. He frowned—his first instinct always being to brace for trouble—but when he opened it, he found a note from Clark, thanking him again for the camera and a chance at his dream job in Hollywood. Jay smiled. A hand-delivered note was a nice, personal touch. The kid would go far.

But then he saw something else in the envelope. He pulled out a black and white photograph and his heart began to beat double time.

Clark had developed the shots from the coffee shop. All that fussing and moving of paper cups and changing of poses ever so slightly had really paid off. If a picture was worth a thousand words, this one about two people who looked really, really good together. Erin was so pretty, beautiful in a way she didn't even realize, because she'd always been so overshadowed by Mila and her movie-star and rock-star brothers. But quiet, unobtrusive Erin was a knockout. And the way she was looking at him, the way he was looking at her... He could feel again the sensation of her shoulder against his chest, how good she felt nestled in his arms.

As he looked at the photograph, he no longer had any doubt he had to try to get Erin to forgive him. To give him a shot. Because he had never felt this way before and he wasn't about to let her slip through his fingers.

But how was he going to fix the mess he'd made?

He needed to clear his foggy head, so he donned sunglasses, clipped an ecstatic Nelson to his new leash, and the two of them set off for a glorious long walk on the beach. Not even his hangover could stop him from enjoying the fresh breeze, the sand, the surfers out daring the waves, the couples strolling arm in arm, and of course, the other dog walkers. It was just a happy place, and when he was with Nelson it was impossible for him not to be happy there too. He couldn't help searching the other dog walkers, wondering if Erin might be among them, even though he knew she wouldn't be. If she *was* walking Buzzy, then she would have found a spot so far away and so secret that newcomer Jay would never have known about it.

No, he wasn't going to be bumping casually into Erin on the beach anytime soon. If he wanted to make it right with her, he was going to have to think of something else. And fast.

Chapter Twenty

By the time Jay arrived home, he'd come up with the beginnings of a plan.

He glanced down at the copy of the *Sea Shell*, the one where he'd been profiled, still lying on his desk.

Telling Nelson that he'd return soon, he called a car service so he could pick up his car. Then, on impulse, he headed for the library. Libraries had been his refuge when he was a kid with no money to buy books. They'd been a safe place where he could hang out and read, escape into other worlds, learn things he never learned properly at school. Even now, donating to libraries to help keep them afloat was one of his biggest charitable endeavors. It made him happy to think about kids like him or people who just didn't have a lot of money being able to access everything from recent thrillers to all the great classics. They also carried newspapers and magazines, and he was pretty sure the local library would keep back issues of the *Sea Shell*.

But when he got there, the library was closed because it was Sunday. He felt like banging his head against the closed door.

Back home he was greeted by Nelson as though he'd been gone a year, then found the library website. They had online services, and to his delight all the issues of the *Sea Shell* were available. He put on his glasses and settled down to read, searching out only Erin Davenport's byline. He read everything she'd written in the last two years. Every single thing. There were profiles of important people and celebrities who'd moved to the area, her Dog of the Week feature— which was probably his favorite thing she did—articles about school plays and funding, and he noticed that a few times she referenced romantic comedy movies. That was funny, because it was one of the things she'd asked him about in their interview: Why was he always making movies like *Shock Tactics* and not putting his actors into rom coms? Now he realized that, as well as calling him out on some blatant sexism, she had also been showing him a side of herself he hadn't seen before—a softer, more girly side, that loved to cozy up with a rom com.

He took off his reading glasses and settled in his chair. He'd spent a couple of hours getting to know Erin in a new and intimate way. He'd been inside her mind, he understood her wry sense of humor, and most of all, he understood what moved her, what caught her heart.

And he knew another thing for sure: she was a damned good writer. She could set her sights a lot higher than the *Sea Shell* if she wanted to, but knowing Erin, she wouldn't want that at all. If he'd ever known someone who was exactly where she wanted to be, it was Erin Davenport. She was the least wealthy of the siblings, and her ambitions weren't nearly as lofty, but she lived with a kind of contentment that was rare to see. Spending so long with Erin's voice, absorbing every story and every word, he could feel her sliding deeper and deeper into his heart.

Maybe Smith was right. Maybe this *was* what love looked like. He shook his head in disbelief.

He was in love!

And now that he had finally faced the truth, he knew exactly what he could give Erin to show her how much he cared.

As quickly as his fingers could type, he messaged his assistant.

Pull every romantic comedy script that's come in and send them to me asap.

Even though it was Sunday, Gina was far too much like him. She responded within seconds. It was one of the reasons he employed her and paid her an extremely healthy salary.

Is this some kind of joke? Or are you delirious with fever?

Great. Even his assistant thought he was a one-trick action-movie pony. He assured her he was serious, and within an hour, she'd emailed him half a dozen scripts and told him he'd have paper copies by courier first thing in the morning. He felt better than he had all day and, his plan in motion, settled back in his chair with his tablet.

Soon, though, he began to frown. In his opinion, they were all terrible.

"I could do a better job than this."

Nelson opened one eye skeptically, then sighed and went back to sleep.

★ ★ ★

On Monday morning, Erin was still seething over Jay Malone's embarrassing juvenile tactics to get her into bed. How could he not have seen that she was already there and didn't need some cheesy, tried-and-tested line? She had been showered, shaved, primped, wearing her best underwear and her prettiest dress, her body already tingling, imagining how the evening would end. And in her wildest dreams she'd never imagined he'd make such a spectacular mess of it all. If he'd just kissed her, gently and softly, if he'd just showed her that he cared, he'd have had her. Instead, he'd treated her like a woman he'd just picked up in a bar and figured she'd fall for his stupid lines.

On some level, she still felt that he'd deliberately sabotaged himself, that he didn't know how to be himself instead of the deal-sealing Hollywood agent character he'd so carefully crafted over the years. But knowing that was one thing, forgiving it another entirely. She was still too angry to really consider the psychology of what had gone down on Saturday night. All she knew was that she felt insulted, furious—and if she never saw Jay Malone again it would be too soon.

Even more irritating, all day Sunday she'd expected some feeble apology from him, but nothing. Not a phone call she could have ignored, not an email she could have deleted, not even a text message she could have refused to open. He hadn't even given her that satisfaction.

And she felt like the world's greatest fool for checking her phone every five minutes just so she could ignore him.

To take her mind off it, she and Buzzy had gone for a long walk on Sunday that turned into a six-hour hike, exhausting the pair of them. She'd thought about calling Mila and suggesting they go out for dinner, but she would have blabbed the whole story to her sister and, as mad as she was at Jay, she didn't want to do that. Maybe it was to protect herself from embarrassment. Maybe it was also to protect Jay. Because she couldn't shake the feeling that she was right about him—that he was a good guy, deep and caring and thoughtful. And sometimes he was an idiot. A great big idiot.

And then she got angry all over again.

After her long hike, she'd cleaned her apartment from top to bottom, cooked herself dinner, and sat and watched *Four Weddings and a Funeral* for the umpteenth time. At least romantic comedies never let her down. Even if they were fantasy. She went to bed exhausted, but found she slept badly.

Now she was at the office, tired and irritable, trying to get her Dog of the Week feature finished according to her own high standards. But as she finally made it to the last line, the newspaper's receptionist, Stacey, called, "Erin?"

She sighed in annoyance, her concentration broken.

"Something's just been delivered for you. It's from Jay Malone."

Even the sound of his name filled her with fury. Whatever it was, it was too little, too late. She didn't even turn around. "If it's flowers, please take them to the library so everybody else in town can enjoy them."

"It's not flowers." Stacey sounded puzzled. "Um. . . I think these are movie scripts."

That got her attention. She spun around in her chair. "What?"

Since Stacey obviously had no intention of bringing them to her, Erin got up and stomped to the front desk.

Stacey held up a sheaf of papers with a big, fat binder clip holding them together. Bemused, she took the packet and glanced down. A handwritten note lay on top.

From the desk of Julius (Jay) Malone
CEO, Exceptional Talent Ltd.

Dear Erin,

I really screwed up on Saturday night. I knew that if I sent you flowers you'd just give them to somebody else who'd appreciate them more, so I thought about a way I could show you how sorry I am. I'm sending you half a dozen romantic comedy movie scripts from some of the top writers in Hollywood. You said I never put my actors in romantic comedies. Well, thanks to you, I'm willing to do that. Pick the one you like best. Whichever you choose, I will get it made. You have my word. This is my way of saying sorry.

Sincerely,
Jay

Erin stood there in the middle of the busy office, too stunned to move. He'd done it. He'd actually done it. Better even than a sincere apology on bended knee, his agreeing to make a romantic comedy showed that he got it. That he got *her*. She wasn't sure how long it took to make a movie, but that was a lot of grovelling he was prepared to do. *For her.*

Her anger drained away. In fact, she was more than

a little bit charmed. She read the note again and appreciated how he wasn't too proud to actually say sorry. That was a hard word for anyone to get out, but he had let his guard down and had apologized to her in the most genuine way he knew how. It was so much better than flowers. She also couldn't help but be impressed that he knew her well enough now that he'd guessed she would give any flowers away.

At last, he'd scored another point on her internal emotional scoreboard, which was good, because after Saturday night, she'd been tempted to take away all of his points forever.

Chapter Twenty-One

Erin had to wait a whole tantalizing afternoon before she could go home and read the pile of scripts. She began the first one over dinner, then moved to her favorite armchair.

She started out full of anticipation, but by the end of the evening, she was horrified. *This* was what people thought was romantic comedy these days? The scripts sucked. She was going to message Jay, or maybe just email him—she didn't want to seem too eager. But then she decided that the personal and yet formally couriered note had a certain distance to it that she liked. She didn't want Jay to think she'd completely forgiven his appalling behavior. Still, he'd managed to get her interested enough to want to respond.

She went to her desk and retrieved some of beautiful stationery her mom had given her one Christmas, but which she hadn't yet had the opportunity to use. The paper was cream, with a small posy of pink wildflowers at the top. Perfect, Erin thought, for correspondence about romantic comedies. She sat for a good while, chewing on the lid of her pen, before she finally committed ink to paper.

Dear Mr. Malone,

Thank you for your correspondence and the attached screenplays. I have to say that each one was more trite, lackluster, and disappointing than the last. I cannot recommend that any of these be made. Only someone who has no idea of romance would think these could be made into decent romantic comedies.

Sincerely,
Erin Davenport (Ms.)

She grinned when she finished. It struck exactly the right note.

Taking Buzzy along for the ride, she hopped in the car and drove to Jay's place. She was about to get out when she saw him leaving, Nelson in tow, heading toward the beach for an evening walk. Note in hand, she scampered up the path and placed the stack of scripts in front of his front door. Before she headed home, she couldn't help but watch Jay and Nelson for a few minutes as they ran and played on the beach. Those two had definitely bonded, and so quickly.

For just a moment, she was tempted to join them, but then she decided against it. Even if it seemed as though his heart was back in the right place, she was still pretty mad at him. He had not nearly finished groveling.

She drove home, full of gleeful anticipation at Jay's reaction and wondering whether she'd receive another note tomorrow, and finally got a good night's sleep.

* * *

Jay had wondered all day if he'd hear back from Erin about those screenplays. He'd kept checking his phone and was bitterly disappointed not to have received a message. She must still be angry with him, grand gesture or no, and frankly, he couldn't blame her. He'd acted a complete fool.

At least he had Nelson, who was always happy to see him, happier still when he took him to the beach and he could play with the other dogs, as he was now. Jay had begun to look forward to these evening walks across the white sand as the best part of his day. He smiled and threw the ball again and again. Nelson seemed to have boundless energy. If only he could have some of that pure puppy contentment. But his heart was heavy and every time he thought about Erin, his stomach lurched with shame at the way he'd behaved.

Finally tuckered out, Nelson followed him back to the house, where Jay found the stack of screenplays on the ground outside his front door. Was this her way of telling him to get lost? And then he saw the note.

As he read it, he began to smile. Okay, she hated

them all—frankly, so had he. But at least she was
talking to him, and if he wasn't mistaken, she was also
being a little playful. The relief that coursed through
him was like one of those huge waves he'd seen her
ride the evening he'd gone to her with a warm towel
and made her hot chocolate. He took this as a good
sign, and decided there and then to write to his assistant and ask for more scripts.

Still, reply or not, he was out of his depth with
Erin. She was so different from the women he usually
dated, and although he was willing to put a lot more
effort into making her happy than he had with anybody
else, how to do this exactly was proving tricky. He
wished he had someone to confide in.

Wait. He did. One woman had been a kind of mentor and mother figure to him for years. He checked his
watch; it wasn't too late.

He called Betsy Davenport.

She picked up after a few rings and sounded
pleased to hear from him.

"It's not every day I get a call from one of my favorite agents," she said, a teasing warmth to her voice.
"How have you been, Jay? I'm glad Mila found you
that house. Carmel's lucky to have you."

He explained he'd been keeping well and loving his
new place. "There's something I'd like to talk to you
about. Can I drop by tomorrow? Maybe for coffee in
the morning?"

"I'm just grading papers, if you want to come by tonight. You're in the neighborhood now."

Jay grinned. Trust Betsy to guess he was itching to talk to her as soon as possible. He was so happy that she was willing to see him. He was burning to unburden himself to her.

And so, fifteen minutes later, Jay found himself sitting in the Davenport kitchen with Betsy. She made them both a mug of herbal tea and asked him how he was settling in, and he told her all about Nelson and how much he loved having a dog.

"And you're enjoying the new house? I was in it once," she said. "I remember it had a lot of bedrooms." Her tone had a questioning inflection that Jay couldn't miss.

He opened his mouth to give his usual answer about having extra bedrooms for friends and clients who wanted to stay, but this was Betsy. She had given him the perfect opportunity to discuss what lay so heavily on his mind. Shyly, he admitted, "I know this might come as a surprise, but I really do want to have children." He added quickly, "With the right woman."

Betsy reached over and patted his hand. "In spite of all those shallow women you've chosen to date, I've always known you were a family man at heart."

And now he had to get to it, the thing he most wanted to talk to Betsy about—even though the prospect of it scared him half to death. The Davenports had become very much like a family to him and the thought of upsetting them in any way was terrifying. But the thought of losing Erin was more terrifying still.

So, he took a breath and plunged in. "You might kill me for saying this, but I think I've fallen in love with your daughter." Then he added, "Erin," because he didn't want her thinking he'd fallen for Mila. Betsy said nothing, just looked at him with her steady gaze and kind eyes, until he added, "But we all know I'm not good enough for her." There, he'd got it out.

Now, instead of looking shocked or slapping his face, Betsy looked as though she was trying not to laugh. Finally, she said, "Jay Malone, you are so much better than you think you are. Besides which, I saw this coming ten years ago." She gave him the broad smile of a woman who has been proven right.

Not only was she not giving him the boot out the door, she was all but welcoming him into her family. He couldn't believe it. *He'd* never seen this coming. How had Betsy seen what he couldn't see?

Jay shook his head. "Erin was always just Archer's kid sister. But since moving to Carmel and getting to know her more through the *Sea Shell* profile and getting a dog at the rescue center. . . well, it's like I'm finally seeing the real Erin for the first time. And I'm finally the real Jay."

"I'm not sure that's true. I've always had a feeling about you and Erin. I've noticed the way you pay attention when she speaks, which not everyone does because she's so much quieter than her siblings. You encourage others to make space for her when they're busy hogging the conversation. And when I saw you two dancing at Archer's wedding, I thought maybe that instinct I'd had ten years ago was proving true. You just looked right together."

Jay wanted to hug Betsy and ask her if she could put in a good word for him with her daughter. But he had another confession to make. If he was going to be the right man for Erin, then they had to know the real him, too. So, he took a deep breath and told Betsy all about his terrible past, his difficult childhood, his addict mother, the hustling, the stealing of food. It was everything he'd told Erin and felt so torn about afterward.

Interestingly, now he'd let that story out once, it was easier to let it out again.

Once more, Betsy didn't seem shocked, or even particularly surprised. She looked really, really sad, though. And when he'd finished, she said, "I'd already guessed some of this. I've had students who've had difficult upbringings—not as bad as that, but there's a kind of wariness that people exhibit when they didn't have stable childhoods. When Archer first brought you here, you were on alert all the time, never quite relaxing. I hope you don't mind my saying this, but I also noticed that you were unsure about table manners, but you watched the rest of us and you picked it up fast."

Jay felt as though he'd been thrown back in time to that raw young man who was barely house trained. He remembered watching Betsy, and now he realized she must have been making an effort to put her napkin on her lap and use her knife and fork correctly. To pass the food rather than helping herself right away. And so he'd copied her.

He let out a long sigh as the tension left his body. He felt better, as though an enormous weight had been lifted off his shoulders, not only because he'd told her about his awful past and she accepted him anyway, but also because she now knew about his feelings for Erin and didn't seem to disapprove. In fact, she had actually said he was a better man than he gave himself credit for.

Jay was silent for a while as he let this all sink in. As they sipped their tea, he felt how comfortable it was in this house, and how much he adored Betsy.

Finally, he asked, "Are you giving me the green light with Erin? I have your blessing?" He had to be sure.

Betsy shrugged kindly. "Yes, but it's not up to me. It all depends on my daughter and what she wants."

He got that. "I think I might have messed things up on the weekend and she's freaking out. How do I let her know I'm completely serious about her and that I love her?"

"I can't tell you that. But I think you've been in love with her for years. You just didn't know it. You'll figure it out. You need to trust yourself, Jay. Listen to your heart."

And then Jay had a terrible realization. He might have Betsy's blessing, but that didn't mean the Davenport men were going to be on board as well. "What about Archer and the others?" He hadn't forgotten Arch's terrible warning about going anywhere near his sister, and he couldn't bear the idea of upsetting his friend and oldest client.

Betsy shook her head. "That's between you and Archer and the rest of the boys."

"Including your husband?" Betsy might be open to the idea of him and Erin, but he was terrified that Howie, who'd been a father figure to him all these years, might hate him after he learned about it.

Betsy smiled at him. "You're worrying too much about what everyone else will think. The only people who matter here are Erin and you."

Jay's eyes widened. She was right. "I guess none of the rest of it matters if I can't get her to fall for me as hard as I've fallen for her. I made such a mess of things."

Betsy didn't look a bit surprised. "Then you'll clean up your mess. My daughter's pretty smart and she respects the truth. If you're honest and open about your feelings, she'll let you know if she returns them."

"So you think there's hope?"

She chuckled. "I definitely think there's hope. Good luck. I'm glad you came to me, Jay. I know it couldn't have been easy. It shows integrity and grit—two other qualities I know my daughter admires."

Jay pulled Betsy in for a huge bear hug and promised he'd attend the next family breakfast. He refused her offer to walk him out, insisting she finish grading the papers, and let himself out of their front door feeling a whole lot better than when he'd arrived.

★ ★ ★

As the door closed behind Jay, Betsy Davenport leaned back in her chair and sipped her chamomile tea, a delighted smile playing across her face. When she was certain Jay was too far away to hear through the open windows, she called, "Howie? You owe me ten bucks."

Her husband wandered in from the office, where he'd been working on his business accounts. "What did you say?"

"You owe me ten bucks."

"For what?"

"Erin and Jay."

Howie's eyebrows shot up. "What are you saying?"

"Jay was just here, and he's just told me he's in love with our daughter. Remember? The bet was ten dollars."

He rooted around in his wallet. "Do you have change for a twenty?"

She grabbed the bill and tucked it in her pocket. "For this, I'm taking the whole thing." Then Howie swept her up in his arms and kissed her. Laughing, she said, "Don't you have accounts to finish?"

"The accounts can wait." And, still holding her as though she were a new bride, he swept her off to the bedroom.

Chapter Twenty-Two

When Jay got home, he was grinning from ear to ear. What a revelation. All those years he'd known the Davenports and Betsy hadn't been fooled by his act— yet she'd neither called him out on it nor embarrassed him. She cared about him, despite everything. Cared deeply enough to believe he was a match for her daughter. He'd have to deal with the Davenport men, not to mention convince Erin he was serious about her. But after his talk with Betsy, Jay felt so much better, as though maybe he'd never needed to pretend so hard to be someone he wasn't.

Nelson was predictably delighted to see him, even though he hadn't been gone an hour, and happily followed him as Jay paced from room to room, letting his idea percolate until he could see clearly how to execute his plan.

Jay went to his library, pulled down every book he owned on screenwriting—there were quite a few—and carried them into his office. Then he fired up his laptop and sat down. Nelson immediately curled at his feet.

"If it's a romantic comedy," he said to him, "you have to start with the meet cute." Nelson wagged his tail in agreement.

He thought about Erin the twenty-year-old university student he'd first met. She was quiet but so smart. And then he pictured his young self, all brash and acting bold, when really he was just trying to disguise his insecurities and impress people. He could see those two younger versions of himself and Erin so clearly he felt as though he were time traveling.

He remembered vividly the first time he'd entered the Davenport home, walking in behind Arch and meeting the rest of the family, who were already crowded around the kitchen counters, helping out. He remembered seeing Betsy and thinking he'd never known a mother could be that beautiful and so well put together. And she combined her undeniable beauty with genuine niceness. He fell for her immediately.

Howie had treated Jay like one of the boys from the second he arrived. He handed out jobs to everybody, Jay included, so he immediately felt like one of the family—the kind of family he'd read about and watched in TV sitcoms, but until then had never really thought existed. Now that he could see what a real family could and should be like, it opened up a whole new world.

He'd been blown away by statuesque, sun-kissed surfing goddess Mila, and then he'd met Erin. She didn't dazzle him the way Mila had, but he'd liked her right away. He'd found himself talking to her a lot. He'd probably just been boasting, he thought with a cringe, but she had listened and given him the time of day regardless. That was probably the thing he'd noticed about her most at first—that she was such a good listener.

Suddenly inspired, he began to type. He'd never win an award for his screenwriting, but if every word came from the heart, as these did, then he was halfway there. He thought again of his young self and instead of cringing, tried to laugh at himself. He crafted the scene in a humorous light. Erin as the quiet, smart girl who saw right through the brash showoff trying so hard to impress her. Both of them a little clueless about how they could connect. And now here he was, a whole fifteen years later, taking the plunge and planning to reveal his true, innermost feelings to Erin.

What was even more frightening was that it would be in print. If Erin was still mad at him, she could publish his first attempt at a screenplay in the newspaper, laugh about it with her friends, or post it on social media if she wanted to. He paused, wondering if he was on a fool's errand, but then he shook his head. There wasn't a chance in hell Erin would ever behave like that. She was the most gracious, most understanding, most thoughtful human being he'd ever met. And that was why he loved her.

Still, he felt a little woozy when he finally pushed Send.

* * *

The trouble with living in a small apartment was it was so easy to clean. Everything was organized, her laundry was up to date, her bills paid, Boswell fed and walked. After taking the scripts back to Jay with the note, Erin hadn't heard a word. That had been a couple of days ago.

Until now, she'd been trying to deal with her emotions by herself, but there was one person she could always turn to when she was in a mess, and that was her sister Mila.

She called, and then worried that she was interrupting Mila and Hersch doing something lovey-dovey and fabulous, but after just a few words of greeting, Mila said, "What's up, Erin? You sound weird."

That was the nice thing about having a sister as close as hers—there was so much she didn't have to bother explaining. "I feel confused and restless and I need your help."

"You want to come up here? Or I can come to you. Or maybe you'd prefer to go surfing?"

Erin knew *up here* meant Hersch's beautiful new home in Carmel Valley, and much as she liked Hersch and felt as though he was already part of the family, she didn't really want to be in an unfamiliar house right now. Erin loved Mila's cute cottage, but for some reason she wanted to stay put, right here in her safe place. She suggested that Mila drive down, and within half an hour her sister was knocking on her door.

Better still, she was holding a Tupperware container. "Don't even start with me. Yes, I baked muffins this morning. That's how badly I am in love with Herschel Greenfield. I, Mila Davenport, baked muffins. Blueberry muffins. What's more, they're delicious."

Erin took the container and ushered her sister inside. She was happy that Mila had been lucky in love, and if her confident, athletic, and wildly independent sister could become a homebody and start baking muffins, who was to say that Jay Malone couldn't also make a huge change in his life? Okay, maybe his change was a little bigger than baking, but she'd work with what she had.

After Mila had finished making a suitable fuss of Buzzy, who adored her second only to their mom, Erin started the coffee machine. "Coffee?"

Mila nodded, taking a seat at the kitchen table. No matter the time of day, she was never one to turn down caffeine. Erin put the muffins on a pretty ceramic plate and then poured them both a cup of steaming hot coffee.

Mila took a deep sip and waited for Erin to begin. Except now that it came to it, she didn't know where to start. Because the whole story went beyond Jay, way back in time, and it was one she'd never told before.

She took a muffin and bit into its still-warm center, then exclaimed in delight. "Hey, these are really good!"

Mila laughed. "Don't sound so surprised. I think the secret is a little lemon peel."

"Nice touch." Erin took another bite. "You can come here more often."

"But you didn't drag me down here for my fabulous baking. Tell me what's going on."

Erin steeled herself and took a deep breath. "It's Jay Malone."

Mila all but smacked herself on the forehead. "Call me clairvoyant—I had a feeling it was about him."

Erin gave her sister a wry smile. She took a sip of coffee and contemplated where she wanted to begin. She wasn't like Mila—she didn't rush into things, including conversations. She wanted to choose her words carefully. Since her sister knew her very well, Mila just waited.

When Erin was ready, she let out a long sigh and confessed, "I'm half in love with him."

"Erin, that's no surprise to anyone but you. What I can't figure out is why you're sitting here with me having blueberry muffins and coffee instead of having hot, wild sex with Jay?"

Erin felt torn. She wanted to tell Mila the whole truth, but she didn't want to humiliate Jay by dishing the details of their disastrous dinner. So all she said was, "We've been getting closer, and I think I'm scared. I think he's scared too. I'm pretty different from the women he usually dates, and he kind of fell back on his old tricks."

Mila straightened and her eyes widened. "He didn't pull a line about you having such a beautiful smile your portrait should hang in the Louvre or something, did he?"

Erin cringed and reluctantly nodded. "Close." How she wished that wasn't the truth.

"Oh, Jay," Mila said, shaking her head in disgust.

"I know."

Mila sat back and seemed to mull things over. "I think you're right that Jay is scared too. The thing about Jay is he's so successful, so slick, and dating hot models is kind of like an immature badge of honor for him. But the fact that he so obviously cares about you tells me that he's growing up. That he might be ready to make a change."

Okay, so maybe Erin didn't love the fact that Mila made such a big distinction between Erin and the supermodels, but the heart of what she was saying was true. She nodded.

Then Mila said, "What if you just go for it? It was my advice from the very beginning. He's a hot guy, he's single, you're single, and now there's obviously something much deeper developing between you. Jay doesn't have to be the love of your life, but you'll never know if you don't try. You've been in kind of a rut, dating those geeky guys who follow you around with sad puppy eyes."

Erin winced. This was way too close to what Jay had said.

And then Mila leaned across the table and took her hand. "Erin, why don't you just take a chance? What's holding you back?"

And then that awful dark feeling of shame began rising within her. She'd never told anyone about what had happened in college. Maybe it was time she did. If Jay could confront the darkness of his past, she could face her demons too.

She took another sip of coffee, steeling herself for what she was about to say. "Mila, there's something I've never told you. I've never told anyone. When I was in college, I—I had a date that went bad. Really bad." She began to tremble.

Mila's outrage was instant. *"What?"*

"Don't worry, the worst didn't happen. But when I was in my first year and living away from home for the first time, there was this guy. He was so good looking and so confident. I was thrilled that he chose me out of all the other girls on campus. I felt special. But it wasn't true. He wasn't interested in me. I found out later that he collected virgins."

Mila looked disgusted as she said, "What a total lowlife."

"I can see that now, but at the time I was so confused. We went out a couple of times and then on the third date, he really pushed me for sex. I knew I wasn't ready, and I wasn't ready for him especially."

"Good girl. You showed good instincts, even that young."

Erin shook her head, the memories churning her stomach, and making her feel cold inside. "But he wouldn't take no for an answer. He got aggressive. I felt trapped." It was hard to breathe, still trapped in that memory. "Mila, he called me the most awful names."

Her sister leaned over and held her hand more tightly than before. "Erin, I'm so sorry."

"All I can say is, it's a good thing our brothers taught me some pretty good self-defense moves before I went off to college." She paused. "I never thought I would need to use them, though."

Mila looked murderous. "Tell me you took him down."

"He'd walked me back to my dorm room and then invited himself inside—pretty much barged his way in. I asked him to leave, but he just kept telling me to relax, that he was going to make me feel so good. I'd never had anyone treat me like that and I was scared, but mad too, you know? I was so glad the boys had taught me how to take care of myself. I finally got him out the door a little worse for wear, but not before he turned nasty and called me awful names. He never bothered me again, but he spread some pretty dirty rumors about me. And I guess since then I've just avoided men who seem overconfident and brash. Who take up too much space." She stopped, overwhelmed by the relief of finally telling someone her deepest secret. "So you're right, I spend time with men who don't threaten me. And now you know why."

"Oh honey, why did you never tell me this?"

Erin looked down at her empty plate. "Because I was so ashamed."

Mila sat there for a moment and then said, "I can't believe you didn't tell me. It's like you have a kind of victim shame, and you've lived with it alone for such a long time. But if you've ever felt shame because of that loser, or like you brought it on yourself, then you have to know you most definitely didn't. That guy was obviously the worst kind of human, and you are the best kind there is."

Erin felt unfamiliar tears prick at her eyelids. She whispered, "Thank you."

"And it sounds like you were more than capable of holding your own and getting the hell away from him." She sat back. "I'm not going to tell anyone else what you just shared with me. That's for you to do if and when you feel you want to. But I do think you should give some serious thought to telling Jay everything you've just told me. If you're falling in love, you want to start a relationship on even ground, where you've both told each other truths that no one else has. That's what happened with Hersch and me and I can't imagine it working any other way."

Erin knew Mila was right. The trouble was, Jay *had* opened up to Erin and told her things about his past he'd never admitted to anyone before. But then at dinner, when they could have kept talking in this open, honest way she'd enjoyed so much, he'd defaulted straight back into his brash, cocky mode, which had set off alarm bells in Erin's body.

She and her sister talked more about what had happened, and hearing Mila tell her how proud she was of the way Erin had stood up to a predator made her see herself in a new light. Then the conversation turned to Mila and Hersch and their plans to take a vacation together. Her sister was so deeply in love that Erin had a feeling there would be another Davenport wedding before too long. She was truly happy for her sister, and when Mila left after giving her a big hug, she knew how much she wanted a loving relationship like hers.

But was she ready?

Chapter Twenty-Three

Later that evening, Erin was curled up in her favorite chair, reading, when her cell dinged and a text came in. When she saw Jay's name, she clicked on the message immediately. She was eager to see how he'd respond to her hand-delivered note and had been wondering what was taking so long. She smiled as she saw he'd chosen a font that mimicked handwriting.

> *Dear Ms. Davenport,*
>
> *I hope you're enjoying your evening. Please check your email. My feelings on the scripts I sent you were similar. However, a brand-new writer has sent in a sample. I'd like to know what you think.*
>
> *Regards,*
> *Julius (Jay) Malone*

Erin felt herself grinning. Why did these notes charm her so much? Even the fact that he'd taken the trouble to find a fun font on his phone made her smile. And if she was honest with herself, she wasn't really concentrating on her book anyway, which was very unlike her. So she got up and opened her laptop. The script was titled *A Love Story*. Well, not exactly original, but okay. She opened the file.

```
INT. SUBURBAN HOME - NIGHT

We meet a young man and woman who could
not be more opposites. A young, brash
hustler from the wrong side of the
tracks is invited to Thanksgiving din-
ner at his friend's family home. His
friend's sister, a college student, en-
ters wearing a prim and proper floral
dress that covers her from neck to an-
kles. But the young man can't take his
eyes off her all night. She's petite
and doesn't talk a lot, but he can tell
she's the one in the family who really
listens. He wants to talk to her, but
she's so serious and so smart he's
tongue-tied around her, so he acts like
the class clown, brash and boasting.
And she's such a good listener, she
lets him.
```

The dialogue that followed was sharp and funny. She was surprised how much Jay remembered about their first meeting, because of course she'd recognized every detail of that scene. Sure, he'd made it funnier and cut down the number of characters, but the dialogue he gave them both rang true. It was the perfect opening for a friends-to-lovers romantic comedy.

Her favorite kind.

If *When Harry Met Sally* could end happily, who was to say that *When Jay Met Erin* couldn't as well?

She devoured the rest of the pages greedily, losing herself in the scenes, amazed at how good Jay's writing was. He'd managed to surprise her yet again. No wonder he'd taken a couple of days to respond. He'd been writing a screenplay.

For her.

At the bottom of the last page, he ended with a personal note:

The writer is struggling with one big thing: where to put the first kiss.

Reading those words sent such a rush of lust through Erin that she felt physically weak. She'd been dreaming of kissing Jay. . . and so much more.

She put down her laptop and sat back in the chair, trying to get a handle on her swirling emotions. She began to type on her phone, then deleted what she'd written, started again, then deleted that too. Finally, she stopped overthinking and wrote straight from the heart.

Dear Mr. Malone,

This story shows promise. I have an idea about where it could go next.

Before she could deliberate any more, she pushed Send. Then, jumping up from her chair, she glanced at her watch. It wasn't late. Nine-thirty. That wasn't late, was it? She didn't even let herself think. She printed off a few pages of the script and then said to Buzzy, "Let's do this." Together, they left her apartment.

As always, Boswell was super happy when he realized they were heading to the beach, but he seemed to sense that something was different. So instead of straining against the lead, desperate to run ahead, he stayed by Erin's side, keeping time with her footsteps.

Erin felt as though she were carrying her heart in her hands.

Soon she was standing on Jay's doorstep. She froze for a moment, wondering if she really had the courage to follow through with her plan. But she was here now. On the doorstep of her dream house, where maybe— possibly—her dream man was waiting. She took a deep breath. And then she rang the bell.

When Jay opened the door, he had his reading glasses on and a book of Rumi poetry in one hand. A thrill ran through her. He couldn't have looked hotter in that moment if he'd tried. Nelson couldn't decide whether he was more excited to see Buzzy or Erin, so jumped madly between the two of them.

"Hi," Jay said, looking both happy and a little bashful, trying to restrain Nelson from tripping over his own excitable wagging tail.

Erin smiled, suddenly shy. At least that broke the ice between them. Jay was obviously glad to see her, but he also looked so surprised he didn't seem to know what to do.

He invited her in and they stood there in the foyer, just staring at one another. Erin thought her heart was going to burst from her chest. Maybe Mila was right—maybe it was high time she started taking chances.

"I read the script and I have the perfect suggestion for where to put the first kiss."

And before she lost her nerve, she went up on her tiptoes and kissed him.

Erin had imagined this moment so many times—it was going to be sweet, soft, and slow. Then maybe she'd see if he wanted to take the dogs down to the beach together and they could have a romantic nighttime stroll, holding hands.

But there was no sweet and slow.

The moment their lips met, the heat exploded between them. She wound herself around him—she couldn't get close enough. All she wanted was his skin, his touch, to feel the ripple of his muscles through his shirt. Vaguely she heard him kick the door closed behind her and then he picked her up, propping her against the door, and she wrapped her legs around him. His hands were everywhere, in her hair and on her back, clutching her hips as she squeezed her legs tighter, trying to bring them closer so that not even an inch of air was between them, so that she could feel every part of him. As she drew him in, she felt his arousal and pressed herself against it, a great shudder of pleasure coursing through her as they connected.

It was crazy—so fast and so hot she couldn't believe it was really happening. She paused to gasp for breath and he moved his lips to her neck. The pleasure was almost too much; it was as though he knew exactly what she wanted him to do. She took just a second to check in with herself, but realized she felt completely safe with Jay.

If there was one thing she'd learned, it was that she had good instincts. They'd been right in college when she didn't want to sleep with that pushy, awful guy, and over the years she'd grown more confident in her own judgment. So she cupped Jay's face in her hands and kissed his mouth again, letting caution go and giving herself over to the glorious sensations racing through her body.

In between kisses he said, "Is this okay? I want you to be sure."

She smiled and if she hadn't been so aroused, the thoughtful question would have brought happy tears to her eyes. She whispered, "I'm more than sure."

He grinned. "I want to take you upstairs and make love to you in that gorgeous bedroom, but I don't think I can wait that long."

She pulled his mouth back to hers. "Me neither."

They'd have done it right there on the floor except there were two dogs looking very interested in the whole spectacle. He carried her into the living room and shut the French doors to give them privacy. He set her down and leaned over to flick on the gas fireplace. Erin used the opportunity to pull the polo shirt out of his jeans, lifting it up over his broad, muscled chest until he helped her and yanked it over his head.

He was glorious. Tanned and manly, with a beautiful physique.

Jay undid the straps of her blue summer dress and let the soft cotton fall to the ground. He stood back for a moment as though he was drinking in the sight of her, memorizing every curve and line of her half-naked body. She'd thought she might feel shy with Jay, who had seen so many sculpted and toned bodies. But she could see how much he wanted her, and she wanted him just as badly. She'd never wanted to be naked faster.

She fumbled with the buttons of his jeans until he took over, not wanting to wait a second longer. They were stepping out of shoes, kicking the clothes away, and then he grabbed a beautiful woven throw from the sofa and laid it in front of the fire. The whole scene couldn't have been more hot and romantic if she'd written it herself. She was about to unhook her bra when he said, "Wait," and ran in his underwear to the closest bathroom to fetch a condom. She loved watching him, the way his body moved, and how much he wanted her was very evident from the sizeable bulge she couldn't help but eye up.

As soon as he returned, he kissed her again, exploring her body as though he wanted to know it all at once. He whipped off her bra and panties and thumbed down his briefs and then they were on the floor, limbs entwined, and it was happening so quickly and yet she wanted more—faster—

She moaned with abandon as his hands touched her where she was so wet and so wanting and she exploded almost immediately. She was barely over the wild tremors that shook her body with pleasure when she felt him push inside her, filling her completely. Their eyes locked. She'd never felt connection like this with anyone. She wrapped her legs around him, pulling him deeper inside her, and then they moved with a fierce rhythm, until the pair of them were crying out again and she felt Jay shudder on a long, low moan.

Spent, they fell side by side, and then he pulled her close so that she rested her head on his chest, listening to his heartbeat, following its pounding rhythm until it slowed along with his breathing.

He chuckled. "That was quite the first kiss."

She laughed too, delighted with herself and with them, and with Mila for such good advice. That might have been the hottest sex of her life. "I think I might have skipped ahead a few scenes."

He tapped her nose with a gentle finger. "That was a pretty good starter, but what do you say we take the next course upstairs?"

"I think that's an excellent idea."

Still naked, they rose and walked up the stairs. Jay let her go ahead and she could feel his eyes on her naked back and swaying hips. Once again, she was conscious she had no worry about her body in comparison to a supermodel or lingerie model. She was who she was and he either liked what he saw or he didn't.

So far, all indications were that he liked it very much.

She could still feel his eyes on her as he said, "You're killing me—you know that, right?"

She chuckled, putting a little extra sway into her hips. She was already aching for him. And when they got to his bedroom, he lifted her again, but this time it was gentle and sweet and he laid her down on that divine king-sized bed as if she were a delicate rose he'd plucked from the garden. His movements were slow now, his touch soft and intimate, and her skin prickled in thrill bumps as his fingertips swept over her and he followed them with kisses.

He was taking his time, getting to know her, learning her responses, finding her most erogenous zones and lingering there, tantalizingly. As much as she'd loved the passion of their first time together, this was something else completely. She allowed herself to be swept away by his touch until it felt as though she were floating on some sexy cloud.

Only when the waves began to shake her body did he enter her again, oh so slowly, so that she could appreciate every inch of him. They rocked together as her hands clung to his neck and she begged him for more—to go harder, faster. But, blissfully, he ignored her commands, keeping a slow and steady pace that kept her hovering on the edge of the strongest orgasm she'd ever experienced. Sweat trickled between her breasts and she realized she was shaking when Jay slid his fingers between hers and held her tight as she reached the peak of her pleasure. Only when her breathing calmed did Jay allow himself to let go, moaning her name into her ear, his breath hot.

Exhausted by their lovemaking, Erin closed her eyes, and only when she woke hours later did she realize that she'd fallen asleep curled up in Jay's strong arms. She smiled into his chest, feeling warm and safe.

Then she realized she hadn't given a single thought to the dogs. Were they okay?

She raised up on her elbow and looked down to see two very happy dogs flopped on the bedroom floor, side by side.

She'd never known a heart could be so full.

Chapter Twenty-Four

Jay was always an early riser, but that Thursday morning he stayed in bed as long as he could, just watching Erin sleep. She looked so beautiful with her hair, gloriously tangled from a night of passionate lovemaking, streaming down on the pillow beside her. There was a little smile on her lips. Did she always smile when she was sleeping, or had he given her something to smile about? He liked the fact that he didn't know yet, but over time, he hoped to find out.

He felt eyes on him and then realized their two dogs were standing, staring at him expectantly. How had he gone from a carefree bachelor to a man with a woman to make coffee for and two dogs to take care of?

He grinned. He didn't know how, but he was darned happy and grateful it had happened. And it was all down to Erin.

He slipped out of bed so as not to wake her and whistled cheerfully as he headed downstairs to let the dogs out and put the coffee on. He was trying to decide what to make Erin for breakfast when he heard her footsteps behind him.

As Erin walked into the kitchen, her tousled hair falling around her shoulders, he saw with pleasure that she was wearing one of his shirts. It reached to mid-thigh and he was pretty sure she didn't have anything else on. He was instantly aroused. He wanted nothing more than to take her again, there and then, on the kitchen island.

But as he looked into her beautiful eyes, he saw a slightly uncertain expression that made him suspect Erin wasn't in the habit of waking up in someone else's bed. It made him desire her even more, but he also found himself filled with a kind of tenderness. He was suddenly determined to protect her from all of life's troubles, which was crazy. No one could do that, but the urge was so strong he was taken aback. He'd never felt like that for anyone before.

And then the urge to hoist her up onto the granite counter and say good morning in a very carnal way returned and he almost laughed at himself. Being in love was so confusing!

Keeping all those urges in check, he simply said, "Coffee?"

Erin visibly relaxed into a smile. "Only if you want me to live."

Once they'd fallen back into that easy banter, everything seemed natural between them.

Both dogs came in and wished her a good morning, as though they hadn't all spent the night together, and she took a moment to bend over and pet the pair, who practically swooned in ecstasy at the attention from their favorite woman. The second Jay finished making her coffee, he handed her the cup and kissed her. Her lips were soft and still warm with sleep.

She took a sip, murmured, "Yummy," then set it down on the counter so she could kiss him again. This time, it was more urgent, as though sleep had kept their bodies apart for too long. He tasted the coffee on her lips and pulled her in tight.

"Good morning," he said, low and sexy.

"Good morning." Her smile was a little shy but very sweet.

He had a feeling breakfast was going to be delayed.

And then his phone rang. He was about to switch the ringer to silent, but then he saw it was Archer.

His stomach lurched. Here he was, kissing Arch's half-dressed sister in the kitchen after his very clear warning to stay the hell away, but he had to pick up. Some habits died hard.

He made a slightly scared face at Erin as he answered. "Arch, my man, how's it going?"

Erin's eyes widened and a flash of panic crossed her face. She waved her hands in front of her, clearly signaling to him not to let her brother know that she was there. Of course he had zero intention of doing that, and was now feeling incredibly guilty about what had probably been the hottest and most beautiful night of his entire life.

He had done the very thing that Archer had ordered him not to do. And yet he could no more have stopped himself from falling for Erin Davenport than he could have stopped himself from adopting Nelson, or, come to that, breathing. Still, he would have to talk to Arch man to man. But not right now. This was far too new and fragile and he needed to make sure he and Erin were on a good footing before he went blabbing to Archer that he was in love with his sister. Erin should be the first person to hear those words said properly.

Okay, he might have hinted as much to Betsy, but that was different. Talking to Betsy was like talking to an ancient Greek goddess. Some kind of family Oracle. She was so wise and knowing and she just wanted the best for everyone.

And then he nearly dropped the phone. Love. He was so *deeply* in love. He needed to tell Erin exactly how he felt about her. He couldn't keep it in any longer. But they had only spent one night together. He didn't want to scare her off.

His thoughts were running away from him so fast, he was almost having trouble hearing what Archer was saying. Lucky thing it wasn't complex wording over a new contract. Archer was inviting him to poker night with the boys. He had to focus. Fortunately, Erin had slipped out of the room. She'd taken her coffee and both dogs with her. Even Nelson, the turncoat. At least without her right there clouding his mind, he could focus. He'd deal with how to face Arch about it later.

Pulling his brain cells together, Jay said, "Right, poker. Friday night. I'm in."

He was about to finish the call as abruptly as he could when Archer said, "So, how's it going with the mystery woman?"

Jay gulped. He hadn't a clue how to respond. He was a hustler, so he knew how to tell a story, but he was no liar. Especially not to someone as close to him as Arch. And yet, a new kind of joy was blooming in his chest as he owned up to the fact that he was in love with the greatest woman in the world. He wanted to run down to Archer's house right now, face him man to man, and tell him what was going on. But not yet.

He circumnavigated the question by saying he'd tell Archer more in person and then changed the subject, claiming he needed to get back to a script he was working on. That much was true—there were several more pages that he and Erin could write upstairs in the bedroom.

But for some reason Archer was in a chatty mood today. It turned out that Tessa was out painting and the actor clearly had time on his hands. So they talked more about *Shock Tactics* and how soon he'd have to fly to Utah, where they were doing some of the filming. Jay promised to fly up and hang out on the set for a day. The script was coming along nicely for the Herschel Greenfield biopic and Archer also had some notes on that. Jay told him to send them over and he'd take a look. Then, finally, Arch ended the call himself.

Jay leaned back against the counter and let out a low whistle. His heart had been beating double time for the entire call. In choosing Erin to be the love of his life, he hadn't made that life easy. Not with Archer, and he suspected not with the rest of her brothers either. They knew too much about him and his past relationships. But the point was, all that was in the past. He just had to make it very clear to everyone that being with Erin was a brand-new start for him. Like coming to Carmel-by-the-Sea, and buying this house, he felt as though he'd finally grown into himself. Finally arrived.

He couldn't wait to tell Erin how he felt. With all that feverish lovemaking, he hadn't got a chance to tell her he had to go back to LA for a couple of days. Now the thought of being separated from her for even an hour seemed unbearable. He considered telling her he loved her. Were either of them ready for that yet? He wasn't sure. He'd play it by ear.

He raced upstairs, eager now for some intense and passionate farewell sex, after which she'd go to work and he'd get on with his day. He entered the bedroom, full of desire and excitement, only to find no one there.

Not even the dogs. He frowned and looked around the room, wondering if she was in the shower, but the ensuite was empty too.

And then he realized there wasn't a single trace of Erin left. No clothes, no watch, no hair tie. She had even made the bed. On the table beside the Barbara Hepworth sculpture was a handwritten note.

Dear Mr. Malone,

I apologize for leaving without a farewell. If you could please grant me a few days to ruminate on the latest development in the script, I would greatly appreciate your patience.

Sincerely,
Erin Davenport (Ms.)

He shook his head in disbelief. She'd gone!

He read the note again. As much as he loved their cute notes back and forth, the formal tone of this one made his heart sink. They should have been closer now they'd made love, but it felt as though their becoming intimate physically had made her pull back emotionally. That couldn't be good.

A man with a smaller ego might have worried that she was trying to give him the brush-off. But Jay was pretty comfortable with his ego and with his appeal to women, and he also knew Erin very well. This was exactly like her—to take a moment, a step back, to think things through. It was one of the things he loved about her: she was a thinker. She didn't rush into action, but instead took her time and contemplated the different aspects of every scenario.

He was going to have to make peace with the fact that she needed some space, when all he wanted was to put as little space between them as possible. The sooner he got used to not having things as quickly as he wanted them, the better.

That was the old Jay. The new one was patient and understanding.

He couldn't help a tiny smile as he thought about last night. No wonder she wanted a moment to reflect—they'd rushed into intimacy with one another, and he imagined that acting on impulse was probably uncomfortable for Erin. She could use words like *ruminate* all she liked, but she'd been as hot and desperate for him last night as he had been for her. He didn't have to worry about whether she was into him or not.

Although he'd obviously rather be having some seriously hot good-bye sex right about now, he gave the rounded top of the Hepworth a little pat and whistled a tune from an old Western movie as he got into the shower. Erin wasn't fickle. If she'd turned up at his door, kissed him, and then had a glorious night of sex with him, it was because she had feelings for him. And if he could be the man she gave him the courage to be, then just maybe she could fall as hard for him as he had for her.

Besides, there were ways he could show her that she was on his mind without encroaching on her space.

So, bag packed and Nelson in tow, Jay left for the airport with a plan to make a quick stop at the *Sea Shell* office. His private jet was waiting at Monterey, and he was very curious to see what Nelson would think about his first flight. At least, he assumed it was Nelson's first flight; Nelson wasn't big on sharing his past and Jay respected that. He suspected Nelson's past and his own were kind of similar. They were both scrappy outcasts who'd managed to make good, mostly by the sheer force of their personality.

Entering the newspaper's office, Jay was glad that in the haze of all that sex, he'd remembered that Erin said she was working from home in the morning to finish an article. He was carrying a handwritten note, one he hoped would show her he understood her need for space, but was also very much available when she was ready to talk.

The office was exactly as he'd pictured: small and cozy, with piles of paper and huge computer screens on each desk. The receptionist greeted him warmly and he told her he was just leaving a note for Erin Davenport. He fished the envelope out of his pocket and was about to hand it over and leave, when he saw a tall woman with cropped hair walking purposefully toward him, her gray slacks making a slight swish as she crossed the room.

She extended a hand as she neared and said, "Pat Sinclair, the *Sea Shell*'s editor. Nice to meet the man behind the profile."

Jay smiled and shook her hand. She had a firm grip. Everything about Pat Sinclair was alert—from her sharp, clear eyes to her military posture—and he liked her immediately. "A pleasure to meet you," he said, meaning it.

"Thank you for allowing the *Sea Shell* to profile you. I know you're a busy man and we appreciate your taking the time out of what must be a busy schedule."

"Anytime," he said, realizing he meant it. He'd be happy to help out the local paper in any way he could. "Erin Davenport did a fine job."

Pat nodded briskly. "The *Sea Shell* is lucky to have her. I've offered to introduce her to people at *The New York Times*, or even one of the big magazines, because she's one of the finest writers I've ever come across," Pat confided. "But she doesn't want to move. She likes it here, and you have to respect somebody that young knowing so clearly what they want."

Since Jay had read every article Erin had written in the last two years, he absolutely agreed that she was a fine writer and could turn her hand to any assignment at any number of places. But he was secretly pleased to have his own observations confirmed. Not that he couldn't work pretty much from anywhere, but when he looked ahead at a future where Erin and he were together—ever since this morning he couldn't seem to think of anything else—Carmel felt like the perfect place for them to call home.

He asked Ms. Sinclair to give Erin the note when she arrived, and the woman said she would. She might have the instincts of a hard-nosed news reporter, but he was fairly certain she wouldn't open the note and read the contents. Even if she did, it wasn't the end of the world, but he liked Pat and trusted his instinct about her. And then, with a final wave, he walked out.

As the door was closing behind him, he heard the receptionist say, "Who was that?"

Pat Sinclair chuckled. "Down, girl. I think he's taken."

He bit back a smile. Pat Sinclair didn't miss much. And he very much hoped she was right.

Chapter Twenty-Five

Erin was more flustered than she cared to admit. A long walk with Buzzy, a hot shower, taking her time getting ready for work—none of her usual routines calmed her. She felt giddy. It wasn't a word she would ever have used about herself. It was a word used in novels where young ladies met their beaux and all common sense flew out the window until they had a ring on their finger and their happily ever after was just around the corner. But there wasn't a better word for how she felt. *Giddy*. As though her world were spinning and the ground didn't seem quite stable under her feet. She was in love with the world and wanted to giggle.

And Erin Davenport had never been a giggler.

Under all that lightness, though, something seismic had happened. She had never been casual about sex, and after her incredibly wild night with Jay, she'd never felt so vulnerable either. She'd given him everything. Did he have any idea? Since she knew perfectly well he had a lot more experience in that area than she did, did their night mean anywhere near as much to him as it meant to her? She needed a little time to make sense of what had happened. Of her feelings. Because right now she felt head over heels.

And she couldn't quite believe it was with Jay Malone.

She couldn't concentrate on her article at home, so she decided to head into work with Buzzy, where the office atmosphere might do her some good.

By the time she arrived, she was still feeling disoriented. Only a couple of minutes passed before Pat Sinclair, who had obviously been on the lookout for her, came out of her office and perched on the edge of her desk. "That handsome film agent, Jay Malone, dropped by this morning to see you. Since you weren't in, he left you a note."

Erin hoped she had sufficiently controlled her expression at the mention of Jay's name. Inside, it felt like a little bird was tap dancing in her stomach. Not much got past Pat.

"Thanks." She took the envelope with her name scrawled across it in Jay's looping handwriting. Even the sight of his handwriting made that little bird dance a little faster. Oh, she had it bad. Pat shot her a knowing look and then went back to her office, leaving Erin to stare down at the envelope, almost afraid to open it. Had she offended Jay by making her escape while he was on the phone to her brother?

Because at the mention of Archer's name, it had all become too real. There was zero chance of her brother approving of the match, and she wasn't ready to face the rest of her family with all their big opinions. She needed to get her own thoughts straight first. Hopefully Jay knew her well enough to realize that was what was going on—not that she had any regrets about the night they'd spent together. In fact, she wished they'd had some hot morning sex before she left.

She fiddled with the envelope, still not tearing it open. Maybe it was just a crush. The kind that teenage girls got sitting in dark movie theaters watching Smith Sullivan in some role where he was heroic and gorgeous and spoke lines that had been written for him by experts. Maybe it was that kind of crush and it would pass quickly.

But somehow she suspected that wasn't true. She had to face facts. This went far, far deeper than that.

She took a breath and opened the note.

Dear Ms. Davenport,

Thank you for leaving me a note before you departed. I will grant your request, as I shall be leaving for LA shortly and will be there for the next few days. I'm bringing Nelson this time. If I weren't leaving, however, I would do everything I could to convince you that what we have together is every kind of right.

With fondest regards,
Julius (Jay) Malone

P.S. *I know you'll miss me, but you'll survive. I just hope I will, because I'll be missing you like crazy the whole time.*

Erin sat back in her chair. She read the note again, slowly, as though savoring the best kind of chocolate. She'd felt a momentary spike of despair when she read that he was leaving, and taking his dog with him so she wouldn't even have the pleasure of being in his home. But *every kind of right*? So he had felt it too. And she really loved the part where the charming formality dissolved. *I'll be missing you like crazy.*

She resisted the urge to kiss the note, and instead tucked it into its envelope, then into her bag. Somehow, his note had calmed her. She would have some space to process this new development between them, now that she knew she was as much on Jay's mind as he was on hers.

But right now she had work to do, so she would have to put those sumptuous, sexy thoughts in a box and get back to it.

When she finished her article, there were a few obituaries to update. She loved how the elder residents of Carmel-by-the-Sea liked to keep her updated on all the goings-on in their lives, ostensibly so that at the time they passed, their obits would be pretty much written and approved by themselves. But also she thought they sometimes liked to boast to her about their newest grandchild or the latest family marriage.

Finally, when she was on top of her work and it was time to break for lunch, she composed an email back to Jay. She could have texted, but somehow email felt more formal.

Dear Mr. Malone,

Thank you for letting me know you will be out of town. I suspect I shall be very busy with my duties at the newspaper and will not have the time to miss you. But I will definitely miss Nelson. Give him a scratch between the ears for me, please.

Wishing you great success in Los Angeles and a safe and speedy trip back to Carmel-by-the-Sea.

Your friend (with some quite breathtaking benefits),
Erin Davenport

She paused. It felt very bold to have written *breathtaking benefits*, but she decided to leave it in. She hit Send.

Then she tried to put Jay Malone out of her mind and took herself out to lunch. She loved to treat herself to a fancy focaccia sandwich from time to time, and this was the perfect day to allow herself that distraction.

She walked out into the brilliant sunshine, trying to keep her hands from pulling out her phone every five minutes. It was a gorgeous day. A nice, long surf out on the waves was what she really needed to clear her mind, but that would have to wait until evening. Maybe she could text Mila and see if she wanted to join her. But then Mila would want to know what had happened with Jay, and Erin wasn't sure she was ready to talk about it yet. Not until she had her thoughts clear.

As she stood in line waiting for her mortadella sandwich, her fingers twitched and again she resisted checking her phone.

But by the time she'd left the sandwich place and strolled to a nearby bench to enjoy lunch in peace and quiet, she couldn't hold out any longer. She slipped her phone from her pocket and then felt a huge grin spread across her face.

Jay had already replied.

Dear Ms. Davenport,

I assure you that you will miss me. I also assure you that I will miss you. Very, very much.

With loving regards,
Julius (Jay) Malone

A series of tiny shivers shimmied across Erin's entire body. She couldn't believe how sexy these semiformal, ridiculous notes felt. *With loving regards?* That was a million steps higher than *fondest regards,* which was how he'd signed the previous note.

She sighed and bit into her sandwich, which oozed happily with fragrant herbed oil and cheese. She was torn about Jay's trip to LA. On the one hand, she wished she could spend every second with him (in his bed for the bulk of it, thank you very much), but on the other hand, it wasn't so bad that he'd gone away for a few days. She needed to sort out her feelings, which were still jumbled.

She couldn't be in love with Jay Malone, could she? Sure, the sex was off the charts and he'd surprised her by not being brash and pushy in bed, but instead giving and looking after her needs. But now that she'd had the best sex of her life, she wanted more. So much more.

But what was there beyond that for the two of them? Could he possibly be good for her? And what was she going to do when he got tired of the girl next door and wanted to go back to his hot and glamorous models?

Besides, he still didn't know about her past run-in with a bad man, a past that had hovered over her like a dark cloud since college. Maybe Mila was right and she should tell him. After all, he'd told her his own dark secrets. It suddenly didn't seem right that she hadn't done the same thing for him, because whether or not they became a couple, they were definitely already friends. In order to be a true friend to him, and to have any possibility of a lasting partnership, she needed to come clean about her own demons.

Even telling Mila, putting what had happened out in the open instead of tucked away in some shamed part of her, had made her look at that awful relationship with the eyes of an adult. She felt a lot more forgiving toward her nineteen-year-old self, who had been so innocent, so trusting. The downside of coming from a family like the Davenports, if there could be one, was in believing that people were good and a man and woman wouldn't become intimate if they didn't truly care about each other. But luckily, she had big brothers who had let her know that it was a tough world out there, and they'd made sure to teach her some pretty useful self-defense skills. Still, deep down, she'd always believed that she'd brought that horrible near miss on herself. And the awful things that guy had said about her in private and in public had suggested that he'd believed it too—that she was at fault for leading him on.

She shook her head and tried to clear those awful memories from her mind. She was older now, much wiser, and sitting on a bench in the world's most beautiful town with her favorite sandwich. And an email inbox containing sexy notes that made her feel like a character in a Jane Austen novel.

Chapter Twenty-Six

On Saturday morning there was a family breakfast at the Davenport house. Erin was glad to be immersed in her crazy family. It stopped her from missing Jay, for one thing, and it was always nice to catch up with everybody over a plate of steaming pancakes and a glass of fresh orange juice.

The house was full of noise, each sibling talking over the other, except Erin, of course, who was listening to Archer and Herschel bonding over the movie they were planning about Hersch's life. She remembered how that whole deal had gone down—Jay adamant that the astronaut's life would make a gripping as well as moving film, Mila cross at Jay's insistence. Now that she knew him a little better, Erin could see why Jay had been like a dog with a bone trying to get Hersch on board. He had seen the man behind the astronaut's fame, a man who had experienced something traumatic and come out on the other side—albeit with some emotional scars and bruises.

Although Jay's story was different, there were similarities: a connection between two people who had both overcome the odds, but buried their stories deep, deep down until—and she realized this now for the first time—a Davenport woman had come along and they'd confessed their darkest secrets. Of course, Erin could imagine how annoyingly certain Jay had been while pitching to Hersch. It was understandable that Mila had felt protective and been defensive on his behalf.

But ultimately Jay had been right. He had good instincts. And that made Erin feel a lot better about the fact that she was falling in love with him.

While Mila and Erin set the table, Arch was frying bacon and Hersch had been tasked with making toast.

Mila said, "Can you believe those two are BFFs now? They all played poker last night at Archer's house, you know."

"Really?" Erin tried to sound surprised, even though she'd overheard Arch inviting Jay. Presumably, he'd had to cancel, since he was still in LA. She missed Jay. Were they just going to be friends with benefits? Or could there be something more? The one thing she knew for sure was that the air didn't spark as much for her when he wasn't around. Nothing did.

Her mom had the radio playing softly in the background, and then the love song Damien had written for Arch and Tessa came on. Betsy raced across the kitchen to turn it up. No one was prouder of her children than she. Whether her rock-star son had created another top-selling hit, or Erin had written a particularly poignant article in the local newspaper, she was just as proud.

Damien looked a little sheepish as the song played. He was always modest about his success and favored privacy over fame. Erin had often thought that if Damien could find a way to play his guitar and write songs with no one ever knowing his name or recognizing his face, he would.

Finn suddenly said, "Listen—Did you guys know that this *love* song is one of Damien's top-selling songs ever?"

Everyone burst out laughing, because Damien was famous for not ever writing a love song.

Dad said, "Are you going to write some more love songs, son? You clearly have a talent for it."

Damien just shrugged and carried on slicing melon. Erin took in her brother, his head bent, intent on his task. "Maybe you have to be in love before you can," she said.

Now Damien turned around for the first time. He looked over at her and nodded. "I think you might be right, little sis. When I watched Arch and Tessa, I felt their love, but I don't think I've ever had that pleasure myself." When Finn made a gagging motion, Damien backtracked. "Okay, lots of *pleasure*, obviously, but I don't believe I've ever been *in love*."

"You'll know it when it happens," Arch said, reaching out to touch Tessa. "And it's the best feeling in the world."

"Sure is," Mila agreed. And then she put down her handful of butter knives and walked over to hug Herschel.

Finn said, "I don't feel so good, Mom. I think I'm going to be sick."

Erin smiled, but behind it, she wondered if, while Arch and Mila had both been lucky in love, she might be destined to fall for the guy who was totally wrong for her. She picked up the butter knives and resumed setting the table, but then she heard a familiar voice.

"Hope it's okay that I dropped in," Jay boomed as he entered the room.

Erin looked up, aghast, and the last knife landed on a plate with a crash. For a second, each family member turned from Jay to Erin. It wasn't like her to drop things.

Nick said, "Okay there, butter fingers?"

A flush bloomed in Erin's cheeks, but she fought hard to retain her composure. No way was she going to let everyone know how wildly bothered she was by Jay's unexpected entrance, his crisp white shirt and jeans, his freshly shaved head and sexy stubble. He hadn't left her mind in two days and she could still feel the imprint of his touch all over her body.

Mom calmly finished plating the scrambled eggs

and then went straight over to Jay to hug him hello. "No invitation needed," she assured him. "You're always welcome for breakfast."

He said a general good morning to everyone and then glanced at Erin. Nelson was with him and bounded straight over for a cuddle and a scratch. She laughed and bent to oblige him. She'd missed Nelson too.

She looked back up at Jay and casually, he said, "Morning, short stuff."

"Morning, big shot."

Something teasing and sexy flickered in his eyes and then it was gone. All chummy now, he turned to Arch, clapped him on the back and said, "Sorry I had to miss poker last night."

Arch smiled. "Aw, I'll fleece you next time."

Speaking of poker, as they all settled down for breakfast, Erin wondered how she was going to keep a lid on her feelings. She had the most useless poker face ever. To make matters worse, Jay made sure he got the seat next to her. As everyone began passing plates and discussing their days ahead, Jay helped himself to eggs and said in a low voice, under the babble of all the rest of her siblings, "You missed me, didn't you?"

Erin forced back the smile playing around her lips. She wanted to stay cool at all costs—because they were in front of her whole family, but also because she was used to keeping her cards close to her chest and doing otherwise felt odd. Then she remembered her decision to talk frankly with Jay, to start things—if that was what he wanted—with a clean slate.

Instead of answering, she whispered, "Did you miss me?"

Without a second's pause, he shot back, "More than you can imagine."

She all but melted. "I missed you too." Then, with a little grin, she added, "But mostly Nelson."

Nelson was currently getting acquainted with Buster, the Davenport family dog, with Buzzy bounding around the two of them, happy to have both his friends hanging out together.

Erin and Jay watched their dogs play, and for a second Erin caught herself imagining their own children playing. She shook her head, half laughing, half terrified, by the strong and enticing vision that had popped into her head. She took three pancakes from the stack and decided she'd eat her feelings until she got them under control.

Jay suddenly said, "Damien, have you ever considered doing the musical score for a film?"

Silence fell as everyone waited for Damien to answer. He looked a little bemused. "Not really."

Erin wondered what Jay was plotting.

"I see your love song is number one—congrats. I've got a little romantic comedy project on the go. We should talk."

Erin almost choked on a blueberry. If she hadn't

already got it, the way his knee was intimately nudging hers made it clear which romantic comedy he was referring to. The one he was writing about *them*.

With regret, Damien said, "I'm not sure I have it in me to write any more love songs. As Erin pointed out before you got here, I might be the kind of artist who has to experience love before they can really write about it."

Beneath the table, Jay's hand came to rest on Erin's knee. Again, she felt the beginnings of a flush spread across her cheeks, so she grabbed her mug of coffee and dived right in.

"Erin is a very smart woman," Jay said.

She gulped. The coffee was too hot and so was Jay. Her heart was beating so hard she could barely think straight.

The rest of breakfast passed in a blur. Normally Erin loved their big family meals, but this morning she might just leap to her feet and blurt, "I had sex with Jay." That's how messed up she felt. Mila was sending her glances that made it clear her sister had read the room.

Would this breakfast never end? She wanted to get to Jay's place. And fast!

When all the food had been polished off, Erin declined another cup of coffee, shared what she hoped was a secret look with Jay, and said she had to get going. Jay got up to help with the dishes and said he'd be making tracks soon, too.

After hugging everyone good-bye, including Jay (which sent a thrill through her body), she headed for the front door. To her surprise, her mom walked out with her. She pulled her in for a big hug and then whispered in her ear, "I just want you to know that I approve."

Erin pulled back, shocked. It was like her mother had some extra sense where her children were concerned. Had she seen that Erin was crazy about Jay? Just from seeing the two of them side by side at breakfast? She thought they'd been discreet, but maybe there was no being discreet when it came to her mom.

She wasn't sure how to respond—after all, she still hadn't got her own feelings in check—so all she managed was, "Thanks."

Her mom gave her another warm, knowing look and then said she'd see her soon.

Erin walked to her car with Buzzy. If her mom thought Jay was good for her, maybe her instincts about him were right after all.

Though Jay hadn't said more than a casual good-bye, Erin got in her car and drove straight to his house. She waited in the drive, all her senses tingling, the anticipation building. Just when she couldn't wait another moment, his Lamborghini pulled up alongside her.

They both opened their doors at the same time and

raced toward one another. His hands circled her waist, pulling her in tight, and his lips found hers hungrily. She stroked the nape of his neck and then allowed her fingernails to rake down his back. He moaned into her mouth. Without speaking, they pulled apart, stared at one another with a shared deep, intense lust, and then he grabbed her hand and half dragged her through the front door, the dogs bounding behind them.

Just like the first time they'd made love, they kissed as if their lives depended on it, and couldn't get naked fast enough. He grabbed her hand again and they ran up the stairs together. Jay managed to close the bedroom door before the two dogs got there.

"I'd prefer to make love to you in privacy," Jay said, smiling at her so tenderly she thought her heart might burst.

She definitely agreed. What she was about to do with Jay Malone was not for anyone else's eyes—not even canine ones. He came toward her and then they tore each other's clothes, laughing as buttons popped and zippers stuck. A shoe flew across the room. She had never felt so good in her own skin. Jay laid her back on the bed and kissed her deeply, tongues intertwining, bodies writhing, and then such a feeling of wanton desire coursed through her that she hooked her legs around his back and rolled on top of him, straddling his muscular thighs. He grinned up at her, delighted at the move, and she smiled too, feeling confident and sexy as she took the lead.

She rolled her hips, teasing him, never breaking their gaze until he cried out that he couldn't take it anymore and reached over to the bedside table for a condom. She watched him put it on, delighted by the size and swell of his arousal, and then she lowered herself onto him and all thoughts left her head. They were nothing but two bodies, enjoying each and every most intimate inch of one another. At first they were fast and furious. And then she slowed down, trying to make the pleasure last. But instead it became stronger, rolling and rising, and as she felt the first glorious tremors of her climax, she cried out, louder and louder until it peaked and she shouted his name—and heard Jay's orgasm echoing right behind hers.

She rolled off him, spent and sweaty, and caught her breath, watching the way the sun played across the high ceiling. She turned to face him, and he to her, and they shared a satisfied smile.

"So," she said, still smiling, "How was LA?"

"Lonely," he said, pulling her closer. "I missed you. Even Nelson was off his food. I think he missed you too."

She kissed his bare shoulder. "I missed you both as well."

Quietly Jay said, "I can't tell you how happy it makes me to hear it."

Erin kissed his lips this time, which tasted now of

salt, and then sighed happily. Jay rolled onto his back and she nestled into the crook of his arm.

They remained in contented silence, their bodies recovering, until she noticed his gaze trained on the Barbara Hepworth sculpture. "That really is the best place for it."

He nodded. "I can't stop looking at it and thinking about whether you could recreate that position."

She studied the Hepworth in surprise. It was all round and sinuous, but she knew what he meant—it was the impression of a passionate embrace rather than actually being one.

Then, to her delight, Jay swung his feet to the floor and leaped out of bed stark naked. "Come here. Let's see if we can make it work."

She had to shake her head at him. "Are you kidding me? You're going to try and use the sculpture as a sexual position?"

"Sure. We'll make our own artsy Kama Sutra. Come on, you're so athletic from surfing, you could easily twist like that, if you're game?"

Erin burst out laughing. It was so ridiculous she had to give it a try. However, she should have known Jay had some devious plan in mind. He bent her over, arching backward so her feet were on the floor and her hands were on the bed and every part of her was curved and exposed to his view and his touch. He leaned over her, with a sexy, wolfish grin. He kissed each of her breasts, his tongue circling her nipples so she trembled, and then kissed his way slowly down her arched belly. He knelt before her, his breath heavy and warm, and pushed her legs apart tantalizingly slowly and then kissed the soft, tender flesh of her inner thighs.

Her trembling turned to shakes as he made his way up and then inward, using his tongue now to draw letters on her skin. Through the haze of pleasure she realized he was spelling her name. As his tongue grew more insistent, he moved its position and began to love her with his mouth. Her legs shook so badly she could hardly hold herself up and he gripped her thighs as she cried out in pleasure.

As her breathing subsided, he said, "Sorry. I got carried away there." He glanced again at the sculpture. "Let's see now, if you're bent over like that, then I should be bent over this way." He contorted himself and then bent her back over his body, and as she allowed herself to be twisted this way and that, she found herself tumbling and the pair of them collapsed on the rug, laughing.

When she got her breath back, she said, "I think it's fair to say that sculpture was not meant as a how-to guide."

He pulled her in for another kiss. When they parted, he said, "Let's do something fun today."

She thought they were already having a lot of fun,

but absolutely agreed. She wanted to spend the whole day together. "But no overpriced restaurant where everything is unpronounceable and served with foam."

He smiled, but kind of winced too. "You're never going to let me forget that, are you?"

She raised herself up on her elbows and tossed her hair over her shoulders. "Nope."

He turned over and kissed her. "I get it. You're special. Unique. Down to earth. How about I take you out into nature, with the dogs?"

She smiled at him, her heart full. "That sounds perfect."

Chapter Twenty-Seven

Erin loved the feeling of the wind blowing through her hair as they drove out to Point Lobos in Jay's SUV. The dogs were in the back, and a sense of deep contentment she'd never known before spread through her as she contemplated an afternoon walking the dogs along the nature trails.

They walked hand in hand, chattering about work and mutual friends, and then books they were both enjoying. At one point, Jay stopped and pointed down to where a trio of otters were playing in a cove. They were as playful as puppies, untroubled by the world. Just the way she was feeling. They kept walking, the trails familiar to Erin, and she pointed out her favorite trees and views. They squinted, looking out over the ocean, where she told him sometimes you could see whales sounding as they traveled back and forth, but no such luck today. It was a beautiful hot day, and they passed families, other couples holding hands, and a group of three women, obviously close friends, chatting up a storm.

At an especially picturesque viewpoint, hot from the afternoon sun, they took a seat on the wooden bench and drank deeply from their water bottles. Jay pulled out a collapsible water dish for the dogs and they lapped happily, then Buzzy and Nelson curled up at their feet, panting.

Because it felt right and she knew it was time, she said, "Jay, you told me a lot about your past and I really appreciate that you trusted me."

He looked slightly surprised at her serious tone. "Of course. And I'll trust you to decide when you want to write that story."

She took a breath of the salt-tinged air. She needed to get this out, needed to tell him. "It's not that. . . it's that, well, I have a story too."

Almost as though he knew she needed his support, he put an arm around her and pulled her against him. "Okay. I'm listening."

The cocky, joking Jay was truly gone, and in his place was the thoughtful one, the guy who read poetry and chose a scrappy rescue dog and made love to her as though she was the only woman in the world who mattered.

She said, "When I was in college, I had a really bad experience, and I think it affected me for years. No, I know it did." She paused. "Remember when you claimed that I always choose geeky guys who don't challenge me? There's a reason why."

He didn't say a word, just squeezed her shoulder. His eyes on hers were serious, clear, understanding. She had to glance away. She watched the ocean while she told him, haltingly, everything she'd told Mila. The charming, cocky student. The three dates they'd been on, and then how he'd forced his way into her bedroom, how he had tried—and failed—to force himself on her.

"All these years I've felt like it was somehow my fault," she concluded. "Like I'd led him on—I've been so ashamed."

She didn't cry, but her voice shook a little. He turned her to face him, tipped her chin up until she met his gaze. His eyes were clouded with emotion—a mix, it seemed, of tenderness toward her and anger at the man who had tried to harm her.

His voice was rough. "First, no man who has the right to call himself that would ever, ever treat a woman the way that no-account piece of crap treated you. I've known men like that. They give the rest of us a bad name. You are honest and decent and nothing that happened was your fault."

Even though she now knew how true that was, with the benefit of hindsight, it was still good to hear him say those words.

Then he said, looking now like steam might start coming out of his ears, "What's his name? Whoever he is, I'm going to find him and kill him."

The note of deep sincerity in his voice almost made her think he might. She shook her head and then gave him a soft, sweet kiss on the lips. "You're too good to even go near a guy like him. He's not worth going to jail for. He's nothing."

"You're right there," Jay agreed. "He's less than nothing."

"Besides, I managed to fight him off myself."

"You sure did." He looked proud for a moment.

Erin sighed, but it was a happy sigh. She had felt much better after she'd finally shared her story with Mila, but now that Jay knew too, she felt a thousand times lighter. "I honestly had no idea how much keeping this inside hurt me. How much it held back my heart."

And then he kissed her, a soft, sweet, understanding kiss. They wrapped their arms around each other and just held on. They didn't talk about it anymore. They didn't have to. What had begun with Mila, in a kind of letting go of the awful shame and self-loathing Erin had felt all these years, was feeling even more significant now that she'd shared her story again, with Jay.

They stood and walked on, and then Jay said, "I can't believe the guy's still alive anyway. How did Howie and your brothers not take him apart?"

"Because they never knew. I never told anyone, until I told Mila a few days ago."

Once more he stopped and turned her to face him. "Are you saying I'm only the second person you've ever told?"

She nodded mutely. He pulled her in again for a hug and whispered in her ear, "I am so honored."

If she'd had any doubts about her feelings for Jay, they all melted away in that moment.

She loved him. Wholly and completely, unlike anything she'd ever experienced before. But after the day's confession, she wasn't ready yet to tell him so. Things between them were already moving too fast. Besides, there was the not insignificant issue of her brothers, especially Arch, all of whom would have something to say about their choice of each other.

For now, she just wanted to enjoy their newfound intimacy. Now there was nothing she couldn't say to him. Nothing he wouldn't understand. Nothing he couldn't say to her and know that she would also understand. It was bliss. Pure and simple.

By the end of their walk, they were both famished, so he took her to Cannery Row for lobster rolls. She loved his suggestion, which was about as far as they could get from an uptight, exclusive restaurant.

As they took a seat, he told her that he'd been doing a little more research on romantic comedies, even talked to a couple of screenwriters he knew. And here she'd thought the script he'd begun was more of a joke or a kind of a romantic gesture than something he was actually taking seriously. But she should have known that once Jay got an idea in his head, he didn't let it go until he'd brought the thing home. It was, she realized now, one of the qualities she most loved about him.

She smiled to herself at the thought, and then took a fry from the basket that had arrived along with their lobster rolls. They shared a pool of ketchup, both dipping their French fries into it, and when he chomped into his lobster roll, he got a little mayonnaise on his cheek. She leaned forward and wiped it away with her thumb. This meal probably cost about a hundredth of what the fancy one had, and she enjoyed it so much more.

In fact, everything felt so right and so easy it scared her a little. She just hoped that Jay's feelings for her were as strong as hers for him.

After dinner, they agreed that they didn't want the day to end, so they drove back to Jay's place and the pair of them settled in the library. She couldn't decide which was her favorite room in the house. Was it the upstairs bedroom, with its amazing view and the Barbara Hepworth sculpture? Or in fact this room, with its beautiful bookshelves crowded with so many amazing books, and the stylish but comfy furniture that simply insisted a person curl up, flip the gas fireplace on, and read. She was looking along the shelves for something new, picking up books, some of which she'd either read or always meant to, and putting them back.

And then she spied a shelf of board games.

She turned to him. "I love Scrabble."

He took off his reading glasses and grinned at her. He'd been reading the *Sea Shell*. Adorably. "Ever played strip Scrabble?"

She put her hands on her hips and stared at him. "Strip Scrabble? Is that even a thing?"

He said, "I don't know. Should we find out?"

It turned out they were both pretty good at Scrabble. He came up with *exudate*, which gave him the X and a whole bunch of points. But she countered with *nexus*, using both the X and a U. They figured the best way to play strip Scrabble was to take off a piece of clothing every time they tried to play a word that didn't exist in the Scrabble rulebook.

She added a little extra spice by suggesting that whatever part of herself she revealed, he should crawl over and give it a kiss or lick. There was the inside of her wrist when she took off her shirt, her ankle when she took off a sock. Then he had to help her off with her jeans, kissing his way from the bottom of her foot, to the inside of her knee, and up her thigh. But even though she was wet and aching for him, he stopped when he got to the barrier of her panties. She was dying to come up with a new, unheard-of word. And then her imagination, along with her body, fired up and soon they were both naked. She got everything she wanted as they made love on the floor, then with her bent over one of the leather club chairs, until finally, exhausted, they collapsed in a heap on the sofa.

He bent to pick up some of the letters scattered all over the floor. He found an *E* and placed that on one of her nipples. The *R* went on the other nipple. Then an *I* between her breasts and an *N* right on top of her navel.

She glanced down at herself. "Is this so you can remember my name?"

"That's good. We should use this scene in our movie."

She laughed, then had to stop and gather up all the boldness inside her. "Jay, I'm scared. I'm not your usual girl and you're not my usual guy."

He turned and kissed her softly. "I'm scared too. But what I feel for you is unlike anything I've ever felt in my entire life." He was so much more open in his response than she'd ever thought he'd be that she softened.

She would trust them both to follow their hearts.

They collected their clothes and Erin realized she was hungry again. "All that lovemaking really works up an appetite."

Jay agreed and said he'd throw together a light supper. In the kitchen, he was in his underwear opening a bottle of white wine, when the doorbell rang. "I'm expecting a delivery—do you mind getting that?"

"Not at all." Since they kept tearing off each other's clothes anyway, she hadn't bothered putting all hers back on again. All she wore was Jay's shirt, which she loved because she had to roll up the cuffs and it hung down on her like a dress. She figured she was decent enough to answer the door.

She opened it, ready to sign for whatever Jay was expecting, when she got the shock of her life. Her brother Damien stood on the step. It was all she could do not to slam the door in his face and run back inside.

Chapter Twenty-Eight

Erin knew this looked very, very bad to her overprotective older brother. She forced herself to be calm. "Damien. What are you doing here?"

After a stunned moment, he said, "I think the better question is, what are *you* doing here?" His cheeks were turning red and his eyes were taking on a wild look. He was clearly already losing his mind at discovering her here in a very compromising outfit.

Obviously having heard the rock star's voice, Jay appeared at the door behind Erin. He'd somehow quickly thrown on his T-shirt and jeans.

"Damien, my man," he said coolly. "What can I do you for?"

Damien stepped inside, managing to slide in front of Erin so that she was forced behind him. Not going to play nice, then. He looked at Jay and then at Erin and back at Jay again. It took about three seconds before Damien completely lost it.

"How dare you touch my sister!" He rushed Jay as if he meant to knock him to the floor. Jay didn't move an

inch, and let Damien push him up against the wall.

Erin was aghast. "Damien! Cut it out!"

At the commotion, the dogs began barking.

Jay said nothing, clearly feeling bad. As if he deserved to be beaten up by her brother. What, was he going to let himself be pulverized? Nelson rushed to his side and barked even louder. Buzzy appeared at Erin's feet and circled her in canine concern.

When she saw Damien pulling back his fist, she threw herself on his back.

"Stop it!" she yelled. "Stop it *right now*." She tried to physically pull him off Jay. Obviously, she wasn't strong enough to succeed, but something in her voice must have got through the sound of blood ringing in her brother's ears.

He lowered his arm and stood in front of them both, panting with fury. Fists clenched, that glorious singing voice of his molten, he said through his teeth, "What were you thinking?" He drilled Jay with his eyes.

Erin balanced on her toes, ready in case she had to jump in again.

Jay's earlier calm had melted and now his temper flared. He yelled back, "I happen to be in love with your sister."

Erin's mouth dropped open. She cried, "What?"

Jay looked at her, suddenly sorry. "This is not how I wanted to tell you."

But Damien wasn't interested. Jay might not have spoken, never mind professed his love. Her brother turned on Erin. "How long has this been going on?"

How dared he? She wasn't a little girl anymore. He couldn't boss her around or demand anything from her—not even an answer. She put her hands on her hips, lifted her chin, and glared at him. "None of your business."

Damien growled, "Yes, it is."

She stood firm, in Jay's shirt and in his love. Almost too calmly, she said, "Have I ever interfered in your love life with your groupies? Even though—yuck."

Damien shook his head like a bull. "I don't hang with groupies." Then, seeing her raised eyebrows he said, slightly sheepishly, "Not anymore. And anyway, that's beside the point."

"It's totally the point. Damien, go home. I'll deal with you later."

He was so shocked at her tone that he stepped back. No doubt he could see the fire in her eyes and got his first clue that his normally quiet, agreeable sister was not about to back down on this one.

As though he didn't know what else to do, he shook his finger at her. "This is not over. I'm telling Arch." It would have been funny if he hadn't been so angry. And then he turned on Jay. "Arch is *so* going to fire your ass. And Smith Sullivan. Oh yeah, you can cross him off your list of clients too." And then, as though he didn't know what more he could do, Damien stepped outside and said to Erin, "And unless you leave Jay's house right now, I'm telling Mom and Dad!"

Was he still in fifth grade? Her only answer was to slam the door in his face. For real, this time.

Sudden silence filled the house. Even the dogs stopped their barking. After all the yelling and the aggression and the testosterone flying around, it was so quiet she could almost hear the dust motes drifting. She glared at the closed door for a moment and then turned to Jay.

Feeling almost shy and, despite the drama of the last few minutes, a little in awe, she said, "Did you mean what you said? That you're in love with me?"

Jay looked pensive. "Yes, I am. Completely head over heels." But instead of pulling her into his arms, he shook his head. "But it doesn't matter. We both know you deserve better than me."

How could he even *think* something like that? Jay was a catch. Big time. Not only was he a top Hollywood agent worth millions, he was so well-read and intelligent and good at everything he did. And he *was* good, in the purest, truest sense of the word. A good man.

Her eyes wide, she replied, "Why would you say that?"

He slumped against the wall in the foyer, his hands

behind him as though he had to stop himself from touching her. In his most serious voice, he said, "Your brother was right. I've got no business loving you. All along I've known I'm not good enough, but I couldn't stop falling in love with you, even though I knew I should."

She said, "You're good enough for anybody. More than good enough. I—"

From the library came the sound of her phone. She was going to ignore it, but Jay said, "Go ahead. I think we both need a second here just to breathe."

She could see that Jay really did need a minute, so she went to retrieve her phone. "If it's Arch, I'm telling him to go to hell." But when she picked up, it wasn't Arch. It wasn't any of her nosy, interfering family.

It was Pat Sinclair.

Erin frowned. It was unlike Pat to call her on the weekend. Or even email, for that matter—she believed in keeping one's work and personal life separate. She said a quick hello and asked Pat if everything was okay.

For once, her editor sounded like she was working at a hard news daily. "Erin, I need you here at the office. We have to remake the front page."

"We do? Why?" She had a terrible feeling that one of their main landmarks was on fire, or there had been a terrible road accident.

"That animal shelter you've been writing all those heartbreaking articles about? Instead of that final plea for money, the lead story is going to be about how the community pulled together and saved it."

Erin felt her jaw drop. Trust Pat to make it sound like the zombie apocalypse was upon them when really it was good news. But still, the shock was real. "But we were a million bucks away from being able to save it."

She heard Pat click a pen. "I know. An anonymous donor gave the whole amount." Her tone lightened and Erin could almost feel her smile beam down the phone. "Erin, we did it. The shelter's saved." Pat Sinclair could be hard and tough on the outside, but as much as Erin loved dogs, Pat loved cats more. She had four at home. One was blind, one was missing a leg, and two were just plain ugly. She rescued the kind of cat that nobody else wanted.

In spite of all the drama that she'd just lived through in the past five minutes, Erin was filled with delight. She told Pat she'd be right in and then hung up. She couldn't wait to tell Jay.

Bounding a little like the two dogs, she found him still standing in the foyer, his feet bare, his head bowed. "Jay! I've got to head into work because—guess what? The shelter's been saved at the last minute. An anonymous donor just gave a million bucks. Can you believe it?"

His expression was hard to read. "Really? That's great news. Congratulations. I think it was all those heartrending articles you wrote. You rallied the community."

But something in his tone made her look at him again more sharply. His gaze reached hers for a moment, then he glanced away.

"Jay?"

He scratched his chin. "What?"

And with absolute certainty, she knew the identity of their anonymous donor. "It was you, wasn't it?"

He sent her a baffled look, as if he had just forgotten what they were discussing. "What was me?"

She pointed a finger at him, not unkindly. "You're the anonymous donor." He started to shake his head, but she said, "I can always tell when you're lying, mostly because you hardly ever do. But you have a tell. You scratch your chin."

He looked shocked. "I do?" He glanced down at his hand as if it had betrayed him. "I clearly need to work on losing that if I'm ever invited to another of Archer's poker nights."

"Stop avoiding the subject. You gave that money to save the shelter, didn't you?"

He shrugged as though it was no big deal. Like people just donated a million dollars every day. "Those dogs and cats needed something better. I have the money, so if I can't adopt them all, why not help them out?"

As much as she loved him for saving all those dogs and cats and rabbits and birds, she almost loved him more for doing it anonymously. Mr. Boastful had learned the power of quiet kindness. And she loved it. She loved him! She was going to figure out a seriously romantic way to tell him—she didn't care what her stupid brother had to say on the matter.

She ran upstairs to get dressed and when she came down, she said, "Jay, even though I have to go right now, this isn't over. We've got a lot to talk about."

★ ★ ★

Jay watched Erin leave with a heavy heart. He had been looking forward to the rest of their date, and had been halfway through making a delicious fig and goat cheese salad for them both when Damien had upended it all. The ice-cold feeling that had gripped him when he saw the depths of Damien's fury hadn't thawed. He'd always known that he wasn't good enough for Erin.

Damien's furious eyes only proved it—and so had his flying fist.

Erin was, well, Erin Davenport, and he was just no-account scum. He'd proved that too—instead of giving Erin some time and space and then finding the world's most perfect and romantic way to tell her he loved her, he'd blurted it out in a rage. Not even the donation he'd secretly made earlier that day to the animal shelter could lift his spirits. Or change his conviction.

Nelson must have known something was up. He

pushed his nose against Jay's leg. He took the dog into the back garden for a run and was about to find his favorite yellow ball, when his phone rang. He was so worried that it was Archer or Smith calling to fire him that he almost didn't retrieve the thing from his pocket. But he had to face up to what he'd done.

To his surprise, it was Betsy. "Jay, I'm inviting you for breakfast tomorrow."

"But we had breakfast this morning."

She had her tough mom voice on. "I think we need another family get-together."

He knew what she was getting at. "I'm assuming this means Damien has told you that he saw Erin here?"

"Sure did. And now he's got his brothers riled up. It's all nonsense, of course, but I usually find that facing these things head on is the best way to put them back on an even keel. See you tomorrow. Ten o'clock." She paused. "And get some rest this evening, Jay. Don't stay up worrying. I can assure you these things have a way of working themselves out."

She hung up before he could come up with an excuse not to come—like an urgent flight to the Arctic.

Later that evening, he phoned Erin. It was Saturday night, and she should have been there with him. Instead, she was at home curled up with Buzzy, and her voice down the line sounded tired and a little unsure. His heart clenched. Even though he didn't deserve a woman as good as Erin, he couldn't stand the idea of losing her simply because her big brothers didn't like it.

He tried to make light conversation, make things feel normal and natural between them again. "How did the article turn out?"

"Pretty well, considering I had to hide the fact that I know who the anonymous donor is."

He liked that some spirit was coming back into her voice. He grinned. "So you didn't out me?"

"Of course not. You already know I'm not going to sell someone out for the sake of a story. Anyway, who doesn't love a closet philanthropist? Frankly, the dogs and cats don't care. So long as they get the money, they'll wag their tails for anybody who seems friendly."

There was a pause and he gathered his nerve. "Your mom phoned and invited me for breakfast tomorrow."

"*Invited* may not be the correct word. That was a *summoning.*"

He chuckled. "Yeah, I got that too. Are you going?"

"Of course. Aren't you?"

He thought about it. "Honestly, I don't know. I'm not sure my health insurance will cover getting beaten up by an A-list celebrity, a chart-topping rock singer, a billionaire app developer, and two guys who build houses for a living. They might say that walking into that house was assuming far too much risk."

Erin was silent for a few beats, but he could tell it was because she was considering her words. Finally, she said, "Whatever you do, I support you. But I want you to come."

There was an awkward moment when it came time to hang up where Jay wanted to say, "Okay, love you, good-bye." Instead, he settled for, "I'll be missing you tonight."

"Me too. More than you know." And then she was gone and he was left alone with his thoughts.

He tried to settle down and read. It was useless. He couldn't focus on a single word, especially when he found an *R* from the Scrabble game under the chair and could think of nothing but how that little square of plastic had gleamed against her beautiful breast. How had they gone from sex to Scrabble to his being hauled in front of the whole Davenport family to account for himself in so short a time? He'd barely done half the things he wanted to with Erin in bed, and now he wondered if he'd get another chance to see her at all, never mind see her naked.

So, it was in a very pensive mood that he finally gave up on his book and went to bed. His big bed seemed awfully lonely without Erin in it. Even Nelson seemed to be missing her and Buzzy. He leaped up on the bed and curled up beside Jay.

Jay didn't have the heart to push him off. Frankly, he needed the comfort.

Chapter Twenty-Nine

When Erin got to breakfast the next morning, deliberately arriving a little late, it would have been easier to cut through the heavy rye bread her mom had picked up at the bakery than through the atmosphere in that kitchen.

All her brothers had ganged up in one big, angry cloud. There was no sign of Jay yet—clearly he aimed to be even later than Erin. Or not turn up at all.

Her father came over and gave her one of his bear hugs. With a kind expression, he asked, "How you doing, kiddo?"

How was she doing? She had barely taken in the knowledge that Jay Malone loved her and she loved him right back. Now she had to defend that love, so new and so precious, against four angry men.

She shrugged. "Okay, I guess."

Her dad patted her back. "You'll be fine."

Betsy made time to come over and give Erin a hug, and then Mila made it clear she was siding with Erin. "I'm proud of you, sis. You gave Jay a chance." She glared across the room at their brothers, who had already taken their places at the table.

Erin followed her gaze, crestfallen. "And look how that turned out." All the lightness and happiness of the last days was being crushed under the thunderous gray cloud of her brothers at their protective worst.

"Is it serious? Because from the expression on your face, it looks serious."

Erin swallowed. "Mila, I told him. I told him about college."

Mila nodded, her mouth set. "That tells me everything I need to know. It was the right thing to do."

Erin managed a small smile. Even though her quiet, people-pleasing self was feeling like she might curl up and crawl away from all the dark looks being thrown at her, Mila was proud of her. And that was huge.

Tessa appeared from the back garden, where she'd been supervising Buster. Her eyes compassionate, she hugged her hello before taking a seat next to Archer at the table. Erin could see how torn her sister-in-law was. She had known the truth about how Erin felt about Jay and kept it to herself, knowing that it wasn't yet any of her husband's business. But she also loved Archer and could see that he felt betrayed by his friend and agent. It put her in a tough spot. Who would mild-mannered and fair Tessa side with when they all finally began talking?

Still no Jay. She understood, and she didn't blame him, but still, she'd have really liked to see him.

Betsy set down the last breakfast dish and then everyone was seated at the table, still in stony silence. Erin avoided everyone's eye but Mila's. Faced with their judgmental looks, her mouth would run away with her and she'd say something she'd regret. It soon became clear to her brothers that Betsy was also expecting Jay to turn up.

Damien's lightning bolt struck first. "I see Jay Malone isn't man enough to show up this morning. Why doesn't that surprise me?" He paused, looking around the table, and then narrowed in on Erin, as though the words wouldn't stay inside any longer, "I cannot believe you let him take advantage of you like that. Haven't we taught you any better? We know what he's like. We've all been to Vegas together."

All the boys nodded solemnly, glancing anywhere but at their mom.

Mila snorted. "And you're all a bunch of choirboys. I guess you four never got into any trouble on your boy trips, hm? Only Jay?"

"That's different," Damien said. "Besides, this isn't about you. This is about Erin." He got to his feet to face her now. "There's no way you can keep seeing him." All her brothers nodded like a bunch of puppets being pulled on the same string. "No way. And furthermore—"

For once in her life, Erin wasn't going to sit there meekly and take it. She jumped to her feet and leaned forward, getting right into Damien's face. "No. You listen, Damien. Shut up and back off. Right now."

He was so startled that after a stunned second, he sat down, his mouth gaping open.

Now that she was standing, she might as well go on. It took all her courage, but she wasn't about to let them know that. In the steeliest voice she possessed, she looked each of her brothers in the eye and said, "Now, all of you listen to me. I know you care about me and you're doing this out of love. That's the only reason I showed up today. My relationship with Jay Malone is *my business*. I'm an adult. Not a little girl you need to protect. Not anymore." She looked at Archer now. "Nobody's firing Jay because he's with me. Are we clear?"

Everyone was so shocked by meek Erin's outburst that they didn't have a single word to say. Erin sat down, inwardly delighted with herself and her little speech. With the argument concluded, she said to her dad, "Could you please pass the eggs?"

He obliged with a small smile, and she realized that while he might not wholly approve of the match, he was proud of her for finally sticking up for herself.

Then, before the silence grew too deafening, Betsy said, "I read your front-page article in the *Sea Shell* this morning, Erin. It's great to know that the shelter's going to be saved. And what a beautiful gesture from whoever donated that million dollars."

Her dad, who always liked to be in the know in the community, asked, "Do you have any inside information? Do you by chance know who it is?"

She huffed. "Even if I did know, I wouldn't tell this family. *Some* of you don't respect my secrets or my privacy."

No one rose to the bait. Instead, her brothers became intently focused on buttering their toast or adding milk to their coffee.

At that moment, the doorbell rang and Betsy excused herself to answer it. Erin hoped beyond hope that it was Jay and not some random delivery. When Jay did enter the kitchen a few steps behind her mom, Erin thought her heart might burst from her chest. She'd never been so happy to see anyone in her life. She would have understood if he hadn't showed up, but she was proud of him for facing down her brothers and being here for her.

The minute they saw him, her brothers jumped to their feet. Four pairs of meaty hands formed into tight fists and they looked ready to take him out back and pound the stuffing out of him.

Jay couldn't have missed the aggressive stances, but he only had eyes for Betsy. "I'm so sorry I'm late. But thanks for inviting me for breakfast. I'll do the dishes to make up for my tardiness."

She slipped an arm around him easily. "Nonsense. I'm just glad you could make it."

"If you've finished hugging our mother, you've got some explaining to do." Archer didn't get angry often, but he sure was now, his tone ice-cold. "I told you to stay away from Erin. I warned you. You've got a hell of a lot more than being late to make up for."

Looking straight at Archer, Jay said, "I know, and I'm sorry. But you see—"

Why should Jay have to apologize or explain himself to her brothers? Bristling with outrage, Erin interrupted Jay's unnecessary apology. "Did I not make myself clear? My love life is *none of your business*. And if you don't like it, frankly, I don't care. You can take your opinions and shove them."

Mila said, "I agree. And I like the new you, sis."

Though Erin appreciated her sister's support, she said, "It's not new. I've always thought these things, I've just never felt the need to say them until now."

Mila gave two thumbs up as she nodded. "Tons of respect. Tons."

Erin caught Tessa's eye and then smiled as she saw her sister-in-law mirror Mila's two thumbs up.

Jay was about to take a seat next to Erin when Finn said, "If you ever make her cry, this is what we'll do to you." He broke a piece of toast into little pieces with his big hands.

"If you ever cheat on her, your life will be over."

Damien brought his fist down on a croissant, flattening it.

Arch wasn't about to be left out. "You so much as look at a lingerie catalog—" With a knife, he sliced a grape in half.

All the men winced.

They looked at Hersch, who was sitting beside Arch. He shook his head. "I'm staying out of this, if you don't mind."

Nick, who had remained quiet through the rest of her brothers' outbursts, said, "Erin's vulnerable and easily hurt."

Erin opened her mouth to defend herself one more time, but Jay got there first. "I don't know what you're talking about, Nick. Not the Erin I know."

Then he gave Erin a smile that warmed her right through to her heart. Still standing, he reached down for Erin's hand and addressed the whole family. "Erin is one of the strongest people I've ever known. She's a brilliant writer, an incredible surfer, and a first-class human being. Over the past weeks, I've come to see her not as everybody's kid sister, but as this incredible woman whom it has been a privilege to know better."

Mila spoke into the silence. "Jay, you're right. I think we're all beginning to understand now that Erin is a grown woman who has always been much tougher than we ever knew."

Just when Erin thought Jay would finally sit down

beside her and pile his plate with food, he said, "I know I'm not good enough for her, but I love her. And I love all of you. You're the family I never had. I'd hate to lose that, but ultimately it's up to you." He took one more longing look at Erin. Then to her shock, he called Nelson and turned to leave.

The two of them walked out of the kitchen.

"*Now* look what you've done," Erin cried once Jay had shut the door behind him. "If I lose the man I love because of you guys being so overprotective, I will *never* forgive you."

And then she did something she'd never done in her life. She stormed out of a family breakfast.

"Erin, wait," Arch called after her, but she didn't. She was done with waiting. She called Buzzy and at the door, he turned and barked—once, but with meaning.

It was good to know her dog was on her side too.

Chapter Thirty

When Jay arrived home, he felt as though everything he cared about was hanging in the balance. The woman he loved, the family he'd come to feel a part of, and some of his biggest clients might be walking out on him—all because he'd fallen in love. In truth, he couldn't blame them. He paced the house, shaking his head at all the beautiful rooms that might never be filled with the sound of happy laughter, the spaces where he had dared to hope that children might lay their heads at night.

He went into the kitchen and made himself a cappuccino to take his mind off it all, but then found he didn't want it. Staring into the frothy cup, he said to Nelson, "In a book or movie, this is what you call the *black moment*. When the guy not only doesn't get the girl, but also loses the only family he's ever known."

The black moment. Hm. He decided to try to ease the pain in his heart by writing about it. He took the coffee and set it down beside his computer, then stared at the stack of screenwriting books. But he didn't even open them. He'd watched so many movies, been part of the making of so many, that he knew the structure instinctively.

And he hadn't lied to Nelson. This was his black moment.

Just as before, when he realized how much he needed to win Erin back, he began to type, his hunt-and-peck style barely keeping up with the words tumbling out of him.

He had no idea how much time had passed when the doorbell rang and jolted him back into the real world. He came to with a start, gut clenched.

He knew who he really wanted to see at the door—Erin. But it could also be four angry Davenport brothers who had decided to ignore her warning to stay out of her love life and had come to pulverize him. He headed for the foyer, Nelson following, and hoped he'd find Erin. But if he confronted Archer, Damien, Finn, and Nick, he'd let them treat him like a punching bag.

In a way, he understood their anger. In a way, he deserved it.

He took a deep breath and opened the door.

And there she was: the woman of his dreams. "Erin," he said, as love and pain collided.

Erin stepped inside and closed the door behind her. He wanted to go to her and cover her face, her body, in kisses, but he held back in case the scene at breakfast had caused her to change her mind about him. He was more relieved than he could express that she'd come here, as he'd prayed she would, but he was worried too.

"I hope I didn't embarrass you in front of your family," was all he could find to say. She was so beautiful and so precious he wanted to pull her into his arms, but it was the truth. He didn't deserve her. Maybe she was seeing that now.

She laughed, but there was no humor behind it. More irritation and frustration than anything else. "Are you kidding? You finally helped make my overprotective brothers see me as a grownup. I've tried for years, but they've never listened."

Jay allowed himself a small smile. "They're right, though. I'm the trailer trash who doesn't know how to do anything but hustle. You're smart and beautiful and educated. You're a great writer. You could do anything. You don't want to be stuck with me."

To his shock, she walked forward and threw her arms around him. He breathed in the scent of her skin, stroked the soft hair flowing down her back. She felt perfect in his arms.

She touched his face with a tenderness he'd never known before. With a smile, she said, "I love you. I love you for bringing me a towel when I'm cold on the beach, for making me hot chocolate with marshmallows, for the way you get excited about books and telling stories that will reach millions of people and touch their hearts. Jay Malone, you may be loud and brash, but you're always fair and honest. And you have the biggest heart of anyone I know."

Jay was so happy that for once in his long, loud life, he was lost for words. Finally he remembered to say, "I love you too, Erin. More than anything in the world."

They kissed deeply, and in seconds he was hungry for her again.

There was so much love and lust in her eyes he knew she was feeling the same way. "Plus you adopted this rescue dog who would have been a goner by now if it hadn't been for you." Nelson was listening to every word and wagging his tail. "Sorry, Nelson." She kissed Jay again. "And I found out for sure that you're the anonymous donor who saved the shelter."

Even though he'd already admitted it to her, he was slightly upset. "That donation was supposed to be confidential."

"I'm a pretty good investigative reporter when I want to be." She smiled. "Plus, I went to high school with the head of the shelter. She couldn't hold back about the 'great-looking man who brought us a huge check.'"

Uncomfortable with being painted as such a good guy, he swiftly changed the subject and asked how the rest of the family had been after he'd gone.

"I didn't stick around for long, but my brothers are still pretty mad. If I know Mom and Dad, they're still at the table, talking them down. My folks seem really supportive of you and me together."

He kissed her again because he couldn't help himself. "I went to Betsy when I knew I was falling for you, but thought I'd messed this up. She told me she saw this coming ten years ago."

Erin's eyes went wide. "What? I can't believe how intuitive my mom is."

"That's where you get it from."

"I kind of love that you confided in her first."

"She really is like family to me. And so kind and understanding." He paused. "You are a lot like her."

Erin smiled shyly. She was about as good at accepting compliments as Jay was. They walked hand in hand to Jay's office so he could switch off his computer.

She eyed the script and the screenwriting books on his desk, intrigued. "Were you busy? Did I interrupt anything?"

"Believe it or not, I was working on the romantic comedy script. This thing better sell, because it looks like I'm losing my biggest clients."

"They'll get over it. After all, where are Arch and Smith ever going to find an agent who hustles like you do?" She turned to face him with an expression so sweet and serious. "*And* who loves them like a brother." With that, she moved into his arms at exactly the same time as he pulled her into them.

They went up to his bedroom and made love, their

bodies communicating without any need for words, with all the sweetness and tenderness growing between them. Maybe the fact that he had stood up for her, believed in her, told her family in no uncertain terms how strong he thought she was, meant that she was beginning to see herself in that light too.

★ ★ ★

Kissing his shoulder, still breathing fast, Erin turned herself onto one elbow. "Jay Malone, you are good for me. I never thought of myself as being that strong."

"Are you kidding me? You are one of the strongest people I've ever known."

"Maybe you're right," she agreed. She had made a beautiful, happy life for herself and now she was in bed with the man of her dreams in the house of her dreams. It was time to put the past firmly behind her and look forward to all the future held.

Tracing patterns on his chest with her fingertips, she said, "You know, Mila was also Team Jay from the start."

"Wait, she knew about us?"

"I told her I had a crush on you before anything happened. Tessa, too. They both thought we'd be a good match." She laughed. "Way before I did, actually. They encouraged me to give you a shot."

Jay picked up her wandering hand and kissed her on the wrist, where her pulse was still slowing. "I owe those two dinner." He kissed her palm. "Man, I love the way you support each other. If only your brothers felt the same way as the women in your family."

"I love my family too," she agreed. "But I'm also pretty irritated with them for butting in the way they did."

"It's only because they love you so much."

"I know. But there's a difference between love and thinking they know what's best for me."

He nodded. "Believe me, I don't think anyone is underestimating you now. Least of all me." He paused, and something shifted behind his eyes. He seemed suddenly lighter. She was beginning to recognize that look as Jay's lightbulb moment. She waited, excited to hear what he was about to say.

He grinned. "Write this romantic screenplay with me. I'm serious about it and I think I'm on to something."

"What?" She was stunned. "Seriously? I'm a journalist, not a screenwriter."

Jay's grin widened and then he looked a little sheepish. "I have a little secret. I read everything you've written in the *Sea Shell* for the past two years. You've got all the chops a screenwriter needs. You managed to make a high school musical sound riveting, and how there's still an unadopted dog in all of California with you writing the Dog of the Week, I do not know."

She was absolutely floored. "Seriously? You read my writing in the paper? All of it?"

"Sure did. Even the interview with that clown who lost a big shoe and just kept on performing. I laughed so hard."

She joined in, and when they both finished chuckling, she said quietly and seriously, "Just in case you missed me saying it earlier, I love you, Jay Malone."

And then he told her, yet again, that he loved her too. Words she would never tire of hearing.

Chapter Thirty-One

Erin spent the week feeling as though she was living in her very own romantic comedy movie. Nothing could have prepared her for how much fun writing a screenplay with Jay would be. In between his agenting commitments and her job at the paper, they worked together feverishly on the end of the screenplay. Of course, sometimes they argued: her ideas were often quite different from his, and that would cause them to sit back—usually naked and in bed—and discuss the way she saw the world versus how he did. Sometimes she felt it was a female perspective versus a male one, but they always seemed to come up with something better together than either of them would have been able to on their own.

By Friday night, the script was almost done and they were reading through the final draft, when Jay said, "Every one of the scenes you wrote—and the scenes of mine you've edited—just fly off the page. I can see these scenes onscreen already. Where did you learn how to write a romance?"

She thought about it for a minute. "From life, I guess. I watch my parents, and every day they show each other in little ways how much they're still in love." She gazed into her memories. "And then I watched Arch and Tessa fall in love. Smith and Valentina have had a pretty rocky time of it, but they're so happy now and having a baby. Even Mila and Hersch. Mila was never going to fall in love easily."

He laughed. "You didn't either. But I think we're the kind of people who, when we do love, it's forever."

She couldn't help it. Tears filled her eyes. "Forever. I feel that too."

They kissed deeply and then smiled at one another. "What about you?" she asked. "Where did you learn about romance?"

"From loving you. I finally get what all the love songs and movies and novels are about. I'm ready to be the kind of man who can truly love a woman." He looked into her eyes, "I will only ever love you, Erin. I'm making that promise to you now."

In her heart, Erin knew it was a vow he intended to keep. She'd never felt happier.

Then Jay smiled sheepishly and swept out his arm, gesturing at the room. "You know, I said I bought this place so friends and clients could stay, and that's still true. But deep down it was also because I'm ready for a family." He chuckled. "A big one, clearly."

Erin's eyebrows shot up in a mild pang of alarm.

"How big?"

"As big as you want it to be," he said. "But I do have six bedrooms, and I'd love a big family like yours. And, as soon as you're ready, I hope you'll consider calling this place home."

Erin was speechless. Everything was moving so fast and yet it felt so right. Gently, she moved the computer off her lap and kissed him. And then they were moving instinctively, their bodies taking over. Jay took the lead this time and she was happy for him to do it. She could barely contain herself as he spent what felt like hours caressing her, kissing her breasts and her belly. He discovered how aroused she became when he licked around her navel and once he found that tender spot, he lingered there until she couldn't take it anymore. She let herself melt into his arms and moaned as he loved each part of her body with his tongue, gently licking, making his way down farther and farther until she was trembling all over, feeling worshiped and adored.

As much as she loved the attention he was lavishing on her, she wanted to do the same for him. She took his head in her hands, pulling him back up to eye level, before rolling them over so that she was on top.

"Hey," he moaned into her mouth, "I was enjoying myself down there."

"Me too," she murmured back, "but it's your turn now."

She felt his excitement swell against her leg and decided that he too needed teasing right to the very edge. So she took her time exploring him, allowing herself the pleasure of feeling *his* pleasure. His body was divine. Tanned and sculpted and oh so manly. She loved the shape of him. He smelled clean and fresh, a subtle whisper of the sea-salt air and sun in his warm skin. When he cried out that he couldn't take it anymore, he needed to be inside her, she straddled him and guided him into her, and together they rocked to a mutual climax, hands entwined, sticky with sweat, completely and utterly spent.

★ ★ ★

The next morning, Jay left Erin sleeping in what he was coming to think of as *their* bed. He walked Buzzy and Nelson on the beach, which was already becoming a routine, as though it was his morning job, along with making the coffee and usually breakfast. Erin needed more sleep than he did; besides which, she had developed her own routines and roles. She was, he had to admit, much better at tidying things away and making the house look prettier. A carefully arranged vase of flowers she'd picked from the garden, a bowl of enticing-looking fresh fruit on the kitchen counter— small touches he'd never have thought of, but that made the house feel more like a home.

Most of all, it felt like home because she was in it.

Out on the beach, with the ocean air blowing away the cobwebs, he cringed to remember that he'd even admitted to her last night that he had bought a house to fill it with children. She hadn't exactly looked thrilled at the idea. She'd brought it up again after they'd made love, her eyes wide. "Six children? You're really planning to have six children?"

"Well, not all right away," he'd replied and then laughed. "Okay, I could compromise. How do you feel about five?"

"That's your idea of a compromise? I was thinking two."

"How about we split the difference and call it four."

"How is splitting the difference between two and five four?" She was quite irate. "Isn't the compromise between two and five more like three?"

He laughed and pulled her to him. "You know what I love about this conversation? We're not arguing about whether we're going to have children together, but how many."

She twinkled at him. "That's true."

But, he hadn't made his living brokering great deals for his clients for nothing. "I'd just like to remind you that your parents have six, and it's worked out pretty well for them."

She kissed him on the nose. "To be negotiated."

He had been itching to leap out of bed, drop to one

knee, and ask her to marry him right there, but something stopped him. The time wasn't right. When he and Erin announced their engagement, he wanted every single person in the Davenport family thumping him on the back and offering congratulations. He definitely did not want her brothers glaring at him the way they had at breakfast last week. Not only for his sake, but for Erin's. She was the nicest person he'd ever known and she deserved the full support of her family when she took that momentous step.

It was a momentous step for him too, but he was ready. He had a feeling that Erin had gotten under his skin a lot earlier than he'd realized. Well, Betsy had seen it, but he'd been too busy thinking he needed to prove himself by showing off the women on his arm like they were trophies. His behavior embarrassed him now, but, as in every decent romantic comedy, he had to accept that loving Erin had made him a better man.

He stood for a moment at the water's edge, watching the dogs splash along the shore, and came to a sudden decision. He couldn't move forward and ask Erin the question he was burning to ask her without clearing the air with Archer and the others. Archer was not only his client, they'd all but made each other, and for more than a dozen years had been close friends as well as respected colleagues. It had to start with Arch.

Leaving a note for Erin, who was still enjoying her Saturday morning sleep-in, he left the dogs at the house and then headed straight along Scenic Drive to Archer's home. He walked deep in thought, his mind working a mile a minute, trying to figure out a way to convince his friend that he was the right man for Erin, and she the right woman for him.

By the time he rang the bell, he knew what he was going to say. He also knew perfectly well there was a video camera at the door. So he wasn't all that surprised when he got a text from Archer.

You're not wanted here. Go away.

Jay shook his head and then stared up at the camera. Was Arch really going to play this game? They weren't children. Arch couldn't just hide away. While Jay stood there, trying to decide whether he should go around the back and try to find a window he could shimmy through, the front door swung open and Tessa Taylor-Davenport stood there. She shook her head and rolled her eyes, and whether she meant to chide him or her husband or, as he suspected, the pair of them, she gestured for him to step inside.

In her soft voice, she said, "You need to work this out."

"I agree," Jay replied and followed her into the great room. He watched, a little bemused, as Tessa got busy texting someone whom Jay had to assume was her husband. After a minute or so, Archer stomped in wearing workout shorts and a sweat-stained T-shirt.

"I don't want him here," he repeated, close to sticking out his bottom lip like a petulant child.

Tessa calmly smoothed back her dark hair. "Yes, you made that clear. And I'm telling you, you need to work this out. Also, I just texted your brothers and told them to come over right now."

Arch looked incredulous. "You did *what*?"

"You guys need to sort this out and deal with it. I am going to have coffee with Mila and I've asked Erin to join us." Then she shook her finger at the pair of them. "And when I get back, there'd better not be anything broken—not an arm, not a head, and not so much as a *vase* in my house. Do I make myself clear?"

The pair of them nodded mutely. Jay had never seen Tessa so tough. He'd always assumed Arch was joking when he said she was a hard taskmaster when she made him do his workouts. Now he realized Archer hadn't been joking at all. Tessa had a core of steel in her and he admired it enormously. He was also grateful, because if there was anyone other than Betsy who could help sort this mess out, it was Tessa.

Archer didn't look happy, but with a grumpy shrug, said, "You'd better sit down." He trudged into the living room with its grand view of the ocean.

Tessa stretched up and kissed Jay on the cheek. Quietly she said, "I really like you and Erin together, and I believe in you. Make this right."

He whispered back, "I intend to. And if it doesn't work out with Erin, I am going to steal you away from

Arch and run away with you."

She laughed, delighted, patted him on the cheek, and then left.

Despite his host's invitation, they didn't sit. Arch stood glaring, his arms crossed over a chest even more formidable since he'd been bulking up for *Shock Tactics*. Jay was no slouch in the workout department, but if Archer decided to take him down, he was pretty sure he wouldn't stand a chance.

"Tessa left us a pot of coffee," Arch said, and begrudgingly walked to the kitchen to pour Jay a cup.

He gulped the hot stuff down as if it were Dutch courage and then took a seat on Arch's leather couch. Neither of them spoke, just watched the glorious waves through the panoramic window. Jay recalled watching Erin out there on the surf alone, so brave and beautiful. He had just opened his mouth to deliver his speech to Arch when the door opened and in walked Nick and Finn, Damien right behind them.

How had he never noticed how built all the Davenport brothers were? If they decided to gang up on him, what was he going to do? Still, they were also decent men and he doubted very much they intended him physical harm. They barely acknowledged Jay as they joined Arch on the couch.

Jay took a deep breath. It was better they all heard this together.

He had to stand. He'd pitched tougher men than

these four in his life, but never, ever had his pitch been more important. He didn't have notes or a prepared speech. All he had were his feelings.

"First of all, I get that I'm not the guy you'd have chosen for Erin. I wouldn't have chosen myself for Erin either. I absolutely agree with you that she deserves better. But you know what? She loves me and I love her. And maybe at breakfast the other day I felt like I really wasn't good enough, and maybe I was willing to walk away, but Erin has convinced me not to. And I'll tell you what—I would not do one single thing that would make Erin Davenport unhappy. If my walking away makes her unhappy, then that is non-negotiable."

The four brothers looked at each other. Obviously, they figured it was Arch who should do the talking, since he and Jay had always been so close.

Arch scratched the back of his head, as though he couldn't quite figure out what to say. "But I told you to stay away from her. I told you to stay away from both my sisters."

He'd made that argument a few times now, and it was starting to sound a little weak. This was good. Jay hadn't become an expert negotiator without being able to gauge the strength of an argument and the commitment behind it. Archer might be saying the words, but he was having trouble holding on to his conviction.

Jay opened his hands. "You did. And I'm telling you right now, I tried. I never thought of Erin as anything but your kid sister. But since I've arrived here and we've come to know each other, what I feel for Erin is unlike anything I've ever felt before—anything I thought I was capable of feeling. Can you understand that?"

Okay, it was a bit of a low blow and he knew it. Because Archer had walked the same road Jay was walking now, having to accept that Tessa, the love of his life, had been right under his nose for a while before he'd figured it out.

However, Archer wasn't giving in that easily. "What happened with me and Tessa has absolutely nothing to do with you and Erin."

"No. I know that. But you have to admit the situations are a little similar."

Damien obviously couldn't hold himself back any longer. Outraged, he growled, "But she's our little sister. You had to know she was off limits."

Jay turned to the fierce rock star. "I never meant to fall for your sister, and I know what a shock this must be for all of you. I agree that I'm not good enough for her, but I love your sister so much that I would give up my whole life and every dollar I've ever earned for her. She's my everything."

Archer scoffed and then stepped forward, getting right in Jay's face. "Do you really think that after pulling a stunt like this, I would let you near my business?"

Sure, it was hard to face the threat of losing one of his most lucrative clients, but Jay was not going to be intimidated. Not by Arch or anybody else. He didn't flinch or retreat. "Falling in love with Erin is not a stunt. I'd pick loving your sister over running your career any day of the week."

Arch was so shocked he couldn't seem to find words.

Finn muttered, "I never thought I'd see the day."

Arch finally found his voice. "Wait a minute. I'm firing *you*. You can't fire *me*."

Jay looked at his friend, red in the face, nostrils flaring, and softened. In a quieter tone, he said, "I don't want to fire you. I want to represent you and your best interests. I want to keep making money for both of us and finding you movies so great they haven't even been dreamed up yet. All I'm saying is that if I have to choose between the two of you, I choose Erin."

Nick shifted on the sofa. "It's easy to *say* you love her. Can you prove it?"

How did you prove love? How could he show what lay deep in his heart? Did they expect him to pull out that organ and display it for them?

Then an idea struck like a sneaky wave. An idea so embarrassing he wasn't sure he could do it. Would he make himself that vulnerable to four of the toughest guys he knew?

Well, Nick wanted proof. He couldn't think of anything better than this. He pulled out his phone and tapped through it.

"It kills me to do this," Jay said. "I can't even believe I'm showing you." Then he had to close his eyes as he pushed the phone toward Arch. "Read this."

Arch took the phone and stared down at it. "What is this? Are you trying to pitch me a project? *Now*?"

The other three gathered around to look over Archer's shoulder and Damien said, "It's a screenplay."

"I know that, genius," Arch snapped, "but why do I want to read a screenplay now?"

Nick, who was the most computer savvy of them all, began flicking the pages forward. "It's a romantic comedy." Now the four of them were silent, all skim reading. "It's about us. Our family. And Jay and Erin." Nick sounded like he couldn't believe it. Then all the brothers stared at Jay.

Stunned surprise dripping off every word, Arch said, "No way did you write this."

"I did. It started out as kind of a love letter to Erin, but now the two of us are working on it. Together. We just figured out the ending last night."

Archer and Damien stared at each other. "He's not bluffing," Archer said. "He never puts his clients in romantic comedies. If he's *writing* one for Erin, he's got to be in love with her."

"That's what I keep telling you. I love your sister and she loves me. Deal with it." And as they all stood there, looking more like they wanted to laugh at him than kick his ass, he said, "Can I have my phone back?"

He had done everything he possibly could here and had nothing left to give. Jay said a curt good-bye and left the room, wondering if Arch would ever speak to him again, never mind let him represent him any longer.

He was almost to the door when Archer yelled after him, "We're watching the video of the Scottish wedding tonight at seven. Make sure you and Erin come."

Chapter Thirty-Two

Erin could barely swallow her coffee, she was so nervous. She played distractedly with a button on her linen shirt, losing track of the conversation entirely. She thought Tessa was talking about her painting, but then realized she was trying to persuade Mila not to spend a small fortune on a pair of gold sandals. But once Mila got an idea in her head there was no talking her out of it, so she tuned out the conversation again and let her thoughts to return to Jay and her brothers. She'd nearly fallen out of bed with fright that morning when she saw his note and realized he'd gone over to Archer's to sort things out between them.

For the last hour, Tessa and Mila had been trying to calm her down, but for about the seventeenth time she said, "Do you think I should go over there? I feel like I should go and make sure everything's okay."

And for about the seventeenth time, Mila said, "No. You are not going to run to a grown man's rescue. He'll be fine."

Erin stared at her sister. "Okay for you—Hersch

isn't in danger of being beaten up by four of the strongest men in Carmel-by-the-Sea. The odds aren't on Jay's side."

"They're not going to beat him up." She took a bite of an apricot pastry and then swallowed. "At least, not very much."

Erin jumped to her feet and just in time, Mila grabbed her hand. "Joking, joking. Sit down. Have you even met Jay? That guy could talk his way out of a firing squad. He's going to be fine."

"Why don't you tell us about the two of you to take your mind off things?" Tessa suggested. "What's really going on with you and Jay?"

Despite her anxiety, Erin found herself beaming. "I love him. That's really the whole story. I could not be more shocked that I fell for someone so brash and loud, but I did."

Tessa nodded, looking delighted. "You're just glowing with it. I remember you saying not so long ago, when Mila suggested you hook up, that you thought you'd get lost when he was around. But you don't. You stand up to him and he listens. And when you told Damien at breakfast to shut up and sit down, it was amazing."

"I thought I heard angels sing," Mila agreed.

"I surprised myself," Erin admitted. "In a good way. I guess I've been surprising myself a lot lately."

Mila looked so smug it was maddening. But Erin

supposed she had a right, since the idea of Erin and Jay had been hers first. Finally, Mila couldn't hold it in anymore. "Didn't I tell you? I told you so!"

Erin had to laugh. When she was with her sister, sometimes it was like they were teenagers again. "You did, and I didn't believe you. But you weren't the first. Jay said Mom got there before any of you. She told Jay she's known we would get together for more than ten years."

Mila scoffed and flicked back her long braid, which was still wet from her surf session earlier that morning. "She did not." Then she looked kind of thoughtful, and Erin could tell she was accepting the fact that their mom had beat her to it. "It's kind of spooky how Mom can see things."

Tessa smiled. "It's because she loves you all so deeply. She's the heart and soul of your family. And I think she and Howie have such a strong marriage that she understands how love works."

"You're not doing so bad yourself," Mila teased. "You've got a glow about you that says 'I'm married to a hot movie star and getting lots of great sex.'"

Tessa laughed and blushed a little, but she didn't deny it. "Speaking of being a newlywed, Crystal says she's got the edited video from our Scottish wedding. Archer wants to screen it tonight at our place at seven." She leaned over and reached for both Erin's and Mila's hands. "We want you all there." Then to Erin she said,

"You *and* Jay."

Erin's nerves quivered again. She shrugged a little miserably. "I don't know. It depends how things are going at your house." She slipped her phone from her jeans pocket and stared glumly at the blank screen. No message from Jay. She saw Tessa surreptitiously check her phone as well. Nothing from Arch either.

Mila kept up her attempts at distraction as the three women ate their pastries and finished their coffee, but Erin couldn't focus. Not until she knew everything was okay between Jay and her family.

Usually she was sorry when their coffee dates ended, because she so enjoyed her time with Mila and Tessa. But this morning she was almost relieved when Mila stood and said, "I've got to show a house."

Then Erin felt released, as though she could do what she'd been wanting to do for the better part of an hour—run back to Jay's place to wait for him. She hugged Mila and Tessa good-bye and told them she hoped, all being well, that she'd see them both that evening.

By the time she walked back to Jay's, she was almost out of breath. She let herself in and immediately smelled fresh coffee brewing.

He was home.

She rushed to the kitchen, where she found him standing by the sink with a mug of fresh coffee, all in one piece. He turned as she entered and by the happy, relaxed look on his face she knew that everything was okay. She grinned and ran toward him and he caught her, pulling her into a bear hug and then lifting her up onto the counter.

They kissed and then she broke away. "So it went well?" There was still a note of worry in her voice, because she knew how much Jay cared about Arch and how hurt he would be if the relationship were permanently damaged because he was in love with her.

There and then, Erin decided that if Archer gave Jay any more grief, or even hinted at finding a new agent, she might have to talk to him about finding a new sister.

"It was tough," he admitted. "Not exactly what I'd call a slam dunk." He paused and looked a little embarrassed—not an emotion she was used to seeing Jay exhibit.

"What happened?" she asked with some mounting trepidation.

Finally, he said, "The only way I could get them to believe I was truly in love with you was to send them our screenplay."

She almost laughed as the tension broke. "That's why you're looking so green around the gills? Because you sent them a screenplay?"

"It's so personal. It's the first time I've ever put down my feelings on paper that way."

Erin smiled. "Well, I wouldn't worry too much.

There's no way my brothers are going to sit and read an entire romantic screenplay that we wrote. No offense."

Jay lifted a brow. "Oh, how wrong you are, short stuff."

Jay was serious. Her eyes widened. As if reading her thoughts, he nodded slowly.

"You aren't seriously telling me Archer Davenport is planning to read that screenplay."

"I'm seriously telling you he must've started it the second I left. He texted me just as you came in. He says he wants to talk Smith into playing the lead."

She couldn't help it—she burst out laughing. The two dogs, hearing the hilarity, had to get in on the act and raced in from the garden.

"Well, it is a very good story," she said at last.

Jay looked up at her on the counter, his eyes twinkling, full of love. "*And* it has a happy ending," he reminded her, and then leaned forward to give her a long, deep kiss.

It took a minute before she could come up for air. "The best kind," she agreed. "The kind that lasts forever."

Epilogue

Damien Davenport was having a hard time wrapping his head around his kid sister and Jay Malone becoming an item. Sure, he could see they were crazy for each other. First Erin had turned into some kind of *sisterzilla*, jumping up at the breakfast table and telling him to sit his butt down. Demanding that her whole family stay out of her business. It was a side of Erin he'd never seen before and, he had to admit to himself once he got over the shock, she had a point. He was kind of proud of her. He'd been so accustomed to thinking of Erin as their vulnerable kid sister who needed protecting that he'd never noticed she'd become a grown woman making her own choices. It was pretty clear his brothers had felt the same way.

But to find out she cared for *Jay Malone*, the hotshot agent who had spent the last fifteen years boasting about which top model he was currently dating, had made his blood boil. He and his brothers had planned to teach Jay a lesson one way or another. But then Jay had gone and shocked them all.

Jay Malone had written a romantic comedy.

Jay Malone, who famously never even put his actors in romances, had gone and written one. Co-written, it turned out, with their sister.

And the shocks just kept landing. The minute Jay had left his brother's house, Arch had started reading the screenplay aloud. Obviously, all of them had figured it would be terrible, something they could have a good laugh at, but after a couple of pages, Arch had stopped reading the lines in a bad falsetto and started reading it with feeling. The way a professional would do a table read.

Even with only one voice doing all the parts, Damien found himself swept up in the story. At first, he'd thought it was because Arch was that good of an actor, but then he realized Jay and Erin were actually that good as screenwriters.

At the end of the first act, Arch put down the phone and looked at all of them grouped around him in an astonished circle. "He meant it. It is a love letter to Erin."

"And one from her to Jay," Nick had said, stunned. Silence had fallen as the brothers took in this new fact that reshaped their world. Those two most unlikely people were in love. Then Nick added, "I guess we have to be okay with it."

Arch read on, not aloud anymore, but skimming ahead, chuckling a few times, shaking his head. Finally, he glanced up. "And damn, it's good. I think the lead could be perfect for Smith."

Damien had been so shocked he couldn't believe his ears. "You seriously think this movie could be made?"

"Oh, yeah. And it could be big."

Nick pondered the question. "You want Smith to play *Jay*?"

Arch shook his head. "It's not Jay, it's every guy who's ever fallen hard for a girl he thought was just a friend. It's a classic storyline, but they've made it feel completely fresh. It's one of the best scripts I've read in a long time."

While his brothers adjusted to the idea of Erin and Jay, it took Damien some time to process things. He'd always felt extra protective of his youngest sister, but what did he know about love?

He still wasn't convinced later that evening, when he walked to Arch and Tessa's for the screening of their Scottish wedding video.

His entire family was gathered together and the smell of freshly popped popcorn filled the air. Crystal Lopez came forward, glanced behind her when he walked in, and laughed, holding up her watch. "See? He's here just in time. Like he always is." She was wearing a white summer dress and her black hair hung loose around her shoulders.

He hadn't been certain whether Crystal would

show up tonight or simply send the recording along, but he was happy to see her here. He was always happy to see Crystal. She was one of his oldest friends, and probably the reason he'd made it in the music business.

"It's true," Jay said. "Crystal said you'd be here."

"Fashionably late," Arch grumbled.

He lifted his own watch, which changed to 7:00. "Hey, I'm right on time." He was never early, never late. He couldn't stand waiting around, but also never wanted to keep others waiting, so he'd developed an uncanny ability to arrive exactly when he was meant to. Crystal knew that, even if his own family didn't.

Crystal brought out red-and-white striped popcorn tubs and began to fill them with the fresh popcorn. It was a nice touch, Damien thought. She was good at her job as a wedding planner, as well as a good friend to his family. She and Erin had gone to school together and, based on the way Jay and Erin were cozied up, Crystal would be planning another wedding before too long.

Arch was already talking to Jay like they were best friends again, even though Jay had an arm slung around Erin's shoulders. Seeing it made Damien uncomfortable. Everyone was treating Jay as though he was already part of the family. Even Buster and Buzzy had welcomed his dog Nelson into their pack, and the three of them were sitting like three statues watching

Crystal, obviously hoping for popcorn.

Crystal wove around the Davenports, handing out the boxes of popcorn, and then they all gathered in front of the enormous flat-screen TV to watch the wedding.

Damien took a seat as far from Jay as he could get, and then squished up next to Mila to make room for Crystal beside him on the couch. It was a squeeze, and he was aware of Crystal's bare thigh pressing against his. Beneath the smell of popcorn, he caught her scent, spicy and elusive.

Considering the Scottish wedding had been for show after Tessa and Arch had their real wedding at the family home in Carmel, Damien was impressed at how good it was. They'd had so much fun. Howie appeared on screen in his kilt and Finn said, "Dad, until that wedding, I never knew you had such great legs." And they all laughed.

Tessa looked gorgeous in her cloud of white veil, and Arch so proud that it made Damien smile.

"They are so good together," Crystal whispered, as though it were a secret.

"My beautiful bride," Arch said, lifting Tessa's hand to kiss her knuckles.

In comparison to the beaming Davenports, Tessa's family all looked snooty, although the niece was very cute in her flowery dress and hairband.

The wedding video had been cut by a professional

Crystal had recommended, so they just watched the highlights: the bagpipers, the speeches, a quick shot of the meal. And then there were scenes of the dancing.

Waltzing across the screen were Smith and Valentina Sullivan, Valentina visibly pregnant and glowing with it, and there was Jay close dancing with Erin. The camera caught them looking at each other, a look of intimacy passing between them that was anything but subtle.

And suddenly, Damien saw what he'd been missing all along. His sister was all grown up and when she danced with Jay, there was obvious chemistry. "How did we not see that coming?"

"Your mother did," Howie announced, looking smug. "Cost me twenty bucks, too."

Damien had to smile. He loved how his mom and dad placed little bets here and there. His mom always won. No surprise.

He and Crystal were sharing a tub of popcorn that sat on her lap and as he reached into it, his attention back on the screen, she reached in too and their hands touched.

"You did a good job on the wedding," he told her quietly. "Both of them."

"I always do," she told him, laughter in her eyes.

He grabbed a piece of popcorn and tossed it at her. But she opened her mouth and caught it, crunching down.

Next to his family, Crystal was his oldest friend. He hoped she wouldn't go off and marry some random guy anytime soon, because he couldn't imagine what his life would be like without her.

★ ★ ★

ABOUT THE AUTHORS

Having sold more than 10 million books, Bella Andre's novels have been #1 bestsellers around the world and have appeared on the *New York Times* and *USA Today* bestseller lists 93 times. She has been the #1 Ranked Author on a top 10 list that included Nora Roberts, JK Rowling, James Patterson and Steven King.

Known for "sensual, empowered stories enveloped in heady romance" (Publishers Weekly), her books have been Cosmopolitan Magazine "Red Hot Reads" twice and have been translated into ten languages. She is a graduate of Stanford University and has won the Award of Excellence in romantic fiction. The Washington Post called her "One of the top writers in America" and she has been featured by Entertainment Weekly, NPR, USA Today, Forbes, The Wall Street Journal, and TIME Magazine.

Bella also writes the *New York Times* bestselling "Four Weddings and a Fiasco" series as Lucy Kevin. Her sweet contemporary romances also include the USA Today bestselling "Walker Island" and "Married in Malibu" series.

If not behind her computer, you can find her reading her favorite authors, hiking, swimming or laughing. Married with two children, Bella splits her time between the Northern California wine country, a log cabin in the Adirondack mountains of upstate New York, and a flat in London overlooking the Thames.

Sign up for Bella's New Release newsletter:
bellaandre.com/newsletter

Join Bella Andre on Facebook:
facebook.com/authorbellaandre

Join Bella Andre's reader group:
bellaandre.com/readergroup

Follow Bella Andre on Instagram:
instagram.com/bellaandrebooks

Follow Bella Andre on Twitter:
twitter.com/bellaandre

Visit Bella's website for her complete booklist:
www.BellaAndre.com

Nicky Arden (aka Nancy Warren) is the USA Today Bestselling author of mystery and romance who had sold more than 5 million books so far! She's originally from Vancouver, Canada, though she tends to wander and has lived in England, Italy and California at various times. Favorite moments include being the answer to a crossword puzzle clue in Canada's National Post newspaper, being featured on the front page of the

New York Times when her book Speed Dating launched Harlequin's NASCAR series, and being nominated three times for Romance Writers of America's RITA award. She has an MA in Creative Writing from Bath Spa University. She's an avid hiker, loves chocolate and most of all, loves to hear from readers! You'll often find her in her private Facebook group, Nancy Warren's Knitwits.

Newsletter signup:
nickyarden.com/newsletter

Nicky's Website:
www.NickyArden.com

Printed in Great Britain
by Amazon

55966181R00196